More . . . Advance Praise for UNFORSAKEN

"John Dwaine McKenna's *Unforsaken* brings to life the birth of the 20th century in the American West. McKenna portrays the West in loving detail and populates it with interesting, conflicted characters."

— JOHN E. STITH, AWARD-WINNING AUTHOR OF *PUSHBACK*

"*Unforsaken* grabs the reader by the heart from the opening pages. Eloquent prose, a riveting plot, and expertly detailed characters make this western adventure one for the record books."

— CLAIRE GEM, AUTHOR OF *HEARTS UNLOCHED*

"Filled with McKenna's whip-crack prose and extraordinary storytelling skill, *Unforsaken* is a quiet masterpiece . . ."

—PAUL BISHOP, AUTHOR OF *LIE CATCHERS*

Also by John Dwaine McKenna

UNFORSAKEN

UNFORSAKEN

A Novel

by

John Dwaine McKenna

East of the Mountains  and West of the Sun

RHYOLITE PRESS, LLC
Colorado Springs, Colorado

Published in the United States of America by Rhyolite Press, LLC

P.O. Box 60144 Colorado Springs, Colorado 80960

www.rhyolitepress.com

McKenna, John Dwaine
Unforsaken / John Dwaine McKenna
First Edition   April, 2019

Library of Congress Control Number: 2018915289

ISBN 978-1-943829-16-3

PRINTED IN THE UNITED STATES OF AMERICA

Cover design and book design/layout by Donald R. Kallaus

For June . . .
the light of my life

While progress toots its greedy horn
and makes its motor buzz,
I thank the Lord I wasn't born
no later than I was.

— Charles Badger Clark
  The Old Cow Man

Prologue

Sometime in the mid 1890s . . .

The woman looked up from her work and watched, as a murder of crows boiled up from the arroyo that snaked off below the two room adobe and log house she and her husband called home on the far west Texas prairie. It was nestled among the mesquite and cholla, the scrub oak and pinon pine, the yucca and blue grama grass that grew in patches here and there like tufts of hair in an old man's ears. Cursing their displacers in a series of low croaks, squawks and muttered groans, the lot of them arrowed over the cabin and headed for another roost in the hills farther north and west. Diversion over, the woman turned back to her task.

It was laundry day—Blue Monday—and the young wife was bending over a wooden wash tub on her front porch, busy scrubbing a denim work shirt on a metal washboard when the gunshots began. They rolled up like claps of thunder from down in the gulley where the crows flew out. The noise assaulted her ears and chafed her nerves, which were already raw from the squabble she and her husband had had that morning. She started counting the reports, but lost track at seven or eight . . . fired in such rapid succession . . . they came too fast for her to record. A short period of silence was followed by two booms from a shotgun, and she felt the pit of her stomach drop. All the shooting came from down in the draw where her husband had gone earlier that day to cut firewood and fence posts. He'd taken an axe and a couple of saws, a jug of water and some biscuits and cheese for lunch. She'd watched as he hitched up the team and loaded everything in the buckboard, then drove off with their dog, Louie, trotting along behind. She remembered all of those details, but could not recall if he took any guns. She didn't think he had.

Her concern was replaced by a stab of fear when she saw the unknown riders emerging from the canyon's mouth, about half a mile away. They were following the wagon tracks her husband had left earlier . . . three Mexicans and a white man . . . all armed to the teeth.

The woman dropped the washboard and waddled for the front door, just as fast as her aching back, swollen legs and advanced gravidity would allow. She kept both hands on her belly, unconsciously protecting her unborn child as she moved inside and closed the door. She reached for the Winchester rifle that was given to her husband by his father, and jacked a round into the chamber. A lever-action model 1873 with a walnut stock and an octagonal barrel in bear, elk and buffalo stopping .30-.40 caliber, it was a fearsome weapon, and one she was infinitely familiar with. Grabbing a chair and a box of shells, she sat next to the only window in the place and slid it open just wide enough to allow the business end of the rifle to protrude. Resting the barrel on the windowsill, the woman drew a bead on the first rider and fired without hesitation. Ignoring the earsplitting noise and heavy recoil, she levered the action, ejected the spent cartridge and drove in a fresh one, which closed the breech as the lever locked home and allowed her to fire again . . . all in less than two seconds. She knew she was fighting for her life—as well as her baby's—and kept firing, cocking and firing again, while smoking hot brass casings pinged down all around her.

* * *

Ten days later a weathered old Texas Ranger was giving an after-action report to his commander at their headquarters in Austin.

Captain Wiley Newton was in charge of all the Ranger Battalions in the state. "Go ahead, Boyd," he said. "Tell it however yuh want, and Cornelius over there will take it down. He's a court reporter I borrowed from Judge Shipman's chambers, so he'll get everything you say without missing an iota. Take your time . . . and tell it all. I want the case fully documented and on file, so those who come in the new century will know how we operated in the old west. Maybe help 'em become better Rangers."

The hard-bitten lawman who sat across the table from Captain Newton was busy rolling a cigarette with one hand and looking at the west Texas dust that still coated his boots as he listened. He smoothed the smoke with his fingers, stuck it in the corner of his mouth and lit up with a kitchen match he produced from his vest pocket. Shaking the flame out, he looked at the recorder and said, "You ready?"

The young man with the wire-rim glasses nodded yes and the debriefing began.

Boyd Pirtle took a drag of his cigarette and said, "You want me to note the dates and days of the week?"

"Just the events."

Looking off into the middle distance at something only he could see, the tough old campaigner began . . .

On or about the middle of April, another Ranger named Juan Medina and I were on the trail of four outlaws who'd come up from Old Mexico and robbed a bank in Odessa, Texas. During the course of the holdup, two patrons of the bank were assaulted, a cashier was pistol-whipped and the bank manager was shot in the abdominal area. He later died of his wounds after five days of suffering.

Ranger Medina and I were in San Angelo when we got word of the robbery and . . .

Captain Newton said, "How were y'all notified?"

"The Sheriff in Odessa. He sent a wire, sayin' that he was formin' a posse to go after the gang, and requested any available law enforcement assistance. We left immediately and caught up with the group two days later, southwest of the city."

"One more quick question Boyd. Is Juan Medina George Medina's son, about twenty-five years old?"

"Yeah. He is. George was one of the toughest and bravest Rangers I ever served with. And his kid is just like him. He's closer to thirty years old, by the way."

The Ranger Commandant pulled a cigar from one of his desk drawers and proceeded to light up. Puffing out blue smoke, he said, "George died, yuh know, about ten years ago. We fought against the Comanche Nation together."

"Sorry to hear he passed."

"The Medinas have been in Texas for ten generations. Did yuh know that George's father, Daniel Medina, fought at the battle of San Jacinto, under Sam Houston, when Texas won independence from Mexico? They're a proud and patriotic bunch with a long history of public service. I'm glad to hear that another one of their family has joined up with us."

"Me too," Pirtle said, "Juan's tough, dedicated and brave," as he crushed out his cigarette in the ashtray on the desk. He looked at the court reporter, who sat alongside. "You ready?"

The young man nodded yes, and without being asked, referred to his notes and said, *San Angelo when we got word of the robbery and . . .*

Pirtle nodded and resumed his narrative.

We joined the Odessa Posse two days later and set out after the robbers. The gang consisted of three Mexicans, or Comancheros, and a white man who appeared to be leading the group. We later learned that his name was Frank Rogers and that he was wanted for murder and robbery down in Mexico.

"How did you learn this?"

"The Mexican Federal Police. They've got a reward of 500,000 pesos out for him, and this'll give yuh a hoot, it seems Rogers is one of those Mormons with a bunch of wives. The Federales said Rogers has four of 'em and fifteen children that they know of . . . mebbe more."

"No wonder he's up here robbin' banks." Captain Newton said, then waved his hand for Pirtle to continue.

Rogers and his gang were headed to the southwest, making for Mexico. We—the posse—started out a couple of days behind, but we were catching up fast. There was five of us, all experienced lawmen: Sheriff Rudd, two of his deputies, Medina and me. We were less than a half-days ride from bein' in a position to have it out with 'em, and they must have seen our dust comin' up the trail behind them, because that's when they did it . . . Pirtle stopped talking, looked down at the floor—as if searching for his next words—and pinched the bridge of his nose with the thumb and index finger of his left hand.

"Are you okay, Boyd?"

Pirtle was quiet for a moment, then said, "Yeah. I'm fine. The next part caught me by surprise . . . made me think about Genevieve is all . . . and I wasn't quite ready for it."

"Can you finish?"

"Yeah."

Pirtle looked out the courthouse windows, at the live oak trees in the entryway. He took a breath and resumed the debriefing.

We tracked them across the desert, all the way down to the Apache Mountains, and came to a small adobe and log freeholder's cabin in the foothills . . . where we found the atrocity . . . the butchery and the carnage they left behind.

We followed their tracks as the trail led us up a wash, and into an arroyo where we found the body of an unarmed man whose corpse had been riddled with bullets. He wasn't just killed, he was annihilated. Nearby, we found a medium sized dog, freshly killed by a shotgun blast and a draft horse, also shotgunned to death. But, the greatest horror was still to come.

Pirtle stopped talking and got out his tobacco sack, some rolling papers and matches, then rolled and lit another cigarette. Taking a puff, he exhaled and resumed.

We came up and over the canyon rim and spotted the only house within twenty miles and headed for it. There, we found that a prolonged gunfight had taken place.

A dead horse was lying about fifty feet from the house, hit once in the chest with a large caliber bullet. Inside there was a dead bandit, also killed with a big round, it was the same gun as killed the horse by the looks of it. The most obscene sight of all though, was a woman who'd been shot to death . . . as was her newborn infant son. We could see she died defending her family and home, fought until she ran out of ammunition. When we found her, she was surrounded by empty brass casings in .30-.40 caliber, but there wasn't any rifle. One of the bandits or Rogers himself, must have stolen it. It had to be a repeater, probably a Winchester, I'd guess. Whoever she was, she was the bravest and toughest woman any of us had ever seen. And the saddest too . . .

Pirtle stopped talking for the second time.

Wiley Newton waited, but the silence only lengthened. After a bit he said, "What's the saddest . . . what did yuh mean?"

Pirtle looked up with eyes that were suddenly bloodshot and resumed speaking

"From what we saw, the woman went into labor from the stress of the fight and delivered her infant as the marauders broke in. Somehow, she drilled the first one in the door with her last bullet. The next one through must have murdered her. Son-of-a-bitch put one in the newborn too . . . while he and his mother were still tied together by the cord. It's somethin' I can't get out of my mind and won't ever forget. And I won't quit hunting for that murderin' bastard Frank Rogers for as long as I live. So help me God."

Captain Newton thought he saw a tear coursing down Pirtle's face, but turned away and pretended not to notice. He waited a moment for the old Ranger to recover before he said, "Is that all Boyd?"

"Not quite. Put this in the report too." Pirtle looked at Cornelius, whose eyes were on his tablet, but nodded that he was ready.

Pirtle said, *We gave a Christian burial to the woman, her*

husband and the poor little baby who never had a chance. We didn't even learn their names. Sheriff Rudd said a few words over 'em and read from his bible. The dead bandit we left in the cabin, and burned it to the ground. But by the time we were finished, it was too dark to see their tracks, and we were done in anyway. We made camp that night and took up the search at daybreak. By that time though, Rogers and the other two had made it through the mountains. We lost their trail and they escaped across the border and back into old Mexico. We notified the Mexican authorities, but I don't reckon they'll do much of anything. There was nothin' more we could do at that point, except come home. But the case remains open, and I won't ever cease my efforts to bring Rogers to justice. He'll come back up here sooner or later and we'll nail him. He is the spawn of the devil, and nothin' less than a monster who must be killed.

The personal ad first appeared in the July 31, 1899 edition of the
Ft. Worth *Daily Gazette,* and thereafter on the last day of every
month through the summer, fall and winter. In January of 1900,
the word 'REWARD' was added and the classified continued
to run as before; on the last day of each successive month
until May of 'aught-one, when a stranger appeared at Ella
Stringfellow's front door.

Chapter One
1901

It was an almost perfect early spring morning . . . and the thermometer was still in the mid-eighties, a slight breeze rustled the leaves in the live oaks lining the thoroughfare, and the sun stood low in a cloudless, cerulean blue sky that looked as fragile as Chinese porcelain and spread to the farthest edges of the world. That's when a man came up East Second Street in Cleburne, Texas. He was driving a black doctor's buggy with red wheels and seat, and pulled by a small Appaloosa mare. He was looking for Featherston Lane, and a certain gray house with a green tin roof and white gingerbread trim. When he found it, he nosed the mare to the curb, half-hitched the reins to the dash rail and backed out on the short step. Once down, he checked his surroundings, opened the picket gate and strode up the flagstone walk like he owned the place.

The woman who lived there saw him come to her front door. She was watching from the parlor, where she'd just placed a bowl of pink and yellow roses, fresh-cut from the bushes at the corner of her porch. The man, who was tall and thin, had on a white shirt, black wool suit, black tie and gray waistcoat, and moved with the insouciance, grace and confidence of a feral cat on the prowl. She noted the cant of his curled brim Stetson, the scuffed, dusty boots and tied-down Colt pistol at his right hip. She shivered at the sight of his drooping, heavy black mustache. Then he was at the door knocking.

She smoothed her apron and tucked a wisp of hair behind her ear before she went to answer it. "Yes," she said, "may I help you?"

The stranger took off his hat, held it in his left hand and said, "Mornin' ma'am. My name is Boyd Pirtle. I'm a Texas Ranger. Are you the Mrs. Stringfellow who's been runnin' the advertisement in the newspaper, lookin' for her brother?"

"It's Miss, not Mrs., I have never married, and yes, I am she. Do you know of his whereabouts?" She saw the creases in his sun-baked face, the gray creeping into his hair, and all the sadness and steel in a pair of pale blue eyes that looked as faded as old denim. *Gun-fighters eyes,* her father would've said . . . the eyes of a long and hard campaigner. She added, "I'm willing to pay for information if you can help me find him." *And Please God,* she thought at the same time, *don't let this one be another crackpot, full of lies and a spinner of tall tales.*

The stranger in the rumpled suit with the worn cuffs looked off to his left before turning back and gazing straight into her eyes. "No ma'am. I don't. I haven't any news for yuh, but I do have a proposal that I believe can help both of us . . . if y'all'd care to listen."

"You say you're a Ranger. Do you have any proof? There's been many who've come around looking for the reward money, but none of them had any validity. No disrespect, but why should I believe you?"

"That's a fair enough question," he said as he pulled back his lapel with his left hand to display a five-pointed star, convex in shape, hand-hammered and filed from a single silver dollar with the words TEXAS RANGER etched into it. "Here's my badge, and you can wire Captain Wiley Newton at Division Headquarters down in Austin. He'll provide my bona fides for you. And, as you can see, he's the one who signed this here letter of introduction," Pirtle added, and pulled an envelope with the Texas Ranger insignia on it from his inside coat pocket. He removed the enclosed document and handed it to her.

She unlatched the door and took the missive, scanned it with care and handed it back to its owner. She said, "Special Agent. I'm impressed. But what's that got to do with finding my twin brother?"

"I'll get to that. It's part of my proposal to you."

She thought for a moment about asking him to leave. But after a second or two of hesitation, she said instead, "When's the last time you ate anything Mr. Pirtle?"

He looked down and said, "Yesterday mornin', I guess. Some jerky and a couple of corn dodgers."

"Corn dodgers, huh. Haven't heard that expression for a while. Were you in the war?"

"Yes'm. I was. Signed up with John Bell Hood and the Texas Brigade right after Shiloh."

"Oh my . . . you must be brave."

"It was a long time ago. I was seventeen years old."

"Did you fight?"

He didn't answer for a few seconds, then looked off to the side and said in a voice so tight and low that she barely made out his words. "We all fought. I was at Chickamauga. Some of us lived through it . . . most didn't. Truth is, I don't like rememberin' it, thinkin' about it, or talkin' 'bout it."

She took a step backwards as if pushed. With a hand at her mouth, she said, "My apologies, sir. I meant no harm . . . I was born a year after conflict ended and I forget at times, how profoundly those who participated in the War Between the States were affected by it."

He looked at her with the eyes of a wounded old soul. *"De Nada*—as the Mesicans say—it's nothin.'" Then he grinned a lopsided kind of grin and said, "I call it *The War of Northern Aggression,* when all'a them damn Yankees invaded our southern homelands."

She almost concealed her impish smile, but it escaped as she said, "I stand corrected, sir. Northern Aggression indeed. Why don't you have a seat on the veranda over there Mr. Pirtle, and I'll get us something to eat. Would eggs be okay?"

"Yes'm," was all he said before heading over to the wicker chair with a green oilcloth seat.

Chapter Two

As they finished off the last of their breakfasts and made the last of their small talk, Ella Stringfellow pointed in the Rangers direction with her tin coffee mug and said, "So what, exactly, is a Special Agent, and what's that got to do with me?"

Boyd Pirtle mopped up the last of the egg on his plate with a piece of bread and put it in his mouth. Chewing with a slow, methodical cadence, he sipped some of his coffee and swallowed before answering. "It means that I work on special projects. Things that might affect the health and welfare . . . or the peace and security of the citizens of the State of Texas."

She watched the hummingbirds for a moment, as they jockeyed for position among the honeysuckle, morning glory and trumpet vines that grew in exuberant profusion and climbed to the tops of the trellises on both sides of the porch, while she thought about what he'd just told her. She put her cup down and said, "Big issues. You . . . and the ones you work for . . . are concerned with what, exactly?"

"It's complicated."

"Well I'm just a dumb little school teacher and librarian from a small town in north Texas, but I read a lot . . . why don't you go ahead and tell me . . . I'll try to keep up."

"I meant no disrespect, Miss Stringfellow . . . fact is I'm in favor of the education of girls and the Women's Suffrage Movement. The world is changin' and there's forces at work that want to destroy the United States. We can't afford to ignore half of our population any longer if our way of life is goin' to survive and prosper."

"My goodness, you're a forward thinker for such a fearsome character."

"I have to be in my line of work."

She poured them both more coffee and said, "Are you what they call a spy . . . a Secret Agent . . . like the one in Mr. Conrad's book?"

Pirtle took a sack of Bull Durham tobacco and some cigarette papers out of his shirt pocket and proceeded to roll a handmade smoke with one hand. He pulled the string that closed the sack with his teeth and put it and the papers back in his pocket, then smoothed and tamped the handmade before sticking it in the corner of his mouth. He struck a wooden match that seemed to appear out of nowhere on the corner of his thumb, cupped the flame with both hands and lit up. He took a deep drag, pulled in a lungful of smoke and exhaled from both nostrils and his mouth. Then he said, "I'm impressed by your familiarity with Joseph Conrad. He's not the usual readin' material of a gentlewoman like yourself."

"True. It's not. But what about my questions? You haven't answered any of them, and, by the way, I'm impressed with how you rolled your own with one hand."

He flashed his lopsided grin again and said, "It comes from too many hours in the saddle . . . not havin' enough time to stop and rest . . . chasin' desperados, back when I was a younger man, just learnin' my craft."

"I'm confused. What craft?"

"Of bein' a Ranger. Bein' tougher then them we were after, no matter who it was . . . Comanche, Mesican, or plain old bandit . . . wanted 'em to know we were relentless. Put the fear a God in 'em."

She sipped her coffee, looked at him over the rim of the cup and said, "The Texas Rangers have quite a reputation alright, and if you don't mind me saying so sir, it isn't always a wholesome one. Some have said that *"The Rangers are worse than the outlaws they're after."*

Pirtle leaned back in his chair with his arms crossed, hands cupped over his elbows and the burning cigarette wedged between the first and second fingers of his left hand. He looked off in the middle distance at something only he could see for a moment, then took another puff, thinking about his answer. Then he said, "The Rangers are the only thing that's been standin' between civilized folk and annihilation. It was true in eighteen and sixty-seven when I became a Ranger, and it's true today. Them we're dealin' with only understand one thing . . . and that thing is force. Kill or be killed. We've had to be tougher than them. It's just that simple."

She looked down at the table and the food left on her plate. She said, as she lifted her eyes to his, "But, those were the old days. This is the twentieth century now. We're civilized. The Indians are confined to reservations, the gunfighters are all dead or in jail, and the cattle rustlers along the border with Mexico have all been put out of business . . . And just think about the scientific progress we've made. Now we have telephones, electric lights, horseless carriages and there's even talk of heavier-than-air flying machines filling the skies with people before long. This is an exciting time to be living, in my opinion. I think there's many reasons to be optimistic about the future."

Boyd Pirtle squinted and turned his head sideways to keep the smoke out of his eyes as he took one last drag on his cigarette and stubbed it out on the sole of his boot. He put the butt into his shirt pocket and said, "Well, from where I sit, and with what I know, it's impossible to be optimistic and well-informed at the same time. There's exceptions of course, but in the main, humans ain't no dammed good. They'll lie, cheat and steal at every opportunity . . . and a great many are flat-out murderous in nature. Some few're not only killers . . . they enjoy doin' it." His voice trailed off at that point, and he looked away from her. "Sorry to be so blunt in your presence Miss Stringfellow, but that's how it is in my world."

She put the breakfast dishes back on the tea cart she'd brought them in on from the kitchen. She said, "Your apology is accepted Mr. Pirtle. I'm no shrinking violet, but I can only say that I'm truly sorry for you, or anyone, who's compelled to live in such a world and hold such points-of-view."

Pirtle turned his gaze back to her and said, "I have lived a violent life amongst the most brutal and bloodthirsty of men for so long, that I fear at times, I am become like them. Make no mistake Miss Stringfellow, I have visited the ultimate act of violence upon my fellow man, but never outside the sanctity of the law. You asked if I was a spy, and I answered no. But I am an undercover agent. My job is to keep tabs on certain groups and inform Captain Newton back in Austin of their activities."

Pirtle picked up his hat, which had been sitting next to him, crown down, on the porch. He removed something hidden in the sweat band inside, unfolded and smoothed it with great care. He turned toward her and said, "Do you recognize this person?"

Chapter Three

She knew that Pirtle was watching her for signs of a tell, but she couldn't stop her sudden intake of breath. Of course she recognized an artist's likeness of her late father. She said, "It looks like my father, Carl, but he's been dead for twenty years. So, if it's a recent drawing it must be my brother, Chester."

"Look again. Make sure," Pirtle said. "How long has it been since you've had contact with him . . . with your brother."

Ella looked off at her flowers and the feisty little birds and honeybees, all busy gathering nectar and harassing each other. There was a high bloom in her cheeks and a snap of anger in her eyes that she was quick to get under control, before she drew in a deep breath and said, "It too, is complicated."

"I have no doubt of that. Take your time. Tell the story from the start, stick to the facts and don't worry. I'm a good listener." Pirtle told her as he leaned back in his chair, stuck his legs out straight and crossed his feet, then added, "And before you ask me again, your questions will all get answered as we go along. The man in the picture here," he tapped the drawing with his index finger, "was callin' himself Frank Rogers. Does that name mean anythin' to yourself?"

"Not offhand, but maybe it's one of our family names—they're scattered everywhere, from North Carolina, to Tennessee, Arkansas, Louisiana, and Texas. But that's my brother Chester. The more I look at this, the more sure I am."

Pirtle, who was now writing with a short pencil in a pocket-sized leather-bound book he'd produced from somewhere on his person while she looked at the drawing, said, "Why?"

"Because of the mole on his face, over on the left side. You can barely see it in the drawing, but the artist put it there. And I have one just like it on the right side of my temple. We're twins. When we were little, I used to tell him he had a bullet hole there. He'd say, *Better than a wormhole like you got. Worms prob'ly ate your brain.*" She pulled her light brown hair back from the right side of her face and showed the beauty-mark to the Ranger. "Chester's is exactly the opposite."

He looked up as she pulled her hair to the side, noticed she had a heart-shaped face and eyes that were the dark blue of forty-fathom water. *She's a pretty girl,* he thought, *rounded just so, in all the right places too . . . wonder why she didn't have suitors . . . get married.* He said, "His eyes blue?"

"Same as mine," was the answer.

Pirtle wrote in his book, looked up for a moment, then said, "Your mother and father? What about them? Where are they?"

"My mother's name was Ellen. She died giving birth to Chester and me. I'm named for her. My father was Carl Ansil Stringfellow. He was a Mormon. A Mormon Bishop, as a matter-of-fact. He died when Chester and I were sixteen years old."

"What from? He pass here . . . in Cleburne?"

Ella didn't answer right away. She looked down at her lap and twisted her fingers together like a little girl. Then, she looked out at her front yard and the Appaloosa mare, standing by the curb. Finally, she said, "He was murdered. Right out there, where your horse and buggy stand. He was coming home from his church duties one night in early November . . . around seven-thirty. It was just after dark when someone came up behind him and shot him in the back of the head. The town Marshal at that time was Silas Pierce. He said Father was dead before he hit the ground."

"Did the Marshal catch the murderer . . . find out who did it?"

"The killer was never caught. Mrs. Ince and I were in the parlor. She was knitting. I was reading a book, *The Adventures of Tom Sawyer,* by Sam Clemens, or Mark Twain, as he was calling himself then. We heard the shot and looked out, saw Father on the ground, his horse bolted down the street. We ran out of the house together, but when we got there, Mrs. Ince looked at Father and stood in front of him so I couldn't see. She told me to go catch Father's horse and fetch Marshal Pierce, which I did."

Pirtle was writing furiously in his book. Without stopping he said, "Who is Mrs. Ince? And where was your brother when all this happened?"

"I don't know where he was, or what he was doing. He was a male; didn't have to explain his comings and goings. He even had his own horse and saddle. Sometimes he'd stay out all night. *Sowing his wild oats,* my father would say with a grin and nod. I, on the other hand, was a virtual prisoner, kept under lock and key."

Pirtle had stopped writing and was watching her with the intensity of a stalking fox. When she paused he said, "Mrs. Ince?"

"She was an old negro woman whose husband was killed in the war. Her own baby died and she wet nursed Chester and me. She lived upstairs in an attic room Father had built just for her. She had her own back staircase and everything. She cooked and kept house for Father and she stayed with me after he died. She was the only mother I ever knew. She had a stroke and died, back in 'ninety-five. I still miss her everyday."

"Do you know how old she was?"

"As best as we could figure, she was around seventy-two or three. Like most negro ex-slaves, she didn't know her exact date of birth."

Pirtle made more notations in his book. He looked up and found her eyes boring into his. Without looking away he said, "So, what about Chester?"

"What about him?"

"How was he taking your father's death . . . the circumstances of it and all?"

Ella Stringfellow stood up and put the last of their dishes on the tea cart. As she started back in the house with it, she stopped and said, "I haven't any idea what Chester was thinking or doing, Mr. Pirtle because, you see, two days after Father was murdered, Chester disappeared. I haven't seen him since. Not for more than twenty years."

Chapter Four

Boyd Pirtle was pacing from one end of the long wide veranda to the other when she came back. The three-story house, with its mix of building styles and decorations, incorporated a generous porch across the front and along one side in its design, allowing plenty of room for him to stretch his legs, think and smoke another hand-rolled cigarette.

When she saw him, Ella said, "Mr. Pirtle . . . would you kindly come back and sit . . . the neighbors all think it's scandalous that I live alone in such a big house. They'll be having a field day speculating about me entertaining strange men."

He looked up from his musings at the sound of her voice.

"Of course," he said, "I wasn't thinkin'. Been in rough company too long. Why don't you tell 'em the truth? I'm a Texas Ranger, lookin' for your brother."

"That would really open wide the floodgates of conjecture, everyone would believe Chester's a criminal of some kind."

The Ranger sat in the same chair, with the cigarette in his mouth, and pulled the notebook and pencil from his coat pocket. Taking the cigarette out of his mouth with his left hand, he said, "The truth of the matter Miss Stringfellow, is that your brother is a criminal. We just didn't know his right name until you identi-fied that drawin' a few minutes ago. Up to that point, I'd been huntin' for a man called Frank Rogers."

"May I ask why?"

Pirtle hesitated for a moment, then said, "We're lookin' into a series of murderous bank and train robberies is all I can say right now. A lotta folks have been hurt . . . lost their life savin's. Five others lost their lives, includin' a fellow Ranger and a Pinkerton man."

Ella Stringfellow shifted uncomfortably in her wicker chair. "And you think my brother's involved? I don't believe that is possible."

"Based on what you've told me, I know it's the truth. Frank Rogers is the leader of the bunch. There's about four hard-core members of the gang, the brains, the ones who figure out the robberies, and another ten or fifteen who come and go . . . dependin' on the size of the crime."

Ella bit her lip and looked away in shame with her cheeks burning. After a moment, she composed herself and said, "It's difficult for me to think of Chester as the leader of a band of outlaws, and guilty of such heinous acts of violence and murder. His father must be rolling in his grave."

Pirtle hitched forward in his chair, sitting with his forearms up and elbows on his knees, he said, "What can you tell me about your father . . ."

She stiffened, then exhaled and said, "What would you like to know?"

"Everythin' you can remember—it'll help me figure out how your brother thinks—maybe give me some insights about where he might be hidin' out or where he might be goin', maybe even what he's been plannin'."

Her cobalt blue eyes showed flashes of lightning when she

looked at Pirtle and said, "I'll tell you everything I can about Father, and Chester too, if you'll promise me just one thing . . ."

"What might that be?"

Her eyes bored into his with an intensity that was painful to behold, then she said, "I want your promise, your own personal oath, that when you find Chester, when you catch up and capture him, you'll notify me and hold him in place long enough that I might travel there—to where ever you're keeping him and allow me a few minutes of time with him."

Pirtle didn't answer right away. He smoked the last of his cigarette and, as he'd done earlier, snuffed it out on his boot before he spoke, "What if he's wounded . . . or dead?"

"Same thing, I want to see him. I want ten minutes alone. When you send word of your whereabouts, I'll drop everything, and come immediately by the fastest available transportation."

"Must be important to y'all."

"It is."

Ranger Pirtle stuck his hand out and said, "I give you my word, I'll notify yourself as soon as I have Chester Stringfellow in my custody."

Ella took his hand in hers. "Thank you." Was all she said.

"We've got an agreement, so tell me about your father. Was the fact that he was a polygamist, and a Mormon bishop a problem, did he have enemies because of it?"

Anger flashed in her eyes again as she said, "First of all, my father was not ever a polygamist—he never even remarried after my mother died—and the concept of plural, or celestial wives was repugnant to him. He warned me constantly not to allow myself to enter into a plural situation. He also advocated for the church to outlaw polygamy . . . which it did . . . before Utah became a state in 1896. He was proud of that fact. But the truth is, it wasn't common knowledge around town that Father, and Chester, and I were of the Mormon faith. As far as most everybody knew, Father operated in real estate, and he was quite successful at it, as you can see by this house I live in."

Pirtle glanced up from his notebook. "Were y'all the only ones in Cleburne?"

"The only Latter-Day Saints?"

"Yes."

"There's a few others, but they stay scattered around and keep a low profile . . . out of sight and mind and reach of the gentiles, so there's less chance of violence."

"Was there any?"

Ella looked away again, with her hand at her throat, as if she was protecting it, she said, "Have you any idea Mr. Pirtle, any idea at all, what life was like for a young white woman living alone in a great big house such as this, with only a middle-aged negress for companionship and protection during the time of the carpetbaggers, reconstruction and the terror wrought by cross-burning night riders? Yes. Yes. And yes again. There was violence aplenty at times. Lucky for me, Marshal Pierce took a special interest in keeping me, the house, and Mrs. Ince safe and well. More than a few times during those awful years the Marshal spent the night on this very porch with a rifle or a shotgun in his lap."

"Was he a Mormon?"

She smiled. "How very perceptive of you. Yes. Marshal Pierce was a Mormon."

"You used the past tense . . ."

"He died, just about three years ago."

"In 'ninety-eight?"

She nodded and said, "Yes. He was killed trying to stop a bar fight during the fourth of July celebration. Two drunks were going at each other over the gold versus silver monetary question and who would be a better president, McKinley or William Jennings

Bryan. One of them pulled a knife out of his boot and stabbed the Marshal and his adversary. The drunk man survived. Marshal Pierce did not."

"And the one with the knife?"

"Hung by a vigilance committee while awaiting trial."

The old Ranger picked up the drawing of Chester Stringfellow, aka Frank Rogers, and folded it with precise care in preparation for secreting it back inside his Stetson.

I wonder, Ella Stringfellow thought at the same time, *just what he's gonna ask next . . . and I wonder too, just how he perceives me . . . am I pulling it off . . . or not.*

Chapter Five

For his part, Boyd Pirtle was wondering what the woman was hiding. As he stowed the drawing, he said, "I'm curious about Chester. What prompted you to start a search for him after so many years?"

The question appeared to make her uncomfortable. She exhaled, shifted around on her chair and looked down the porch to her left. She took a deep breath and said, "After not having any word from, or about, my brother for more than a decade, I'd pretty much given him up for dead . . . and I was busy trying to survive. Mrs. Ince and I had our hands full keeping the household together, fighting off the carpet-bagging Yankees, land speculators and more than a few unwanted suitors. They were the worst. Moonstruck Lotharios. All of whom were trying to get their hands on Father's assets by marrying me. We were so busy for so long, that the years just melted away like spring snow; and then I looked up one day after Mrs. Ince passed, and I realized that more than fifteen years—in fact, almost sixteen— had elapsed since Father was murdered and Chester disappeared. I was thirty-some years old, past marriageable age and had no idea what would happen next."

Pirtle was watching with the same fierce intensity he usually reserved for interviews with captured criminals. She was leaning back in her chair, staring at the ceiling above, her face frozen into a rictus of pain by her memories. He let the silence lengthen, filling the passing moments by rolling another smoke with his left hand. Three cigarettes in a couple of hours was a much greater intake than his usual habit of one after each meal, and it was making his throat raw, but he needed to keep himself occupied, lest he give away his mounting excitement. *This is the best lead I've had in the last eighteen months of chasin' them sonsabitches . . . don't spook her, she'll tell me more . . . just keep your mouth shut and let her come 'round,* he thought to himself as he lit another kitchen match off his thumb and fired up.

The noise of the flaring sulpher reanimated her. Ella sat up, took a gulp of air and resumed her narrative. She said, "More months went by and I busied myself with school and the library. I was achieving some satisfaction with my quiet life when I received a notice from the Stockman's Bank in Ft. Worth. They'd received a money transfer in the amount of two hundred and fifty dollars in my name. The remitter was my brother, Chester Stringfellow . . . my twin . . . the one I hadn't heard from for seventeen years. I was struck dumb."

Pirtle smoked and thought for a moment, then said in a raspy voice, "What did you do then?"

"I put the money into that same bank. In a savings account in my name. It's what my father taught me. *Always get the money. Get the money first, then hang on to it.* It's what he preached. It's what I did."

"Have you heard anythin' since? From Chester?"

"Not from him directly, no. But from the bank, yes. I'll get to that in a minute. May I get you something to drink, Mr. Pirtle? Some cold tea? Lemonade? Water or coffee? You sound parched."

"Some sweet tea would be fine. I'm a little bit sore-throated," he said as he put out his cigarette and stuck the butt in his pocket. He watched her movements from behind as she went back into her house, thought again about what a fine looking woman she was, and felt a stirring in his body he thought had disappeared with the death of his wife, Genevieve, eight years earlier . . . chastised himself, thinking, *Quit'at you damned old fool. She ain't no Mesican whore* . . . It seemed like a long time before she returned with a pitcher of tea and a pair of glasses.

After she poured for both of them, she sat back in her chair, sipped some tea and, with the glass in both hands, resumed speaking, "There have been sporadic receipts, of varying amounts of funds over the past two years. The smallest was fifty dollars and the largest three-hundred and fifty. Altogether, there's a bit over two thousand dollars in the account as of now. I've never spent so much as a penny of the money. It's all in the bank account."

"When was the last one?"

"Four weeks ago."

"All sent by your brother? From where?"

"Yes—to your first question, I don't know—to your second one."

Pirtle looked up. "Why not?"

"I never thought to ask. But, in truth, I'd rather doubt they'd have told me anyway. I've had an exceedingly hard time getting the people over there to take me serious . . . me being a silly female, and as such, one who can't control her emotions and all . . . thereby unable to understand the complexities of banking. It was quite difficult to maintain my composure when dealing with them."

"I can only try to imagine," Pirtle said with a shake of his head.

Pirtle made several notations in his book, then said, "Is there someone in particular that you talk to at the bank in Ft. Worth?"

"Oliver Witherspoon. He's the manager. I've left written instructions with him to put any funds received in my name into that same account and send me a monthly statement including the amount of interest earned."

"I'd like to see the most recent one."

"Of course." She went inside and came back with an envelope bearing the bank's logo and address.

Pirtle wrote all the details in his notebook and returned the statement to its owner and said, "There's just one other thing I'm curious about. This isn't a place where Mormons are known to congregate. Why was your father—a Mormon Bishop—located here? I can't help but think that fact may have had somethin' to do with his murder."

Ella sipped more tea, stalling for time while she composed her answer . . . and decided how much to reveal.

Chapter Six

After a bit of soul-searching, Ella decided to tell Ranger Pirtle nearly all she could recall about her father; The Bishop, Carl Ansil Stringfellow, elder and luminary of the Church of Jesus Christ of Latter-Day Saints . . . and high-ranking member of one of the largest and deadliest vigilance groups in the United States.

She said, "Ever hear of the Danites?"

Pirtle looked up sharply. He stopped writing in his book of notes and focused his full attention on the woman who'd just spoken aloud one of the most sinister names in all of America. His response was cautious and guarded. "Are you talkin' about The Army of Israel?"

"Very good Mr. Pirtle. That's the name they started out with, back in the 1830s. It was the Mormon militia that was formed to protect the faithful during the Missouri Mormon War and the later Extermination Order issued by Governor Lilburn Boggs. They were properly called *The Armies of Israel,* by the way, and later became known as the Danites."

"I'm no historian, but I thought they were disbanded after the Mormons left Missouri and migrated to Utah."

"That's the rumor, the myth that's been spread by the LDS

church, especially since statehood was granted in 1896. But, the truth is that the Danites are alive and well and operating all over the west. My father was one of them."

Pirtle, who was a ranking member of a respected law enforcement agency, had an awareness and some general knowledge of the Mormon vigilance organization, but was in the dark about specifics . . . the who, where and when of the group whose existence had been denied for more than half a century. He was eager to gather any intelligence on the secret cabal, but anxious not to display his excitement. He said, "And how is it, Miss Stringfellow, that you know this . . . are these facts y'all are givin' me . . . or just conjecture on your part?"

"I'm quite sure Mr. Pirtle. I'll get to it in due course. Do you know the meaning of the term *Blood Atonement*?"

"Sure. An eye-for-an-eye."

"That's close. To the faithful, it means that anyone who causes harm to any Mormon follower—a member of the Latter-Day Saints—will in turn be harmed. The offender will pay in blood. The Danites are the enforcers of that unwritten dictate. My father was instrumental in organizing and enforcing those penalties. He was a sort of high-court judge, jury and executioner."

Pirtle was watching for any sign of deceitfulness or falsehood, saw none, and said, "But your father's been dead for twenty years. How's any of that relevant now?"

Ella hesitated for a moment, looked away at the trellis, before she answered in slow and measured, precise words. "Because he set up a structure which would ensure that the organization will live on in perpetuity. The Danites will always stand ready and able to avenge any Mormon . . . anytime, anywhere . . . who's been maimed or murdered by a gentile. My father made certain that justice would always prevail and no one would be able to use the courts or outright bribery to avoid paying for their crimes."

"You mean justice in the biblical sense then, but to be determined by who, exactly?"

Ella was watching Pirtle as close and careful as he was studying her, looking to see if he believed what she was saying. *I hope so,* she thought, *I know it sounds like something out of a Jules Verne novel . . . I don't know how he's going to take this next revelation. All I can do is try. It's my best chance of ever finding Chester.* She said, "The Mormons have been persecuted mercilessly wherever they have congregated."

Pirtle cut in, "Yes. They have been. But who's doin' the decidin'?"

"I'm getting to that. My father set up a system to protect the Mormon faithful by getting as many Danites as possible appointed as deputy US Marshals."

Pirtle was dumbfounded. He stood, walked to the porch steps and leaned against one of the columns that flanked the stairs, thinking and buying time. He'd heard a lot of confessions in his years as a lawman, but nothing as fantastic as this. *If it's true,* he reminded himself. *If it's the truth, or even some part of it, it's gonna be one helluva bunch of legwork to prove or disprove it, carried out by those with impeccable records in law enforcement, as well as the implicit trust of their superior officers. Otherwise, it could destroy the public's belief in our government . . . and that right after we fought a war which killed 600,000 of our finest young men to keep and preserve the Union . . .*

He turned and went back to his seat by Ella Stringfellow, who watched him approach and waited for him to sit and make himself comfortable before she spoke. "I know it seems fantastic, but every word of it is the truth."

Pirtle looked at her and said, "To be frank, I don't know if I do, or don't, believe such an apocryphal tale. Do you have any specifics about how this audacious plan was going to be put into place?"

"I do . . . but . . . it will strain your belief system even more."

Pirtle, who was busy rolling still another cigarette in order to give himself something to do while he waited her out, said, "I'm all ears Miss Stringfellow. Tell me."

Chapter Seven

Ella poured them more tea. She took a sip and said, "Do you know the name Porter Rockwell?"

Pirtle thought for a moment and said, "A notorious man. I've heard many stories about him, some truth, mostly lies and many legends. Why do you ask?"

"Because he's an integral part of what I'm about to disclose, Mr. Pirtle. His full name was Orrin Porter Rockwell, and he was known among the Latter-Day Saints as *The Destroying Angel of Mormondom.* He was utterly devoted to the prophet, Brigham Young, and a devout member of the LDS church. He never again trimmed his hair, after Joseph Smith prophesized that Rockwell couldn't be harmed by bullets, as long as he kept the faith and didn't allow it to be cut. Porter Rockwell was Brigham Young's personal bodyguard, a relentless tracker, and a stone cold killer. He was also the deputy US Marshal for the City of Salt Lake and all of the Utah Territory, from 1849 until his death in 1878."

Pirtle took a puff of his cigarette, thought, *I'm gonna quit these damnable things before they kill me. My throat feels like it's been set on fire.* Aloud he said, "How does this history lesson have somethin' to do with what we've been talkin' about?"

"It's what gave Father the idea."

"What idea," Pirtle said, growing uneasy and impatient.

"The idea about how to protect the Latter-Day Saints and enrich the church at the same time by getting Mormon Danites appointed US Deputy Marshals in all the western territories."

Pirtle coughed into his hand to keep from laughing out loud. Then the cough took over, and he couldn't stop. Finally, with his eyes streaming, face beet red, and his throat feeling like it was ready to bleed, he managed to get control, catch a breath and take a gulp of cold tea.

"Are you all right?"

"Fine," Pirtle said, "I just had an irritation . . . a catch in my throat from smokin' too much. But tell me, Miss Stringfellow, are you serious? I have heard some wild stories in my time, but yours takes the cake. Do y'all expect me to believe that the US Marshals Service is compromised . . . infiltrated . . . by Mormon assassins?"

"That's exactly what I'm telling you Mr. Pirtle. Do you wish to hear the rest, or do you want to go back where you came from? All I desire is to find my twin brother. Which, I believe is why you showed up here today. I'm telling you about my father, and his schemes, in furtherance of finding Chester. I have not forsaken him, Mr. Pirtle. I will not deviate from my search . . . nor will I be mocked sir. You have my permission to leave at any time."

Pirtle realized he'd compromised the interview with a rookie mistake . . . by allowing his personal feelings to be involved. He said, "I beg your pardon once again Miss Stringfellow, and am forced by the exegesis of the present situation to fall back on my previous excuse of having spent too much time in the company of rough men . . ." He trailed off into silence, hoping she'd forgive his rudeness.

Ella let the silence lengthen and the tension increase for a half-minute or so before she giggled and said, "*Touché*, Mr.

Pirtle, I have heard some wildly inventive and colorful excuses in my time too, but if there was ever a prize for world-class crawfishing, you would get first place. Goodness gracious . . ."

Pirtle put on his boyish, lop-sided grin for the third time and said, "May we go on then, as if it never happened?"

"Of course. And I want you to know that on the night my father was murdered, after Marshal Pierce did his investigation, and Mr. Leech, the undertaker, had come and gone, I spent the rest of the night and most of the next two days reading and making notes in Father's offices. I wanted to know as much as possible before they came and took everything away."

"They who?" Pirtle said, "And took what exactly?"

"Some Federal Marshals and a pair of Mormon Bishops from the President's Office in Salt Lake City. They carried off every document, handwritten note, ledger, deed and scrap of paper they could find. There were half-a-dozen laborers who crated and boxed it all up, put it in a big freight wagon pulled by four draft horses and left. They even took Father's library of hunting and fishing books—which had nothing whatso-ever to do with what they were searching for. When they were done, all that remained in his office was the desk and chair, a student lamp and the bookcases. I was devastated and Mrs. Ince was terrified."

"What was she scared of . . . did she go through his papers with you?"

"Mrs. Ince could neither read, nor write, Mr. Pirtle. She was afraid of anyone who represented authority because she thought that they had come for her. She assumed they would take her somewhere and sell her into bondage again. I tried many times to explain to her that President Abraham Lincoln had freed all of them in 1863, with the Emancipation Proclamation, but she could never understand, poor soul, and lived in terror all the rest of her life."

"May I infer then, Miss Stringfellow, that you have a workin' knowledge of your father's plan and that you'll soon divulge it to me?"

"I do, Mr. Pirtle. And yes, I will."

Chapter Eight

As Pirtle was waiting for Ella to resume her narrative, he heard a scrabbling under the porch and a rustle of leaves among the flowerbeds. Then, a large black and white tom cat came bounding up the steps with a newly-expired mouse in its mouth. The feline made straight for Ella, trilling about its prize, which it laid out at her feet while proclaiming "Mee-row, mee-row, mee-row," and rubbing against her shoe.

Ella reached down and petted the demonstrating cat and said, "Good boy Duke. There's a good boy. Yes you are."

Satisfied, Duke picked up his prize and disappeared around the corner of the porch to enjoy his snack somewhere less public. Pirtle said, "Enthusiastic little critter ain't he."

Ella looked at him and said, "Do you like cats Mr. Pirtle?"

"Can't say I like or dislike 'em, but I do admire them. Nature's compact little killin' machines . . . they know their job and they're good at it, always ready to slay somethin' in an instant. I guess that qualifies me as a cat enthusiast. They're mighty entertainin' to watch go about their business, for a fact."

She sipped some of her tea, then said, "I never thought of them like that, but you're absolutely correct. Cats are not what they seem . . . all cute and cuddly, sitting on your lap purring, or washing their faces by licking their paws . . . in reality they are merciless assassins and dealers of death. My father was like that—not what he seemed—one thing on the outside and something altogether else on the inside."

Pirtle said, "We all have a public and private face."

"My father was a master of deceit. He wasn't even what he was pretending to be."

On full alert, the Ranger leaned forward in his chair. "How's that," he said.

Ella watched him come to attention. *Careful with this next part,* she thought, *be cautious, don't give it all voice.* She said, "I hardly know where to begin . . ."

"Anywhere will do," Pirtle said as he picked up his notebook and turned a fresh page.

"There's several things you should know about him. First of all, he wasn't just a land speculator. He did some of that, but his main job was trading parcels of land that the LDS church had received during the building of the first transcontinental railroad, for US Marshals appointments. It required a delicate touch, firm negotiating skills and the utmost diplomacy . . . for it was of course, an unlawful act."

"Have you any specifics?"

"No. But if I were investigating, I would look into the Governor's Offices of the Colorado, Nevada and Arizona territories—before they became states."

"Not easily done, Miss Stringfellow. I'm not a federal agent. I work for the Texas Rangers . . . officially I'm a state employee."

"Perhaps you could find out about the Marshals themselves. I would guess they're all Mormons."

"Could be," Pirtle said as he made more notes in his book. "Is that all . . . about your father?"

"No. There's more." *A lot of which I'm keeping to myself,* she thought. Aloud, she said, "It has to do with this house. The reason it's so big is because it's part of a Mormon underground railroad."

That piece of information was wholly new intelligence to the Ranger. Shifting in his chair, he said, "You mean like certain abolitionists did before the war, when they helped negroes escaping from slavery in the south get to freedom up north?"

"Precisely. That's exactly what he was doing."

"Helping blacks . . . I don't understand how that could be the war—and slavery—was over."

"Not them. Mormons. Before polygamy was officially outlawed by the church, a great many plural families opted to migrate down to Mexico and continue living as they always had. Ours was a house of refuge for those travelers. Father would bring them in late at night. They'd come up the back stairs, Mrs. Ince and my father assigned them rooms and the refugees would rest for one or two days . . . then disappear in the night, as quietly as they came."

"Why here in Cleburne?"

"Proximity to Dallas and all the train lines. There's many ways to come and go."

Pirtle frowned, looked back through several pages of his notes, and said, "You told me your father was opposed to polygamy, so why would he help them. And, secondly, what you're tellin' me took place at least twenty or twenty-five years before the practice was disavowed. Can you explain that?"

"My father was a pragmatist who didn't let his ideals get in the way of reality. He knew that the church would eventually have to do away with the practice of celestial wifery. But at the same time, he realized that public policy and private activity aren't always the same . . ."

Pirtle cut in, "You mean the LDS leaders could say that they'd outlawed multiple wives for the same man, but go ahead and do it anyway?"

"Well not exactly, and not everyone, but the church could look the other way—allow the fundamentalists for example, to continue the custom—and not enforce the law about it."

"And twenty-some years ago?"

"Father was an absolute follower, as well as an advocate of the teachings of Joseph Smith and the prophet, Brigham Young. At that time, just after the war, the forward thinkers among the brethren were concerned about the survival of the LDS church, and they came to the conclusion that the idea of celestial, or plural wives would be a flashpoint—a justification—for destroying Mormonism, so they decided to disperse some of the Saints in order that the church survive if the unthinkable happened."

"A doomsday scenario?"

"Yes. And Father was one of those who were chosen to carry it out."

Pirtle checked his notes again and put them in his pocket. He yawned and stretched and stood. He said, "Thank-you for your cooperation Miss Stringfellow—and the breakfast. It was the best I've had in quite some time."

Realizing the interview was ended, Ella also stood. "You're welcome," she said, "and you'll let me know if you find my brother . . ."

"As promised, Miss Stringfellow," Ranger Pirtle said, "just as I promised. I always keep my promises, else no one believe my threats." He put on his hat, shook her outstretched hand and started down the front steps.

Halfway there he stopped, turned to her and said, "Do you think your father and the LDS church was successful?"

"Yes. I know so. There's a thriving Fundamentalist LDS settlement in Chihuahua Province and another in Mexico City."

"And the Marshals?"

"I am positive that they are infiltrated by Mormon Danites. I would bet my life on it."

From her vantage point on the front porch, Ella Stringfellow watched Pirtle leave. She gave him a slight wave as he took his seat and untied the reins. He tipped his hat to her, gave the mare a quick slap on the rump with the harness, and just like that, he was gone. As he disappeared, she was left to wonder, *Well, Mr. Texas Ranger Special Agent Boyd Pirtle . . . will I ever see you again? . . . And if I do, will you be my ally . . . or my adversary? And as for you, my darling brother, have no doubt. I'm going to find you, no matter what it takes.*

As he drove away, Pirtle could see the woman watching from her seat on the veranda. She'd given him a wealth of facts and knowledge, but he couldn't shake the feeling she was holding back. *Whatever it is,* he thought, *it'll have a major impact on this case. She's got somethin' on her mind, or up her sleeve. I'd bet money on it.* He urged the mare on, making plans as he headed for the livery stable. He'd have to hurry to make the last train back to Austin.

Chapter Nine

As Boyd Pirtle and Ella Stringfellow were eating breakfast in Cleburne, a thousand miles to the northwest, and an hour earlier in time, the man calling himself Frank Rogers was trying to remember the exact sequence of events from the night before. He'd been mugged—beaten and robbed and left for dead—in the alley behind Gun Wa's Chinese opium den on Huerfano Street in Colorado City, where he'd been taking the pill for the last three weeks. *Whoever did it took my gold watch, my money and even my fucking shoes,* he thought as he rolled over onto his stomach and tried not to vomit from the pain.

He was almost passed out again, spread-eagled and facedown in the filth of the alleyway when a delivery wagon drove up. His route completed, the milkman, whose name was Doug Burke, was short-cutting back to the dairy on Washington Street when he spotted the supine figure. His horse snorted and seesawed its head up and down at the object in its path and the smell of blood on the air. Rogers made it to his hands and knees, just as Doug got to him. He said, "Think you can stand if I help yuh?"

"I'll try," was all Rogers could manage to croak out as the Samaritan helped him to his feet.

"Looks like they worked yuh over pretty good. There's a gash on the back of yer head, and a lump the size of a duck egg. Are ya seein' double or anythin'?"

"No," Rogers said, as he tried to get his bearings and figure out his next move. "Thanks. I think I can stand up now."

The milkman, who was at least a head taller and a hundred pounds heavier than Frank Rogers, let go. He swayed, bent over with his hands on his knees and heaved his guts out against the bricks of the adjacent building. Finished, he wiped his mouth on his sleeve and spit several times, trying to get the taste to go away.

Doug handed him a pint of cold sweet cream. "Here. Drink this. It'll coat yer belly. Make yuh feel better. Always works for me."

"Thanks," Rogers said as he took a big chug. "Do you think you could drop me at the back entrance of The Antlers?"

"It's a little outta my way, and we ain't s'posed to let nobody ride in the wagons. Company policy."

Rogers felt around inside his shirt, where the moneybelt the muggers had missed still rode low and tight on his hips. He dug in one of the pockets and extracted the contents: three silver dollars. He held them out on the palm of his hand. "I'll pay you. Those bastards took my shoes, I can't go very far in my socks without attracting attention. It's only a half-mile or so outta your way."

Doug, thought for a moment about how many glasses of beer those three silver dollars would buy. Then he took the money from the outstretched hand. "Get in the back. Stay there until I tell yuh to get out."

"Okay," Rogers said, and did as he was told.

Twenty minutes later, he stood at the back door of the hotel, watching Doug and his milk-wagon move off at a brisk trot, with a couple of hundred empty milk bottles in their crates, jiggling and tinkling and clinking together in a kind of unholy, out-of-tune

Angelus as an accompaniment. Another five minutes, and Frank Rogers had gained the sanctity of his room, thankful he hadn't been seen. He didn't have a lot of time. He had to get cleaned up and presentable before the pigeon got there. *It's gonna be close,* he thought when he saw how bad he looked in the mirror. He had a good thing going . . . and he didn't want to screw it up. He'd spotted the mark himself, and together with Delbert McKnight, who was one of the best steerers in the entire organization, they'd coaxed and massaged and stroked their patsy every day for the last three weeks. Now, he was ready to pay up, and they were going to make sure he did.

Chapter Ten

Pirtle turned the Appaloosa mare and buggy back at the livery in Cleburne, then made his way to the depot and caught a ride on a work train with some tired, sweaty section hands who'd been working on the track extension south of town and rode it all the way to Ft. Worth.

Pirtle walked a few blocks to the Stockman's Bank Building where he showed his badge and was ushered into the office of the President, Oliver Witherspoon.

As soon as he was introduced, Pirtle came right to the point. "I'd like to see your records for the account of Miss Ella Stringfellow of Cleburne, Texas."

"Rest assured sir, all is in order. I run a fully up-to-date and legal bank," Oliver Witherspoon said.

"Not my concern," Pirtle replied. "I want to know who set the monies in the account and where they came from."

"I can do that. Be happy to accommodate the Texas Rangers." Witherspoon summoned his secretary, gave him an order and the young man left and came back shortly with one of the banks huge leatherbound ledger books. He opened it on the President's desk, turned to the right page and pointed. Witherspoon put his glasses on and said, "Would you like me to read off the amounts?"

"Yes. And the corresponding bank, with an address," Pirtle said as he opened his notebook to the spot where he'd copied Ella Stringfellow's deposits.

"Well the second part's easy. All the monies were sent from the same place: The Mining Exchange Bank in Colorado Springs. All remitted by Chester Stringfellow."

After confirming that all of the deposits matched, Pitle thanked Oliver Witherspoon and took his leave of the bank. He hurried back to the train station and hopped aboard the shuttle back to Dallas.

There wasn't much conversation once the hard-drinking laborers figured out that he was a lawman, which suited Pirtle just fine. It gave him time to think and go over his notes. He'd gone to Cleburne on a hunch after seeing the advertisement in the Ft. Worth newspaper and it had paid off big. He'd garnered a wealth of information about the elusive and murderous Frank Rogers, aka Chester Stringfellow. More in fact, than he'd learned in the previous four years, since the outlaw had dropped out of sight after the botched bank robbery and gun battle in the cattle town of Clarendon, in the fall of 'ninety-seven. Saints Roost, as the place was called by the cowboys, would never be the same.

As the Baldwin 4-4-0 pulled out of Dallas for the four hour trip to Austin, Pirtle was sitting on a pile of letter bags in the mail car watching a pair of clerks sorting the correspondence, and organizing his thoughts. One of the benefits the Texas Rangers enjoyed at that time—in gratitude for all the train robberies they'd thwarted—was free transport on all trains in the country, just by showing their badges and identifying themselves. But the railroad operators were also notoriously cheap, and they weren't about to give away any of the prime Pullman car seats to free riders, Texas Rangers or not.

Pirtle had learned a lot from Ella Stringfellow, but how much of it was truth, and actionable? *It's sure as hell gonna cause an uproar in the Texas Rangers,* he thought, *when I tell Captain Newton that the U.S. Marshal's service may in fact be compromised in four or more western states. Sweet Jesus on a bicycle . . . what a helluva mess . . .* It made his head hurt to think about. He shifted his weight around and leaned into the corner to give his back some relief and fell asleep to the monotonous and repetitive *clickity-clack, clickity-clack, clickity-clack* of the rails. He slept, and dreamed.

Pirtle couldn't see the riders coming into town, as they were backlit by the mid-morning sun . . . but he felt the thundering of sixteen pairs of steel-shod hooves, heard the jingle of eight pair of spurs, together with the creak of saddle and gunleather . . . and he smelled the rankness of unwashed men, old trail dust, and the stinking sweat that comes from horses that've been rode too hard, and too far, for far too long.

All at once, Pirtle had a big single-action army Colt .44 caliber pistol in his right hand as he watched, and waited, and tried to swallow his fear, and felt a single drop of sweat drip from his left armpit, and do a slow waltz down his side, in anticipation of the gun fight that was about to break out like the sudden call of a lost and broken heart.

Then Pirtle was on the street with the risen sun in his face, eight riders were bearing down on him at full gallop, their guns directed his way and about to fire . . .

Pirtle couldn't see, the sun was too bright, and as he tried to raise his pistol, there was no trigger . . . he couldn't shoot at the horsemen, about to run him down . . .

One of the mail clerks was nudging him awake. "Mr. Pirtle. Mr. Pirtle. We're here. It's Austin. We're in Austin."

Pirtle, who always woke in an instant, was slow to rouse. He finally stood, just as the screeching of the drive wheels announced that they'd arrived on home ground. He said, "Thanks. Much obliged," to the clerk and hopped down on the platform like a much younger man. He'd wired Captain Newton of his arrival time, and that he had a wealth of information to sift through. So it was no surprise to Pirtle, when he found his boss waiting on the platform.

Captain Wiley Newton was frowning as he strode down the depot toward his number one Special Agent. "Boyd," he said, "I know its past suppertime and you've had a long day, but you've got me worried. How about I buy you somethin' to eat and you can tell me what the hell's goin' on. Your wire sounded ominous."

"It was in a way, but I didn't intend it to be. The Stringfellow woman positively identified Frank Rogers as her brother, Chester."

The two Rangers exited the train station and walked down the unpaved street to a cafe, where they had well-done steaks with Spanish rice and beans, warm flour tortillas and coffee, while Pirtle disclosed the details of his interview with Ella Stringfellow.

Captain Newton, who was quiet, had no questions, and listened attentively to the first repetition, made Pirtle go over a few of the details on the second time, then started grilling him on the third recital. "Are you sure she was tellin' you the truth?"

"Yeah, as she knows it anyway. I don't believe she was disclosin' everythin' though. I keep feelin' she was holdin' back somethin'."

"Any idea what?"

"No. It's just a hunch on on my part."

"I gotta say, Boyd, your presentiment about that ad in the Ft. Worth paper was a real longshot . . ."

"Paid off though didn't it? It's the best lead I've had about Frank Rogers since the robbery in Clarendon. If only I hadn't been in court with them other three in Ft. Worth, I might'a caught that murderous son-of-a-bitch."

"Yeah, and he might have bushwhacked and killed you up in the Oklahoma territories too."

"It's always bothered me," Pirtle said as he rolled an after-dinner cigarette, "how Rogers just disappeared like that."

"Well you've drawed a bead on him now. I'm sendin' you to Colorado the day after tomorrow and I'm sendin' Will Posey with ya."

"Thanks. Will deserves to be in on the arrest. But, what about the Mormans?"

Captain Newton looked up at the ceiling and blew out a long breath that was an equal part sigh. He looked back at Pirtle and held his gaze as he said, "In all honesty Boyd, I don't have a clue right now. It's so damned sensitive and politically hot, I think I'll go see the governor."

"He ain't exactly the bold and decisive type."

"No. He ain't. But tellin' 'im'll give the Texas Rangers cover for our asses when the shit hits the fan. You do realize don'tcha, how explosive this information is?"

"I do, Cap'n. It's all I been thinkin' about since I first heard it . . . that and catchin' the fugitive sonofabitch who's callin' himself Frank Rogers." *The fact of the matter too, is that I keep thinkin' of his sister, Ella. She flits through my mind at the oddest of times . . . like now.*

Chapter Eleven
1897

Four years earlier, things weren't so good for Frank Rogers or his men. After the gang had been *Shot all to hell trying to rob that chickenshit little bank up in Clarendon,* as Doroteo put it, the survivors split up. Arango and his sidekick, Tomás Urbina, jumped a Fort Worth & Denver City freight train and rode it all the way to El Paso, where they melted across the border into Juarez and disappeared in the vast Sonoran Desert of their native Mexico. Thereafter, they set themselves up as bandits, with headquarters in the northern Sierra Madre Mountains, from where they rode out periodically to terrorize, loot and pillage the banks, *haciendas* and *rancheros* of Mexico's wealthy upperclasses in a dress rehearsal for the soon to come revolution, when the whole world would learn their names.

Two members of the Rogers Gang—Bill Davis and Jack Lacey—were shot dead during the botched holdup. Three others were caught in Ft. Worth, Texas, where they were tried, convicted and hung for the killing of a Texas Ranger named Billy Joe Hasty and Pinkerton Detective Agent, M.E. Fields, in the same attempted bank robbery and shootout.

Frank Rogers himself, thanks to an amazing amount of blind

luck, escaped into the Oklahoma Territory. He had a saddlebag stuffed with the only cash taken in the robbery . . . about nine hundred dollars . . . *And not near enough for all the time and effort, or the blood sweat and tears we put into it,* Frank thought, *let alone gettin' our asses shot off by them Rangers that were layin' in wait for us.*

Frank Rogers was smart enough to know he had to change if he was going to survive. He new that a Ranger named Boyd Pirtle, the man who was in the middle of the ambush that decimated the gang, was relentless, and had a reputation for always catching his man. He thought, *As soon as Pirtle's done testifyin' in Ft. Worth, he'll be after me like a hound on the hunt . . . but twice as mean, and tireless as a demon, straight outta Hell.*

Rogers slowly made his way from north Texas to Oklahoma City avoiding all human contact along the way in fear of being recognized. There was a price on his head and he couldn't afford to take chances. As soon as he arrived, Rodgers started the process of renewing himself from a rough-cut cowboy fresh out of the mesquite and chaparral, into a modern city-dwelling man. He sold his horse and saddle outright, pawned his chaps, spurs and saddlebags and never went back to redeem them. Then he bathed, got his clothes washed and ironed, shaved his beard and trimmed his mustache, and had his hair cut and parted in the middle. He traded his sweat-stained cowboy hat for a fashionable black derby, which, along with the clear lens wire-framed spectacles, made him an altogether different looking man than the uncouth renegade who'd come to town only two days earlier. He bought a large brown leather Gladstone bag and checked into a cheap downtown hotel using the name Ralph Stuart.

The next day, Ralph Stuart went to the best men's haberdashery in the city. There he ordered two suits, four white shirts and celluloid collars, underwear, three assorted silk ties, socks and a pair of kidskin leather high-button shoes. When he was fitted for the suit coat, he requested it to be extra roomy under the left arm . . . in order to facilitate the cross-draw pistol and shoulder harness he'd be wearing there. The tailor was happy to accommodate him. It was an ordinary request after all, and he'd done it on the sly for many others.

While his clothes were being tailored, and still using the name Ralph Stuart, Frank Rogers went shopping for weapons. He went to a second, different pawn shop where he traded his Winchester rifle for an evil little .44 caliber nickel-plated and engraved derringer with ivory grips. The man in the pawn shop, whose name was Levi Flesher, said, "It's the finest belly-gun I've ever had. I should be getting twice as much for it."

"Yeah, sure." Ralph Stuart said, "And I oughta be gettin' thirty times as much for the rifle too."

The conversation went back and forth like that for a little while, with the final result being that Levi threw in a box of ammunition, a nine-inch Balinese throwing knife and a worn ten-dollar gold piece; and then a reluctant Ralph Stuart, aka Frank Rogers, surrendered his 1873 Winchester lever-action .30-.40 rifle with the octagon barrel. In terms of value received, in his opinion, Frank got only slightly more in worth than the Lenape Indians received from Peter Minuit for Manhattan Island. *But, oh shit,* he thought, *I can't carry it around anymore if I'm gonna be a city-slicker . . . I just hate to give it up. It's been a part of me ever since I took it off that lady pilgrim down in west Texas.*

Ralph Stuart's last stop of the day was at Trapper's Guns and Ammunition. After talking with the clerk for the sake of appearance, he purchased a shoulder holster rig and a lightweight .38 caliber Smith & Wesson double-action revolver. The blued steel pistol came with a three-inch barrel and checked walnut grips. It was a piece that came into his hand with ease and concealed itself nicely under his arm. Ralph left Trapper's quite pleased with himself, and wearing his new concealed weapon. He was certain that he was unrecognizable from the furtive and trail-worn desperado who'd come to town only a couple of days earlier.

The following morning, after a greasy breakfast at the adjoining cafe and bar across the street from the hotel, Ralph Stuart paid his hotel bill in full, checked out . . . and disappeared. He was never seen again.

That afternoon a dapper-looking gent named Frank Rogers was dropped off by a hansom cab at the swank Palace Hotel, where he signed in for a stay of two or three days, while he took care of some personal business. He listed his home address as San Antonio, Texas and his occupation as Real Estate Broker. He was given a room on the third floor with a view of the street, and treated as an honored guest . . . not the fugitive who was wanted for robbery and murder in Texas, New Mexico and Arizona. For the time being at least, he was a prosperous businessman and an honest citizen. He had a bit over six hundred dollars to his name and the clothes on his back, as the bellman carried his baggage and escorted Mr. Frank Rogers of Texas to his room. *But, that's all about to change,* he thought, *and soon.* His next goal was to increase the money in his pocket, because Frank knew . . . whatever respectability he now enjoyed would disappear in less than a heartbeat if he ran out of money. He intended to make absolutely certain it never happened. Never again, as long as he lived, would he be broke.

Chapter Twelve

Three days later, Frank Rogers was looking for a score. He was down to his last five hundred in cash, had a thousand-dollar—and growing—bill at the ostentatious Palace Hotel in Oklahoma City, and no prospects for adding to his bankroll. He'd been looking high and low for a game, or a sporting event where he could either *Take 'em at the tables,* he thought, *or catch 'em afterwards and relieve them of the burdens associated with too much money, before this new lifestyle ruptures me.*

That afternoon, the Bell Captain stopped him in the lobby. "Excuse me sir," he said, after looking around, and making sure he wouldn't be overheard. "Are you the gentleman who was looking for a game of chance?"

"I'm a poker player," Frank Rogers said. "Poker's a game of skill, not chance, by the way."

"Sorry sir. My mistake. I believe there are several others who are interested in starting a game—a high stakes enterprise— sometime this evening in the hotel. It'll be a gentleman's game, with drinks and sandwiches, ice and towels all provided by myself and one of my trusted associates."

"How trusted?"

"Very. We've done this before."

"Security . . ."

"Several of the players have their own, and of course the hotel itself is quite well guarded. But in addition, both myself and my associate will take precautions and act as lookouts. I should also tell you, that he's been a professional prize fighter as well. The game—and the players—will be as safe as babes in their beds."

Unless you fuckers are planning on knocking it over, Frank thought. Aloud he said, "What's the buy-in? And is it cash only?"

"Yes. The minimum one should come with is a thousand dollars, cash or gold coin. Either is acceptable."

"Not a problem. Dealers?"

"Two, in alternating two-hour shifts, both provided and vetted, by myself. They are above reproach; both of them are known to me and used before. They're paid from a five-dollar house ante from each pot, which goes to the promoter of the event."

"Which is . . ."

"Myself."

"Count me in."

"Very good, sir. We will commence at nine o'clock sharp. No one is admitted after nine-oh-five."

"Where's it at?"

"Be in your room at eight-thirty. We'll let you know."

"I'm looking forward to it. And by the way, how many other players may I expect?"

The Bell Captain gave him the stink-eye, for the indecorous question and said, "Never less than ten, nor more than twenty. The table itself is limited to seven players."

Frank ignored the slight and asked, "The cards?"

"Provided by myself . . . in fresh, new cellophane factory-sealed packs."

"See you later then," Frank Rogers said, as the Bell Captain came to attention, gave a short bow, turned and went back to his station at the front desk.

Frank watched him walk away, then headed for the street. He needed some fast cash . . . and he knew just where to get it . . . one way or another.

* * *

Levi Flesher was at his desk behind the oak display case that ran down the length of the pawnshop, eating a liverwurst and onion sandwich, when he saw the man come marching up the sidewalk and into his place of business. Wiping his hands on the cloth napkin his wife had wrapped his lunch in, he stood, turned and greeted the man he knew as Ralph Stuart. "Back already? What can I help you with today my friend."

"We ain't friends," Ralph, alias Frank, whose real name was Chester, said. "I need a thousand dollars."

Levi, who assessed everyone coming into the shop for potential threats, knew when he saw one . . . and he could tell that Ralph was pulsing with pent-up energy and anger. Levi pushed the hidden switch that connected to several dry cell batteries, which rang a small bell, and summoned Gort from his office in the back, where he was cleaning and repairing gold and silver jewelry.

Gort Bortosky was orthodox—a Hasidic, observant Jew— and an expert in all facets of gemology. He could grade and cut diamonds, and he was a genius at identifying any precious or semi-precious gemstones on planet earth . . . a most useful skill in a pawn brokerage. But his main assets to Levi were his great size, strength, and formidable appearance . . . plus the fact that he was utterly fearless . . . and a man who was at ease when blood-letting was called for. He'd been captured and tortured by a band of vicious Ukrainian Cossacks looking for treasure during one of the endless pogroms over in Crimea, but Gort was able to escape when he killed several of his captors with his bare hands. After escaping, he made his way to America, where he met and headed out west with Levi, who'd become like a surrogate father. At six-foot-eight-inches tall and three- hundred-and-forty pounds, with obsidian eyes, long unkempt hair and a barbarians lengthy beard, Gort was a fearsome character who commanded the attention of all in his presence. When the bell tolled, he stopped what he was doing, picked up his war tools and headed up front. Levi needed him.

"Well you've come to the right place," Levi said, "I'm in the money lending business. And what may I ask, do you have for collateral?"

"I don't have anythin," Ralph Stuart said, "except for a guarantee."

"I don't make loans . . . to anyone . . . unless they have surety. If you have no item to pledge, than I have no money to lend."

"Well, you ain't heard the guarantee yet."

"There's no assurance you could possibly make that I'd be interested in hearing."

"How about this. Give me the thousand dollars I need, and I'll guarantee that your place don't get burned down."

"Is that a threat? Are you threatening me?"

"No. Threat goes like this: *Refuse me the money and I'll guarantee that your place gets burnt to the ground. Probably in the next day or two.* See now, what a threat sounds like?"

"Oh I know quite well what threats and extortions are Mr. Stuart," Levi Flesher said as he turned and walked to the rear of his shop—under the watchful eye of Ralph Stuart—and threw back a set of three huge deadbolts that covered the face of a robust and reinforced oak door. He opened it, and out stepped the biggest human being that Frank Rogers had ever seen. "Meet Gort. He's my insurance policy."

Chapter Thirteen

"Well, he may be eight feet tall, but is he bullet-proof?" And just like magic, a cocked .38 caliber pistol appeared in Frank Rogers right hand, aimed in Levi's general direction. "Is he tougher than a couple of these, right between the eyes?"

"No. He's not," Levi said, "but I can assure you that before you could make good on your threat, Gort would put at least one, and possibly as many as three, very large holes somewhere between your neck and your nuts."

That's when Rogers, who'd been staring at the huge man's head and face, looked down and saw the big S&W pistol in his left hand, held close to his thigh and a short-handled, double-bladed throwing axe in his right. Without hesitation, Frank shot him in the face three times. Gort was dead before he'd cleared the door to the back room.

Levi was looking on in horror when Rogers put a 125 grain chunk of lead into his left clavicle, where, after breaking the bone, it calved off into two pieces. The smaller one was deflected downward, where it sliced through the upper lobe of the old man's left lung, nicked the aortic arch, and came to rest in the right ventricle of his heart. The heavier, primary particle exited posteriorly, destroying most of his left scapula, and rendering Levi's arm useless. In exquisite pain, with only moments left to live, the last thing seventy-five year old Levi Flesher heard was the voice of his killer: "Shudda give me the goddamned money."

Frank Rogers walked back to the doorway. He needed to be certain that the terrifying *golem* was disarmed, and dead. He took the .45 caliber pistol from Gort's left hand and stuck it in his own waistband, then he pried the axe from Gort's other hand and stuck it in the big man's head. Finally, Rogers administered the *coup de grâce* to Levi with the confiscated hand-cannon and jammed it back in his waistband. He locked the front door, put up the "CLOSED" sign and pulled down all the front window shades. Frank found a near-new black alligator doctors bag among the sale items, and proceeded to loot the pawn shop of all the cash and gold and silver coins he could find. After throwing it all in the bag, Rogers turned his attention to the still warm bodies of his victims. He got only some small bills and change from Gort, but Levi was a whole different story.

Going through the old man's pockets, Rogers found wads of bills of varying amounts and denominations in each one. Not stopping to count, stuffing it all into the alligator doctor bag as fast as he grabbed it; Frank hit the mother lode as he was stealing the old man's gold watch and chain. That's when he discovered the money belt; overflowing with twenty and fifty dollar gold pieces and large denomination banknotes . . . it was a fortune. *And it beats the shit out of robbin' banks,* Rogers thought, as he crammed it in with the rest of the take.

Satisfied, he stepped over the bodies one last time without so much as a glance at them, and exited the back door into the alley. He locked up using Levi's keys and walked down to the street. Frank Rogers was on his way to play poker, with a pirate's ransom in a bag, after inadvertently leaving a fortune in diamonds, rubies and emeralds lying around on Gort's workbench.

Whistling as he walked back to The Palace Hotel, Rogers tossed the keys off the first bridge he crossed, down into a turgid and muddy-looking stream. He made it to his room in time to clean up and take a short nap before enjoying a light, room service supper and changing into his most fashionable new clothes. He was ready and waiting by a quarter after eight and spent the next half-hour filing his fingernails and thinking about the odds of drawing various hands with six other players at the table. Satisfied at last that his fingertips were as sensitive as he could make them, Rogers started fretting about his escort. *Where are those guys . . .*

By eight forty-five he was getting restless. *The Bell Captain said he'd be in my room at eight-thirty, so what's keepin' 'em . . .*

At five minutes until nine, Frank figured it was all over. *I guess they're gonna stiff me. No poker tonight.*

Then someone knocked at the door.

Chapter Fourteen

Not knowing what to expect, Rogers opened the door and found the Bell Captain standing at attention in his red and black monkey suit. He said, "Are we ready sir?"

"I thought you said eight-thirty."

"No sir. I said, *be in your room* at that hour."

Frank had put his time to productive use. The doctors bag with his cash and all the stolen gold and silver coins, three pistols and extra shirts and socks, was locked and nestled inside the Gladstone bag he checked in with. It, in turn, was locked and left in the closet with his freshly cleaned spare suit and the washed and ironed outdoor riding clothes he'd come to town in. He'd learned, in the course of his years on the run, that the best place to hide things was in plain sight. That, plus the fact it was an upscale hotel, led him to believe his goods would still be there when he returned. He was carrying twelve hundred dollars in cash in his wallet inside his suit coat, a like amount was concealed in each tightly-laced high button shoe, and for good measure the flat, double-bladed Balinese throwing knife was taped to his left forearm with adhesive plaster. "Okay." he said, as he stepped into the hallway, hung a 'DO NOT DISTURB' sign on the knob and locked the door carefully. "Let's go. I'm ready to play some cards."

"Very good sir. If you'll follow me," the Bell Captain said, and set off at a rapid pace for the stairs at the end of the hall. They climbed two stories to the Presidential Suite and prepared to enter through an unmarked, and ornate carved rosewood double-door that was flanked by a pair of behemoths in police uniforms who both wore identical handlebar mustaches on their upper lips and scowls on their faces.

The copper on the left told Rogers to hold his arms out to his sides and proceeded to frisk him for weapons. Finding none, because he failed to notice the knife taped to Frank's forearm, the copper nodded to the Bell Captain, and the one on the right opened the door. "Thanks Andrew. This is the last one. Nobody else comes in. You and Denny can sit if you want, and I'll have one of the bar girls bring you some sandwiches and beer in a little while. There's no pisser on this floor other than the one in the suite, so don't go overboard on the beer, 'cause it's five stories down and five stories back up, and I want both'a you on the door. Stay sharp. We ain't expectin' trouble, but you never know. There's a bunch of cash in there . . ."

Andrew, the one holding the door said, "Don't worry none, Mack. We'll do our job."

The Bell Captain nodded. He and Frank Rogers went inside as the big copper closed the door behind them. "Mack?" Rogers asked.

"My name," Mack, the Bell Captain answered. "This will be a gentleman's game tonight, so we'll use chips. Bank and cashier are over there, with the guy in the striped shirt. Bar's on the left and sandwich stuff's right next to it. Enjoy yourself."

Frank Rogers lit a cheroot, walked up to the cashier and bought a thousand bucks worth of ivory playing chips, which came in a wooden rack. He carried them to the end of the bar, where he stood for awhile, drinking a glass of beer and surveying the room, sizing up everyone in attendance.

I'm not sure this place could be knocked off with less than eight or ten men, he thought. *There's three goons that I can see with guns under their arms, plus Mack and his 'associate,' whoever that is, and the pair of coppers out front. And that's just the ones I can make . . . but I ain't got a gang no more anyhow. Better start sizin' up the competition, and remember to stay in character too.* Frank reminded himself as he watched the seven players at the table.

It took another two hours for a place to open up and Rogers to sit down to play. The dealers changed—Dolly, the young blonde woman who'd been dealing—got up, thanked the players and walked over to the bar where a glass of lemon soda pop was being poured over ice for her.

The man who replaced her in the dealers chair was so average-looking, he could have been Frank Rogers brother. *We both have on fake eyeglasses and hair-parted down the middle,* Frank thought as he took his seat. *No surprise either, it's the middle one. I'll lay ten-to-one, both these dealers are card mechanics, and twelve-to-one that I come up a winner for the first hour or so . . .*

Frank nodded to the players as he sat down, got mostly grunts, or no recognition in return.

The dealer announced, "My name is Smitty and we'll play either five or seven card stud. The button man will call one or the other and pass it to his left. This is the button," he held up a round, black stone that had been flattened on the bottom and said, "and he, is the first to call." Smitty put the obsidian token in front of Frank Rogers.

"Seven," Rogers said as he passed the button to the balding man with a clipped military mustache on his left.

"The man calls seven. The ante is twenty dollars and the bets are table stakes," Smitty said as he opened a new deck, took out the jokers and fanned the cards—face up to show that they were a complete set—flipped them back over with a casual flick of his wrist, shuffled up and offered the deck to the man on his right, who was chewing tobacco and spitting in a brass spittoon on the floor. The 'baccy-chewer cut the cards and slid them back to the dealer, who showed the top card, the eight of diamonds, then buried it in the bottom of the deck and dealt the first hand. The game was under way and the chips were falling

A little more than six and a-half hours later, Frank Rogers was broke on his ass . . . *I've been gutted, scalded and plucked like a fuckin' chicken,* he thought, *and without one fuckin' idea as to how they did it.*

Chapter Fifteen

Just past six o'clock in the morning Frank Rogers was back in his room, formulating his plans. He wasn't quite as broke as he'd made himself out to be in the penthouse poker game. He'd lost all the chips he bought and the two hundred in cash from his pocket. The last thing he threw in—and lost—was the old ten dollar gold piece he got in part trade for the Winchester rifle. It was such a convincing act that he almost felt sorry for himself and worked up a tear or two as he took leave of the game he first meant to rob.

Counting up, Rogers still had all the cash he'd stuffed in his shoes, and in addition to that, another eleven-hundred dollars, mostly in gold and silver coins in the alligator doctor's bag. His bill at the hotel was approaching fifteen hundred and change, a sum which he had no intention of paying. He washed and shaved, put on a clean shirt and tie, the shoulder harness with the .38 caliber pistol, and his clean pressed suit. The dirty one went into the hotel laundry bag, which he left on the rumpled and unmade bed. He put on his derby hat, adjusted his eyeglasses and left the room with the small bag in hand.

Downstairs in the lobby, he stopped at the front desk, showed his room key, and said, "Please have the bag of clothes on the bed cleaned and ironed. I'll be all out all day today, concluding my business here, so kindly have my bill ready . . . I'll be checking out tomorrow morning."

"Certainly sir. As you wish," the night desk clerk said, while Frank Rogers turned and left through the front door of the glitzy Palace Hotel. He walked a few blocks down the street to the train station where, after checking the departures he purchased a first-class ticket to Denver. It was on an over-nighter, scheduled to arrive at eleven am local time, the following day.

Frank left Oklahoma City at nine o'clock that morning, enjoying a champagne breakfast with white-glove service in the dining car while the epic poker game went on back at the Palace Hotel—where the bursar was busy calculating a historic bill—and where, a mile and a-half away, in a closed, locked and shuttered storefront pawn shop, the savaged bodies of Levi Flescher and his henchman, Gort Bortosky, were waiting to be discovered.

Chapter Sixteen

Boyd Pirtle and another Ranger named Will Posey both survived the gunfight in Clarendon, but were forever affected by it. Pirtle blamed himself for the loss of two men and the escape of the three ringleaders: Rogers, Arango and Urbina. He promised his dead brothers-in-arms that he'd never give up trying to bring the three escapees to justice. *I'll not stop hunting until they're all dead or in jail,* he thought, *or I'm in the dirt myself.* Pirtle was unscathed in body, but his psyche was affected by what he considered a debt of honor . . . an obligation that could only be paid in blood . . .

Will Posey was a young man in his early twenties and a new recruit into the Rangers. The action at the Farmers and Merchants Association Bank in Clarendon was his first taste of the kind of violence that would infuse the rest of his working life as a lawman, and he rose to the occasion with all the temerity of a young man, but at the same time, the self confidence and courage of an older, more experienced fighter. It was Ranger Posey who held the mortally wounded Billy Joe Hasty as he lay dying and comforted him until he passed.

It was only then, as the pain set in when the shock wore off, that he realized he'd taken a bullet to his left leg. An in and out wound, the slug bounced off his femur, just above the knee . . . and left him with constant pain and a limp, all the rest of his days. But his valor during the attempted robbery and gun-battle earned him the respect of every Ranger in Texas—as well as a permanent soft spot in the heart of Boyd Pirtle. Clarendon was their first action together, and it happened due to pure chance, rather than great management.

The truth is, the Rangers got lucky. When two of them down in El Paso killed a couple of renegade Apaches and a Mexican bandit who'd been attacking, robbing and raping their way across southwest Texas and northern Mexico, they managed to capture a fourth member of the gang alive. He tried to make a deal with the Rangers: information for freedom. With no promises made, he spilled his guts.

The outlaw's name was Malone, Francis Malone, and he said that an eight man gang, headed by an American named Frank Rogers and a Mexican by the name of Arango were on their way up to a North Texas town to rob the richest bank in the state.

"And how is it y'all've come by this information," one Ranger said.

" 'Cuz I was supposed to go with 'em."

"Why didn't you?"

"Got too damn drunk. I was shacked up with a pair a whores. Sisters, they was . . . and what one didn't think of, the other one did. I was havin' one helluva time for myself, 'till I run outta money. Then, them nasty bitches threw me out on my ass. I was broke, hungover and near naked, all I had on was my boots, hat and union suit. When I tried to go back for my shirt 'n' pants, and gunbelt, them crazy wenches laughed and shot at me with my own damn pistol. It was embarassin' as hell. Humiliatin' too.

The Ranger, whose name was Randy Buckner, tried not to laugh. He said, "You ain't much of a desperado from the sound of it."

"Why don'cha untie me and we'll go at it with guns. Or knives," Malone spat. "I ain't drunk now."

"And I ain't stupid neither. What about the Rogers bunch?"

"They left without me. I believe Frank would of had one of them mesicans cut my throat if they'd found me."

"Where's this rich bank they're gonna rob, and when, and how'd they know about it anyhow?"

"Jeeze . . . that's a lotta questions. Can I have a cigarette, and y'all goin' to let me go after I tell, right?"

"Juan," Randy said to the other Ranger, who was putting a couple of sticks of wood on their camp fire, "would you give Malone here one of your hand-rolled?"

"Waste of tobacco if you ask me," Ranger Juan Medina said. But he rolled up a thin smoke, lit it with a twig from the campfire and stuck it in the corner of the captive's mouth.

"There's your smoke. Now talk," Buckner said, "we've got a ways to go yet."

"All I heard was that it's someplace called 'Saints Roost.' Rogers knew about it 'cause of his religious connections down in Mexico. Wherever that place is, they got a lot of money. Church money, farmer and cattle money too."

The pair of Rangers locked eyes. Juan Medina said, "What religious connections, Francis?"

For the first time, anger flashed in the outlaws eyes and he said, "Yuh want me t'talk, don't call me that."

"OK, Malone. Same question."

The outlaw took a last drag on the smoke, inhaled deep and spat the butt into the embers of the fire. Then he said, "Rogers is a Mormon. One a them kind with more than one wife. There's a whole bunch of 'em livin' down in Mexico."

Randy Buckner said, "Last question. When's this big holdup goin' to take place?"

"Don't know 'zactly, but soon. All eight of 'em was headin' up north last I heard. You goin' to cut me loose now? I told you everythin'. There ain't no more. Yuh gotta let me go."

"After what you and them three done," Juan Medina said, as he pointed with his chin at the corpses tied facedown on their horses in a picket line between two mesquite trees. "No. I don't think so."

"Aw, shit. You promised, goddammit. You said . . . awww fuck . . . fuck me runnin', I should of known better than trust a law man," Malone said, as he tried to struggle out of the rope and knots which bound him.

"That's enough," Buckner said and pulled Frances Malone to his feet, and then pointed him toward the waiting horses. "We got another fifteen miles before we make it to El Paso." He stood the captive on the bank of the dry creek they'd stopped to rest beside, while Juan Medina led Malone's horse over in the empty stream bed, so he could mount up with his hands tied behind his back.

Randy Buckner kicked dust on the campfire and climbed up on the big roan gelding with three white stockings on its legs, and took hold of the picket line with the three attached horses and their bloody cargo. He said, "OK Juan. Take the lead, I'll ride drag and keep an eye on Mr. Malone."

"You'd better," Malone said through clenched teeth as Ranger Juan Medina jerked both horses into motion.

As a gibbous and shining moon rose up in a crystalline night sky, it looked down on the silver desert, watching a half-dozen horses set off together on an unknown mission, headed for an unknown destination . . . three of them carried the quick . . . and three were conductors of the dead.

Hours later the moon was setting, and the six-horse caravan was making its way into a still and sleeping town, carrying one less of the quick, and one more of the dead.

The official report of the incident was brief:

> Prisoner under escort, Francis Malone, was shot
> and killed by Rangers Buckner and Medina,
> while attempting to effect an escape . . .

It was signed and dated, witnessed, and stamped with an official embossing seal of the State of Texas, then filed away and forgotten. Juan Medina best expressed the official attitude that night over beers with Randy Buckner when he said, "Shit, them bastards wudda hung anyway. Just think of all the money we saved the state of Texas . . ."

Chapter Seventeen

Boyd Pirtle was in Amarillo when the telegram came from Captain Newton. He ordered Pirtle to go to the panhandle town of Clarendon as fast as possible, and take charge of a pair of Rangers and a Pinkerton man who were awaiting the arrival of a pack of eight or more outlaws, led by the notorious Frank Rogers. Word had been received at Ranger Headquarters in Austin that a holdup was imminent at the Farmers and Merchants Association Bank, and it was just the break Pirtle had been hoping for. He'd pursued the renegade Frank Rogers and his accomplices, Arango and Urbina, for many months without success. He'd been so close—oh, so close—to capturing or killing them a few times, but the outlaws were always one step ahead of him.

Pirtle was on an eastbound train within an hour of receiving the telegram.

Finally, Pirtle thought, as he slipped into the mail car for the ninety mile ride to Clarendon, *I've finally got a chance to get in front of that murderin' bastard. We'll see if the sorry sonofabitch can slip away again . . . with me layin' in wait for him.* Two hours later, Ranger Boyd Pirtle was met at the Clarendon, Texas train station by a man in a white cotton flannel suit.

Pirtle had pitched his small travel bag onto the platform and was climbing out of the mail car when someone said, "I'll take that." Boyd turned and was greeted by a well-dressed young man who stood a head taller than himself. The big boy stuck out his right hand and said, "You must be Special Agent Pirtle. My name is Will Posey."

"How long you been a Ranger son?" Pirtle asked, as he shook the young giant's hand.

"Almost ten weeks, sir."

"Seen any action yet."

"No. I haven't. But I ain't scared."

"You will be, before we're done here. Well, lead on MacDuff. Let's go get those law breakers."

Posey started down the platform with the carpet bag in hand. "Who's Mack Duff? He a Ranger from Austin or El Paso?"

"Naw. He's too old to be a Ranger, but he's a warrior, for a fact. You ever hear of William Shakespeare, or a king named MacBeth?'

"No. I ain't."

"Well, no matter. Can you read an' write? Can you cipher . . . do your sums?"

"I can do a little. Never went past third grade. Pa died. We moved. Had to take a job an' help my ma.'"

"Well, we'll work on that some after we get them desperados."

Will Posey squared his shoulders and walked with pride. He said, "I can shoot good with rifle, pistol or shotgun . . . and I can fight like a sonofabitch with my fists."

"You're just the kind of man we need," Pirtle said as they exited the train station and mounted the pair of horses Posey had waiting for them.

The Farmers and Merchants Bank stood on the corner of First and Jefferson Streets, catty-corner from the First Methodist Church, whose spire could be seen from everywhere in town.

Pirtle said, "Have y'all posted a lookout up yonder, in the church steeple?"

"Yep," Posey said. "Mr. Fields, the Pinkerton man put a couple of local lads up there yesterday afternoon."

"To do what, exactly?"

"Ring the bell, sound the alarm when a group of riders shows up."

"How far is the bank, from the train station?" Pirtle said, as he turned his horse in a slow circle, trying to get a sense of the layout of the place.

"It's about five minutes, walkin' or ridin' slow."

"Where's the Pinkerton man and Billy Joe Hasty?"

"At the bank."

"Let's go there," Pirtle said as his horse snorted and backed up, eager to be on the move. It took just the barest touch of the riders heel to set the pale beast in motion.

A few miles to the south, on the blackland prairie amongst a copse of cottonwood, bur oak and horse apple trees that grew along a small stream, a company of larcenous and rough men settled down for their last night of bivouac together on the trail. They'd attack the richest bank in the state first thing in the morning.

Chapter Eighteen

They came into Clarendon riding two abreast with the mid-morning sun backlighting them, just like Frank had laid it out the night before. With Rogers himself and another bad-ass named Jack Lacey in the lead, the outlaws rode right up to the front doors of the Farmers and Merchants Association Bank, as precise and pretty as George Armstrong Custer leading the Seventh Cavalry to the Little Big Horn. When Lacey and Rogers dismounted and entered the bank with pistols drawn, four of the outlaws peeled off to take up positions at the sides and rear, while the Mexicans, Arango and Urbina, covered them all with long guns from concealed fire posts across the street. It was all going great—until it wasn't—until gunfire erupted inside the bank, and all Hell got tapped with a four-inch auger.

Jack Lacey yelled, "This is a holdup," and fired one round into the ceiling. Frank Rogers crashed into the teller's cage, where he shoved the lone attendant to the floor, scooped the cash from the drawer and stuffed it into a cloth sack he carried. The teller tried to hit Frank from behind with a spittoon he'd picked up, but the bandit shot him in the leg. As the teller went down, the contents of the brass vessel splattered all over him and the floor.

"Next one goes in your guts," Rogers said to the young man who was covered in gore, as he writhed around in the blood and filth on the floor. "Where's the safe?"

"There ain't any," the wounded man said through gritted teeth as he dripped with tobacco spit, held his wounded leg, and tried to stop the blood from spurting, all at the same time.

"Then where's the fuckin' money? I know this is the richest bank in the state," Rogers said as he looked at the stricken teller through the iron sights of his .45 caliber pistol.

"Yuh got the money. It was all in the till you just emptied. There ain't no more. Clarendon's a church town—started an run by Methodists—why some call it 'Saints Roost.' There's folks with land, cotton, 'n cattle wealth, but there's not any cash to be had. Anybody says otherwise is a liar, or don't know what they're talkin' about."

"Wouldja bet your life on that," Rogers said as he thumbed back the hammer and cocked the monster weapon he held.

"Mister I hurt so bad I don't give a fiddlers fart if ya . . ." That's when gunfire broke out behind them as Jack Lacey got into it with somebody.

Frank Rogers looked back at the main floor of the bank, in time to see a large man dressed in a dark suit and string tie exchanging gunfire with Jack Lacey. They were both behind desks, taking potshots at each other from across the lobby and over the tops of the half-dozen customers lying facedown on the floor, praying for dear life as bullets whanged back and forth overhead.

The first couple of volleys missed. Then, as Lacey raised up to take another shot, the big man—whose badge identified him as an agent of the Pinkerton Detective Agency—reached out and fired his next to last round. The heavy 225 grain lead slug from the .44 caliber Colt Peacemaker hit Lacey on the upper part of his right cheek, where it tore off most of his lower jaw, destroying his tongue and half of his face in a splatter of blood, bone and teeth. In agony, the outlaw jumped to his feet in a welter of gore and caught the detectives last bullet in the center of his chest, killing him instantly. The whole exchange took less than fifteen seconds and filled the room with smoke, but left the Pinkerton man unscathed . . . until he stood up, intending to survey the body. That's when Frank Rogers shot him twice . . . once in the neck, and once in the back of the head. Marvin Fields, Pinkerton detective agent from Chicago, never saw it coming, never knew what hit him, and never had a chance.

Gunfire could be heard in the street outside the bank, and bullets were thwocking into the oak front doors. Frank Rogers looked at the teller, writhing around in blood and nicotine-laced tobacco sputum on the floor and said, "Hey you, money man, is there a back door?"

"Around the corner," the stricken man said, "past the manager's office." He pointed with a jerk of his head, and then laid down in the coagulating mess on the floor. But no one was there to see his agony—Frank Rogers had bolted for the door.

When he got into the alley, Frank could hear the battle going on in the street on the other side of the building, and he could see Bill Davis, right where he was supposed to be, watching the alley and holding Frank's horse. *Bill's not much smarter than that hoss he's sittin' on, but he sure as fuck follows orders,* Rogers thought. *Which is why I gave him this job.*

Davis started down the alley toward his boss as soon as the gang-leader came out the door with a smoking pistol in hand. The lookout was crouched low over his horses neck and leading Rogers mount as bullets buzzed around him like hells own hornets. He'd just begun moving when Frank heard a couple of shots and saw the trailing horse flinch as it was hit in the flank, and watched as it started to limp, favoring its back leg.

Frank checked the bullet wound and saw that there was no way the poor animal would make it very far. He pulled his Winchester from its scabbard, ducked under the critters head and looked up at Bill Davis. "Bill, I gotta have your horse."

Davis blinked, hesitated and started to open his mouth in protest . . . which was when he was shot through the heart and killed by Frank Rogers.

Peace re-entered the bank. The gun smoke dissipated and it was quiet, except for an occasional moan from the wounded teller, and a few hiccups and some sobs from the only female patron, who thought she was about to die as the bullets flew back and forth over all of them.

Outside, it was a whole different story. Outside, they were all so busy trying to kill each other, that no one noticed Frank Rogers fleeing to the north on a stolen horse.

Chapter Nineteen

First Street was nothing less than a war zone as Pirtle, Billy Joe Hasty and Will Posey battled it out with the outlaws, who outnumbered them two-to-one. And although they were outgunned, the Rangers made up in grit and determination what they lacked in numbers.

As soon as Rogers and Lacey went in the front doors of the bank and Jack fired the first shot, a fusillade erupted in the street. Boyd Pirtle—on his way back from the Town Marshal's office, where he'd found both the Marshal and deputy absent—saw the gang ride up. He took cover behind the barbershop and fired at one of the bandits, who was wearing a canvas duster and a gray sombrero, just as the man disappeared behind the adjacent building.

Will Posey and Billy Joe Hasty were following the Pinkerton man into the bank when the outlaws came storming up the street with guns blazing, and the pair of Rangers were caught out in the open. A few feet too far from the doors to gain the safety of the lobby, both men were hit in the initial volley. Posey took one in the leg, and Hasty was grazed on the upper left arm. They dove into the hardware store next door, regrouped and started to return fire.

They were both running so high on adrenaline, that neither Ranger noticed he'd been wounded. Stopping only long enough to reload their smoking hot pistols, they continued to pour round after round of .44 caliber, 225 grain lead at the would-be bank robbers.

Pirtle thought he'd winged the bandit wearing the duster and sombrero, but couldn't be sure in all the smoke and dust, and all the confusion and chaos. Peering around the corner of the three-chair haircut and shave parlor, he saw Posey and Hasty duck into the hardware store, where they were laying down a heavy barrage at the bad guys. When Pirtle heard gunfire inside the bank, he guessed that the Pinkerton man was either in control, or dead. He shouted, "This is Special Agent Boyd Pirtle with the Texas Rangers. Show yourselves. Throw down your weapons and surrender."

The reply was gunshots, which whined into the corner, splintering wood and spreading chips all around where Pirtle was crouching, then a mocking voice inviting him to perform an act that was both lewd and physically impossible. He fired blind, across the boulevard, where he thought the voice came from. That touched off several sets of back and forth volleys which ended when one of the gang members, a longtime outlaw named Milt Davis, stuck his face out from behind the wagon he was hiding under and got the top of his head taken off by a random shot from Will Posey.

Davis's death turned the tide. The outlaws pulled out. Arango and Urbina were the first to go, but not before a stray rifle round from one of them took out most of Billy Joe Hasty's right lung. As the Ranger lay dying in the arms of Will Posey, the two Hispanics were hopping aboard a Fort Worth and Denver City boxcar that would carry them all the way down to El Paso. From there, they'd cross into Juarez, Mexico, then disappear into the Sonoran Desert. Eventually, they'd establish themselves in the

Sierra Madre Mountains, from where they would rain banditry and havoc throughout the region.

Pirtle had made an inexcusable tactical error—he assumed the heist, like every other bank robbery carried out by the Rogers bunch, would come at a little before closing time when the most cash would be on hand. But he was wrong—caught by surprise and unprepared, his men out of position—which cost two lawmen their lives. The responsibility for those deaths rested heavily on his conscience, and Pirtle made a silent vow to both souls that he would bring Frank Rogers to justice . . . or die trying.

As Boyd Pirtle looked on in anger, frustration, and impotence, Frank Rogers and what was left of his gang escaped. Two of them were dead, two were gone to another country and three others would soon be captured and put on trial in Ft. Worth. Rogers himself had disappeared. It would take four years of constant searching before Pirtle tracked him down again.

Chapter Twenty

About two days ride southwest of Dallas—in the north Texas town of Cleburne—an attractive, unmarried woman thirty-one years of age was all alone in the three story mansion on Featherston Lane where she'd been born and raised. It was the only home Ella Stringfellow had ever known, and the only place she had ever lived. She was comfortable, kept the house beautiful and well-maintained thanks to the money and properties her Mormon father had passed down to her and her twin brother Chester. Ella was content with her life as a schoolteacher and part-time librarian, but she was lonely and without family.

Her mother died in 1866, when she and Chester were newly born. It had been a long, difficult labor for her, followed by the equally complicated births of two, six-pound babies—one of each sex—the female first, followed five minutes later by the male. The newborns were robust and appeared healthy, but the midwife in attendance was unable to stop the hemorrhaging which followed the afterbirth, and twenty-one hours after the first infant drew breath, Ellen Stringfellow died. She was only seventeen years of age, married to an older man for a mere thirteen months and enduring her first pregnancy. Barely more than a child herself,

Ellen Linn Stringfellow's life was over before it really began.

The doula—a stout Mormon woman with seven children of her own and a longtime practitioner of the art who had attended dozens and dozens of births—was devastated. She had never lost so young a mother, nor seen such prolonged suffering. But her immediate task at hand was keeping the neonate twins alive without a mother to feed or care for them. Six pound twins were larger than usual. They were hungry and squalling for mother's milk.

An emergency, short-term solution was to feed them bottles of warm goat's milk with some sugar added in, but it was only a stopgap. The newborns wouldn't thrive unless a wet-nurse could be found. Otherwise they would most likely die.

The twins' father was a ranked officer and founding member of the Church of Jesus Christ of Latter-day Saints, with many contacts throughout the western United States . . . but they were all to no avail. It seemed that there was a scarcity of babies and mothers in the year 1866 . . . the Civil War had taken more than six hundred thousand men to their graves, a staggering number in terms of the total number of American citizens, one that affected families everywhere. In desperation, the father put an advertisement in the New Orleans *Picayune*. He told of the babies plight, asked for help and got an immediate response.

Five days after the appeal, a buckboard, pulled by an ancient mule and driven by a gray-haired man of color wearing strap overalls, a denim shirt buttoned to the neck and a black frock coat, pulled up to the side of the Stringfellow residence, some thirty miles south of Ft. Worth. It was a place then known as Camp Henderson, but was soon to be renamed Cleburne. Alongside the man sat a light-skinned black woman in mourning clothes, holding a parasol over her shoulder. She stared straight ahead as the man set the brake, wrapped the reins around the lever and dismounted. He walked around to the back of the property, removed the battered top hat he was wearing and knocked on the side of the Conestoga wagon that was serving as a dwelling place while the multi-story wood framed house in the foreground was being constructed.

Just as the elderly man knocked, a bearded white man in homespun clothes came around the other side of the wagon. He'd been working on the skeleton of the new building—where hammers, saws and men talking could all be heard—as were the wails of a pair of hungry infants inside the wagon.

Holding his hat in his hands, and looking at his counterpart, the older man said, "Would you be Mr. Stringfellow?"

"Yes. I am. What can I do for you?"

"My name is Freeman Lyle. I'm from Ft. Worth. I'm here because of your advertisement in the *Picayune*. My sister sent me a telegram from Louisiana, about your babies needing a nurse."

"They do. Can you help?"

Freeman Lyle looked back at his wagon where the woman sat with rigid posture, her eyes looking straight ahead but seeing nothing, her hands clenched on the handle of the umbrella so tightly that her bones showed through the skin. He said, "I'm hoping to help both of us Mr. Stringfellow. That woman's my niece, Abigale. She lost her man to night riders back in March, and her little son died two days ago of a fever. Fact is we just came from burying him. He was but a few weeks old."

Carl Stringfellow could plainly see the pain in the older man's eyes. He said, "I'm sorry for your loss Mr. Lyle, and I would gladly pay you and your niece, if she would take care of my babies for me."

"That's not necessary. I don't need, or want your money. What I do wish, is for Abigale to regain the health of her mind. She ain't spoke a word since her lil' man passed. He was all she had left after those murderous bastards lynched her husband. I want to know that she's comfortable and well taken care of . . . I desire most of all, to know that she's safe. These are dangerous times we live in sir, and we've all had our hearts broken enough."

"Indeed we have Mr. Lyle. If you'll get Abigale, I'll introduce her to Mrs. Kyle, the midwife and the babies. Their names are Ella . . . and Chester."

Less than an hour later, Abigale Ince was sitting in the Conestoga with an infant suckling from each breast, while tears that would not stop flowed down her face.

Chapter Twenty-One

Ella Stringfellow was not only lonesome, she was restless, pacing through the empty rooms of the big three-story house day after day and night after night . . . cleaning what didn't need cleaning and dusting what didn't need dusting . . . doing things that didn't need doing. It had been more than two years since Mrs. Ince had passed, but Ella still mourned her like a daughter for her mother. The dignified old woman of color had appeared at the hour of Ella and Chester's most dire time of need, then nourished, and cared for, and loved them as if they were her own flesh and blood until the day she died.

Since school let out back in May, Ella had put all her energies into the exterior of *The Manor*, as she referred to the place in her mind. The crew of painters had covered the clapboard siding in a medium shade of light gray and accented the railings, shutters and gingerbread trim in white before adding a few gold-leaf highlights to some knobby projections on the eaves. Then they sanded the floor of the porch and covered it in a sturdy gray deck paint. Their last job was to apply a traditional two coats of light sky blue to the underside of the porch roof that delighted her every time she sat out there and looked up at it. With its green tin roof topping it all, the manor was stunning.

She was in the front yard watching Angus Duncan, the neighborhood carpenter and handyman—when he wasn't drunk—who was installing the pair of trellises she'd had him build, on either side of the front stairway. Ella had several buckets of honeysuckle, lace vine and morning glories in a profusion of colors she meant to plant there after he was done. *I'll do it this evening,* she thought, *when it's cooler . . .* aloud, she said "Those are just what I had in mind, Mr. Duncan. Very pretty. Sturdy too. I can't wait to see them covered with flowers."

"Aye. 'Twill be a bonny sight I'm sure."

"Can I get you anything, Mr. Duncan? A glass of water, or some sweet tea?"

"Nivver touch the stuff meself," he said from his perch atop the step ladder. "But maybe you can help the laddie there." Angus nodded his head in the direction of the iron picket fence that paralleled the property and the street, where a boy, who looked to be about nine or ten years old, sat weeping, and holding an old cotton sack between his knees.

Ella thought she recognized him as one of her former students. She opened the front gate, walked over to him and said, "Hello there young man. Are you hurt? What's the matter?"

"No Ma'am. I ain't hurt. Just sad is all," the boy said between sobs.

"What's making you so sad? It can't be that bad, can it?"

The boy looked at her in anguish, with tears coursing down his cheeks and snot running from his nose. He was the essence of pathos as he said, "I found a kitten in the street. It was just about to get run over by a freight wagon, but I ran out and saved it. Ma said we can't feed no more mouths since Pa took sick. She told me to put a rock in there and throw it in the railroad pond, but I can't. I can't do it."

As if on cue, there was wriggling in the faded sugar sack, followed by the yowl of an unhappy little critter trying to escape.

Ella gathered her skirt and sat down beside the distraught boy. She said, "My name is Ella. May I have a look in there," and pointed at the sack.

The boy said, "They call me Skipper," as he handed the bag and its contents over, then watched her while he wiped his face on his sleeve, hiccupped and did his best to regain his dignity. He waited as she untied the drawstring and peeked inside.

When she opened the five pound sack, Ella Stringfellow's heart was captured on the spot by the twenty-five pounds of attitude she found in a furry little black and white body weighing less than ten ounces. A pair of luminous yellow eyes and perked up ears complimented the bandit-masked face. As soon as Ella peered in, the feisty kitten caterwalled several times, as if it were saying, *Well, what are you waiting for, damnit, get me out of here!*

"Have you named her, Skipper?"

"He. He's a boy. I named him Duke, 'cause he looks like he's all dressed up in fancy clothes—sorta royal."

"Like the Count of Monte Cristo."

"Who?"

"It's a story about a man who's sent to prison for a crime he didn't do."

"Oh . . . I didn't know . . ."

"Tell you what. How about I take Duke. He can live here with me and you can come visit him whenever you want. You can let your mother know he's got a home where he'll be happy, and you didn't have to throw the poor little guy in the pond."

"Wonderful. Thank you, Miss Ella. Thank you very much."

"You're welcome Skipper. You're very welcome. And thank you for bringing Duke. I think we're all going to be very good friends."

"Miss Ella . . ."

She looked at the boy without speaking.

"Would you tell me more about the court of Monde Crispo?"

"It's the Count of Monte Cristo, and I'd be glad to. I'll be at the library all day Saturday. You can come by anytime and I will get a copy of the book for you . . ."

"Can't." Skipper interrupted her. "I hafta work all day."

"Doing what?" she said.

"Whatever needs doin'. Haulin' firewood, makin' charcoal for the blacksmith, workin' the bellows for him, muckin' out the stables. Stuff like that. Helpin' support the family. It's why I hadda leave school. But I wanna learn."

"I see. Well, tell you what. I'll get a copy of the book for you and keep it here. Then, whenever you can, come over to visit Duke and we'll read together. How's that sound?"

"Swell, Miss Ella. Thanks for takin' 'im."

Chapter Twenty-Two

Watching the unhappy boy walk away, Ella wondered about a world in which children were worked like adults for a fraction of the pay . . . who were sent out to do it by desperate mothers who had no other alternative. *The very same mothers,* she thought, *who send those very same children on missions to murder innocent little critters like Duke here, because they can't afford to feed them . . . and what must those offspring, the ones forced to commit such murderous deeds at such a tender age . . . what must they grow up to be.* It was a question that had not an answer, but one which raised other issues in her mind.

Where is Chester? She wondered. *Is he still alive? Why did he do what he did . . . where did he go . . . when will I ever hear of him again and what, will become of us then? When I look him in the face after so many many years.*

Her thoughts were broken by another yowl from the drawstring bag in her hands as her unhappy little companion petitioned for his release from confinement. Ella carried him into the house to comply, as their new friendship started to flourish.

* * *

Some forty miles away, a Texas Ranger named Boyd Pirtle was being sworn as the primary witness in the trial of three outlaws who'd been part of a notorious gang that had terrorized southwest Texas and northern Mexico, as well as the Arizona and New Mexico territories for years.

Roy Edrington, Simon Ethel and Jose Dura were all part of the Frank Rogers crew that rode into Clarendon, Texas and shot up the town as they tried to loot the Farmers and Merchants Association Bank. Their information was fallacious . . . they thought they were hitting *the richest bank in the state* . . . instead, the whole haul wasn't enough to pay the expenses of getting there; three persons were wounded and four were dead. Two gang members were killed, along with a Pinkerton Detective and a Texas Ranger named Billy Jo Hasty

The trio of desperados had managed to escape the gun battle in Clarendon and were headed for the sanctuary of the Indian Territories when they were intercepted by a four man posse out of Ft. Worth. They were captured, because Ranger Special Agent Boyd Pirtle had telegraphed law enforcement agencies all along the northern edge of the state, hoping to catch some of the fleeing bandits.

After he was sworn in by the court clerk, Pirtle took a seat in the witness box and began answering the prosecutor's questions, while the twelve men of the jury and the three men on trial watched. The queries were blunt, direct and left no misgivings, qualms, questions or uncertainties as to the guilt of the three outlaws, who were all being tried together. There was no lawyer for the defense, no rebuttal and no doubt as to the outcome. The jury came back with a verdict in less than twenty minutes: *Guilty as charged.*

Judge Drury Hightower polled the jury. Each man stood in turn, and uttered a single word . . . *Guilty* . . . the decision was unanimous. The judge thanked the jurymen, looked at the condemned prisoners and said, "Do any of you have anything to say before I pass sentence on you?"

The three, Edrington, Ethel and Jose Dura, stood mute. Longtime brigands, they knew what was coming, and accepted it with the detachment of those who had long since given themselves over to the idea of a violent and ignominious end.

In a deep baritone voice that was a match in gravitas for the finality of the punishment he was about to mete out, Judge Hightower called each man by his full name and said, "You have been found guilty by a jury of twelve of your peers of the crimes of murdering two officers of the law, attempted murder of two others, as well as the attempted armed robbery of a state chartered banking institution, crimes of violence against the peace and prosperity and welfare of the citizens of the town of Clarendon in the county of Donley, and the state of Texas. The penalty proscribed by law in this jurisdiction is death. Therefore I order that each of you shall be held in a place of confinement for a period of not more than five days, thence you shall be taken to a place of execution and hung by the neck until you are dead.

This court is adjourned."

Chapter Twenty-Three

Boyd Pirtle watched as the three convicted men were led away in chains by the bailiffs. They would be returned across the courtyard to the city jail, where they'd be held in solitary confinement on the top floor until their date with the gallows on the following Wednesday at six o'clock in the morning. He hated attending executions. They attracted voyeurs, agitators and thrill seekers looking to get their morbid and unholy jollies by watching another human being take their last gasp.

Then too, he thought, *they want to see drama. Last minute reprieves, breakdowns of men or equipment; anythin' to relieve the boredom of their ordinary, everyday lives . . . give them somethin' to tell their relatives and scare the bejeezus outta their kids, frighten 'em into bein' good. And I guess there's value to that—a deterrence factor—don't break the law and you won't suffer the consequences. Like prison or death.*

Pirtle's reverie was interrupted by the senior bailiff—a portly, gray-whiskered man named Otto Sherwell who'd seen much hard campaigning back in the 1870s and '80s with General George Crook, as they battled native American Indians from the Rosebud to the Rio Grande, before forcing Geronimo himself to surrender—who said, "Mr. Pirtle, Judge Hightower would like to have a word with you."

The courtroom was empty. Pirtle followed bailiff Sherwell through the door behind the elevated platform from which the judge oversaw the trial proceedings, and on down the hallway to his chambers, where the Ranger was ushered in. And although he was no stranger to the inside of a courtroom, Pirtle had never been invited into a judge's inner sanctum. He was impressed. It was opulent. Not knowing what he was there for, or what was expected of him, Pirtle stood, silent . . . and waited.

Judge Hightower finished writing, looked up at Pirtle and said, "Please, sit," indicating the pair of red leather chairs in front of his carved, quarter-sawed oak desk. Pirtle took a seat, all the while eyeballing the walls. They were crammed—full of leather-bound books encompassing everything from law to the theory of natural selection, philosophy to fiction, and included biographies of the generals on both sides of the Civil War. History, Science and Classical Greek and Latin, it was all there.

As a reader himself, Pirtle was awed by the quality, selection and quantity of the judge's library. He said, "I am honored sir, to be in the presence of so many great minds."

Judge Hightower smiled, "I take it that you are a reader, Mr. Pirtle . . ."

"Voracious. Your Honor. And please call me Boyd."

"Thank you. I will. My friends refer to me as Dru, or Judge. I'll answer to either one. But the reason for having you here is the pending execution of those three condemned criminals I just sentenced to the scaffold." Judge Hightower removed a pair of white porcelain cups from his desk drawer and poured two fingers of bourbon for himself and Pirtle, then held open a box of cigars. After they had each clipped and lit one, smoked and sipped some of Kentucky's best, he continued. "We're gonna hang all three of those felonious sons-a-bitches simultaneously—to make an example of 'em, like when they hung those thirty-eight Sioux Indians up in Mankato, back in sixty-two—and I want you personally, to oversee everything. I don't want controversy, claptrap editorials from absentee editors, or second guessing by woman suffragettes. Think you can handle all that . . . make sure it goes according to plan?"

Pirtle sipped some of his drink before answering, "All due respect, Your Honor, I could do it, but I don't want to. I've attended more than my fair share of executions . . . seen men repent, confess, recant, blubber and piss themselves in fright, until I'm just sick of it Sir. And while I'm here, Frank Rogers is getting' away, coverin' his tracks and buryin' any and all clues leadin' to his whereabouts. He's the ringleader in all this—him and a Mexican named Arango. They're both murderous renegades who've burnt, raped, looted and murdered all over the southwest. Mexico too. I promised I'd bring 'em to justice."

Judge Hightower smiled and drained his cup, poured another, then said, "Your candor and devotion to duty is both admirable and commendable son. If I only had a dozen like you I could clean up Texas, and Oklahoma too, in less than a year. But that's why I have to override yuh on this one. Five more days won't make much, if any, difference in catching up with the pair of them, and the execution proceedings have to be done right. I don't have anyone else."

Pirtle sighed. He said, "I guess that's what we'll do then. But, I have one suggestion to make right now."

I'm all ears son. Talk to me."

Chapter Twenty-Four

Pirtle said, "If you don't want any outside interference, I'd like to change the date."

"The Court Order says five days. I can't alter it."

Pirtle thought for a bit, gazing out at the courtyard below, where the simultaneous hangings would take place. He puffed on the cigar, then said, "Which means *on the fifth day,* doesn't it?"

"Exactly."

"And that fifth day starts at twelve-oh-one a.m. So what about moving the time up until then. We'll be done and tearing the gallows apart by the time the sun comes up."

"That's a hell of an idea Boyd. A lawman who thinks like a lawyer is a deadly combination . . . tough and smart . . . that's hard to beat in my book. You make me proud."

Pirtle left the inner chambers with a letter from Judge Hightower, authorizing him to act as the officer in charge of everything and anything having to do with the pending execution, and a list of all the persons who'd be involved. In addition to Jack Ketch, the hangman, there was a crew of six carpenters and a foreman to build and tear down the scaffold, four deputies to guard the prisoners, a chaplain to administer the last rites and prayers,

Otto Sherwell—the senior bailiff of the court—who would read the charges, the verdict and sentence, then give a silent signal to the hangman, who would pull the lever that released all three traps at the same instant, and send the men to their doom. Last of all was Digger, the undertaker and his assistant Wurm. They were the ones who would cut the bodies down, make the removal and bury them in Potters Field . . . for which the pair of citizen morticians would receive the royal sum of nothing.

"If a public-spirited benefactor hadn't donated five acres, there wouldn't even be a place to bury the indigent," Digger told Pirtle. When they were unsuccessful in getting any of the jail inmates to dig the graves, Pirtle rounded up a couple of drunks, and paid them a dollar per hole from his own pocket to open and close three pits on a desolate piece of ground outside the city. It would be the final resting place of the executed criminals.

After that, everything went smoothly for the Ranger. No one questioned his authority and he was pleased by the competency of the crew he had to work with. Three wagonloads of rough cut lumber, five wooden kegs of nails and an assortment of hardware was delivered, unloaded and in the hands of the six-man crew of carpenters that was run by a beefy, red-faced German foreman named Thorvold, before ten o'clock Saturday morning. When they knocked off for the day at six in the evening, the thirteen-step stairway was constructed and ready to be raised in place first thing Monday morning. In addition, all of the timber framing, braces and cross ties were nailed and bolted together, leaving only the traps, decking and the gibbet itself—from which the nooses would hang—yet to be finished.

Pirtle felt a flush of relief when he stopped by to check on progress at the courthouse. He'd spent the afternoon in the company of Jack Ketch, who'd had a load on by lunchtime, and which he kept reinforcing throughout the afternoon with sips from a flask of brandy inside his coat pocket. The trouble with that was, he couldn't keep the names, heights and weights of all three prisoners straight, much less do the calculations necessary for a humane execution. Use too thin a rope, along with too much of a drop for example, and one of two things would happen. The rope might snap, or most likely, the condemned prisoner would be decapitated. Pirtle shuddered, just thinking about it. He said, "Jack, I didn't ask to be in charge of these proceedings. To be honest, I don't want to be, but since I am, I want everything to happen as planned. No screwups." What he didn't say was that he had enough nightmares, and visits from the dead in his dreams. He didn't want any more.

Jack Ketch looked at Pirtle, his droopy, bloodshot eyes giving mute testimony to his close, personal friendship with John Barleycorn. He said, "I know I'm a souse, but I've been doing this since I was a young man in my twenties. Do'na worry. Those lads are gonna get kilt slicker'n goose shit on ice. You mark my words, Boyo."

"Don't forget to oil the ropes and break them in so they'll work like they're supposed to."

"Aye-aye Cap'n. Aye-aye," was the only response from the dour hangman.

In keeping with his promise to his wife Genevieve, who'd passed away of pneumonia in the winter of 1894, Pirtle attended church services on Sunday morning. Then he ate lunch and spent the remainder of the day reading a Jules Verne novel about the Baltimore Gun Club and their attempt to build a huge cannon that would shoot three men from the earth to the moon. Although it was written thirty years before he got around to reading it, Pirtle was impressed. *That would be one hellacious big gun,* he thought. Then he closed the book, and tried not brood over her untimely death, or think about how much he missed his wife, or how worried he was about the pending execution. *Sundays are the hardest. There's not enough to do. Too much time to ponder what if . . .*

But all of Pirtle's worrying was a waste of time and effort. On Monday morning, at a little after daybreak, the construction crew was hard at work. By six that evening the heavy work was done. On Tuesday morning they finished up all the detail work—such as railings on the stairs and atop the platform, installing the three nooses to Jack Ketch's specifications—and then testing the trapdoors and springs, to make sure that everything was working as it should.

It did.

Wednesday at five minutes past midnight, the three condemned prisoners were brought out, marched up the stairs and stood in place with their hands fastened behind them. Jose Dura, who had been wounded in the left hip by Pirtle during the shoot-out in Clarendon, had to be helped up the stairs with two of the guards almost carrying him. When all three were standing on the trapdoors, their feet were roped and knotted together at the ankles by the guards, who then stood behind each prisoner. The chaplain said a short prayer for them, and Otto Sherwell read the charges, the verdicts and the sentences for each man. His sonorous, deep voice rang with the finality of doom as he uttered each word. Finished, he asked if any of them had any last thing to say. No one did. Long time renegades, the three men all expected to die by the gun or the gallows and long ago made their peace with it. They accepted the fate a life of crime had led them to.

When no one had anything to say, Sherwell nodded to the guards, who placed a black hood over each prisoner's head, followed by the hangman's noose. It was cinched firmly behind the left ear so that the neck would snap clean and quick . . . causing an instant death. After everything was in place, the guards were brought to attention and marched off the platform, down the steps and out of the courtyard. The Chief Baliff then motioned with his right hand. Jack Ketch—who had quietly moved into place while Otto Sherwell read the charges—sprung the traps, and just like that, three souls departed the earth.

* * *

Thirty miles to the south, an attractive young woman named Ella Stringfellow slept in quiet comfort, unaware of the events taking place in Ft. Worth, the persons involved, or the impact one of them would have on her life. Beside her, a young black and white kitten was laying sphinx-like and motionless, his all-seeing eyes wide open . . . staring into the dark as if he could observe unfathomable events taking place elsewhere in the world . . . and purring to himself in quiet contemplation.

Chapter Twenty-Five

Frank Rogers found Denver to his liking. The city was a rip-roaring frontier town, as wide open as a willing woman and stuffed to the gills with money. *What's not to like,* he thought, as he polished off an epicurean breakfast of Eggs Benedict, ham steak, fried potatoes, fresh fruit, sweet rolls and butter, steaming hot coffee . . . and all of it finished off with flutes of orange juice and champagne cocktails . . . served by waiters in black trousers, white shirts, bow ties and short jackets with linen towels draped over one arm.

Rogers had been in Denver for one week. He'd come to the city on an overnight train, been picked up at Union Station by a liveried barouche that was pulled by a matched pair of coal-black horses and whisked down Seventeenth Street to the luxurious Brown Palace Hotel. There, he'd been rubbing elbows with society's best, while at the same time keeping company with an infamous woman named Mattie Silks, and several other notorious ladies of the night. He was acting like a prince and living in the lap of luxury. *The trouble is,* he thought, *it costs like a bastard to live like one a them bastards. I gotta either quit spendin' money like this, or make some do-re-mi.* He'd been ripping through cash like a drunken sailor on shore leave after a two year whaling voyage.

It didn't take long before he found what he was looking for . . . another high-stakes poker game. It came about by accident, while he was sitting in the lobby smoking and reading the *Denver Post*, the daily newspaper with the modest claim that it *Tells Everybody, Everything, Every Day* emblazoned across its masthead.

As Frank was in the middle of an article about a gold strike up in Alaska—at some place called the Klondike—he overheard a well-dressed older man say to his bosomy, gray-haired companion, "No dear, it will be gentlemen only. No riff-raff of any kind. It requires at least one-thousand dollars to attend. I'll be fine, pet. Don't worry yourself. And tomorrow we'll go to the opera. Yes. I promise . . ."

When they strolled off toward the coffee shop and out of his hearing, Rogers folded the newspaper, stuck it under his arm and walked to the main desk, where he sought out the Head Bellman. Looking resplendent in his light gray and black livery, the man came to attention, gave a short bow, and said, "How may I be of service sir?"

Rogers slipped him a silver dollar, watching as the bellman palmed it, then disappeared it into his pocket as if by magic. It was done with such adroitness that it seemed like the coin never even existed. Frank was impressed, but acted nonchalant. He said, "I was told by a friend that a gentlemen's game of poker was being arranged and wondered if you knew anything about it . . ."

"Are you a guest of the hotel?"

"Yes. I'm from Texas, San Antonio to be exact. Name's Rogers. Frank Rogers, I buy and sell land and property. I'm in the real estate business."

"Most of the Texans who come up here are cattlemen."

"It's a big state. There's a lotta things to do."

"So you want to play poker."

"Yes. I've played before."

"Well, if there was such a game—and I'm not sayin' there is— it'd be by invitation only, and cost at least a thousand to play. And they wouldn't take no checks neither."

"That's not a problem. If there is a game, and if I got invited," Frank said, as he shook hands with the bell captain, and felt the silver dollar he held between his index and middle finger vanish, as quick and sure as the first one had.

"I'll check around," was the last thing the bellman said before he turned and walked away.

Frank Rogers spent the rest of the morning and most of his afternoon in relaxed idleness: shopping for clothes, taking the steam at the Denver Athletic Club and sampling the ambiance of several Larimer Street bars and tobacconists . . . where he purchased a handful of Cuban cigars, and a velvet lined gutta-percha cigar case that featured an arrangement of roses in bas-relief on the cover. He was well-pleased with himself when he returned to the hotel in late afternoon. He planned on cleaning up, having a short rest, and changing into more formal attire for the evening. That all changed in less than a heartbeat when he opened the door to his room and found the message on the floor where it had been shoved under the sill.

Chapter Twenty-Six

Frank stepped over the threshold, being careful to avoid the white envelope, which bore only his name. On a folded piece of stationary inside, the hand-written message was clear and brief. *Rogers, be in room @ 8:30pm tonight. Have $1000 buy-in. Cash or gold. Will escort you to the game. Be alone. Unarmed.*

Sounds like Oklahoma City, Frank thought as he stuck the invitation in his shirt pocket and started making preparations.

The first thing he did was count his money. He found, to his surprise, that he only had seventeen hundred and forty dollars, plus a few small bills and change left from the four-thousand he'd come to Denver with, one week ago. *Just how the fuck could you go through twenty-two hunnert and some-odd dollars in six damn days?* His rational self asked. *Drinkin', expensive whores, eatin' like a pig, flashy clothes, expensive presents for whores, and Christ only knows what-all else . . . you dumb-assed bastard.* His emotional other self answered. *Truth is, you've been goin' through a fortune.*

He had twenty, twenty-dollar gold pieces and fifty silver dollars from the pawn shop robbery and murders, a bit over twelve hundred in greenbacks. He pried one of the end caps off of the footboard of his brass bed. Then he spread the coins into four piles of five gold and ten silver each. These he deposited into four of his dress socks. He tied knots in each end, then tied each sock together with twine. The end result looked like links of sausages. Frank lowered the whole string down in the bedpost. Then he looped the twine around the top, knotted it and replaced the end cap. Checking his work, Frank was pleased to see that the twine was almost invisible underneath the brass ornament.

Next, he retrieved the alligator doctor's bag from its hiding place. He checked his guns, making sure they were all loaded, before taking out the .44 caliber derringer with the ivory grips and the Balinese throwing knife. Rogers put the rest of the silver dollars and his excess cash back in the bag, leaving eleven hundred in assorted greenbacks, the knife and belly gun laying on the bed. He closed the bag and stuffed it in with the dirty clothes, then shoved everything in the bottom of the wardrobe. Hoping for another cursory pat-down and weapons search, Frank attached the knife to his left forearm with mustard plaster and, in a burst of insight, taped the derringer to his body, behind his belt buckle. It was a little bit uncomfortable, but within easy—and surprise—reach, because he was betting that no man wanted to touch another man there. Pulling up his pants, tucking his shirt in and buttoning everything up, Rogers checked his appearance, then settled down to wait.

The knock came early. It was only eight twenty-five when Frank opened the door, expecting to find the bell-captain. Instead he was greeted by a big tough looking bruiser in a black canvas duster and derby hat. He said, "Are you Frank Rogers?"

"I am."

"I'm supposed to come getcha an' carry yuh up to the game. My hansom's downstairs waitin'. Yuh got any weapons?"

Frank looked at the man with feigned astonishment. "Me? Oh my goodness. No."

"Okay then. We better get goin."

"The game's not here?"

The man looked at Frank like he was an insect, pinned on a specimen board at the Museum of Natural History. "Didn't they tell you . . . it's at the Oxford. All the way down t'other end of Seventeenth Street. Almost to the train station."

How handy, Rogers thought, as he followed his guide down the hall to the elevator, *how very damned handy.* It was only the first of the many surprises he was in for. Frank Rogers was about to be introduced to big time organized crime in a big way. Denver, The Queen City of the Plains, was about to throw wide her arms and clasp him tight to her breast.

Chapter Twenty-Seven

Rogers trailed after the big man who hadn't bothered to give any name, so Frank called him Bunyan in his mind, after the legendary lumberjack of American folklore. They didn't speak on the elevator ride down to the lobby, where Bunyan crossed the vestibule without looking left or right. He exited through the revolving front entry and opened the door of the one-horse hansom that was standing in the porte-cochere, beckoning Frank to enter. As soon as he was aboard, Bunyan followed, filling the interior with his presence and rocking the carriage with his bulk. The coachman snapped his whip and they set off at a steady pace up Seventeenth Street.

Fifteen minutes later, the cab pulled in to the Oxford Hotel where Bunyan hopped out and headed for the entrance without a word or glance at Rogers, causing Frank to scramble in order to keep up. Without conversation of any kind, Bunyan and Frank Rogers took the stairs up to the penthouse on the top floor. Not yet acclimated to the thin air of the mile-high city, the climb left Frank out of breath, with his heart thumping in his chest and a thin sheen of perspiration on his face. What he saw at the entrance to the luxury suite made him do a double take, while an icicle, born of apprehension formed a cold knot behind his scrotum. Standing in front of the entryway were two beefy, red-faced, clean-shaven Denver policemen in regulation black uniforms, with silver badges, whistles and holstered pistols prominently on display. The only thing missing were name tags, but even without them, Frank recognized Andrew and Denny, who'd been Oklahoma City cops just last week.

Bunyan said, "This 'uns' clean, I checked. I got one more to fetch, probably take 'nother half-hour or so 'fore I'm back." He turned to leave, nodded at Rogers and said, "Luck to yuh, Boyo," then ambled back to the stairwell, where he descended out of sight . . . leaving only the scent of cheap bourbon and the thudding of size fifteen brogans to mark his presence.

One of the Denver PD door guards looked at Frank for several seconds with his eyelids squinted in concentration, then, recognition blossomed as he realized when and where he'd seen Rogers before. He put his big Irish paw on Franks shoulder, turned him to face the wall and proceeded to pat him down for weapons. Finding none because of the laziness of the patdown, the big copper with dark hair and eyes said, "Okay. You're clear. You'll find food and drink inside. Help yourself. The game'll start in about half an hour." The blue-eyed cop opened the door and ushered Rogers inside the gambling den, where the surprises—and shocks—just kept on coming.

As he watched Frank go in, the brown-eyed cop said to his partner, "You remember him, Andrew?"

"Looks sorta familiar, but no, can't say I do."

Andrew closed the door he'd been holding while Denny opened the call box on the wall and got on the house phone. He spoke for a few moments, hung up and came back to his partner who was sitting in one of the wingback chairs positioned on either side of the door, preparing to light a briar pipe.

"I gotta go see Adolph."

"Okay Denny," Andrew said, as he puffed his pipe into life. "I got us covered here. Take your time, but bring me a sandwich and glass of beer, wouldja . . ."

"I look like a fookin' waiter to you?" Denny said as he slipped through the door leading to the gambling tables.

Andrew drew on his pipe, wreathing his head in tobacco smoke. He made an obscene gesture with his middle finger at Denny's back, hawked up a gob of phlegm from the depths of his lungs and spit in the same direction. Andrew Coker watched his sputum as it slid down the polished mahogany door and smiled, as he imagined Denny's face and uniform blouse, superimposed in the red-veined wood.

Inside the penthouse, Denny McCullough was looking for his boss, Adolph Duff, known in some places as "Kid Duffy," and in a few others as "Smitty," the loquacious, friendly card dealer at their annual high-stakes poker games. Unknown to all but a select few close associates and confederates, Smitty was the ruthless leader of a vast underground network of con-artists, bunko-men and cheats at any kind of game of chance. Smitty—good old smiley-faced, sympathetic Smitty, the guy who made everyone feel so good while he was cheating them out of a fortune that they left him a tip on their way to the poor house—was one of the best card mechanics and bottom-dealers in North America.

When Denny located him, Smitty was telling jokes to a group of lambs he was about to shear. Catching the silent high sign, Smitty excused himself and met up with the man who was masquerading as a Denver policeman by the rest room. "This had better be important Denny . . . I'm in the middle of basting those turkeys."

"Yeah Boss. It is. We've got a problem."

Chapter Twenty-Eight

Careful to stay in character as 'Smitty,' Adolph Duff checked for eavesdroppers, then said—in a voice only Dennis McCullough could hear—"Spill it. What's the trouble?"

"You remember a mousey-lookin' jasper with a good suit, round wire-rim glasses and blonde hair parted dead center of his head that we clipped for twelve hundred and a ten-dollar gold indian head last week in Oklahoma?"

"Yeah. Sure. I've got the lucky gold piece in my watch pocket."

"He's here."

"You certain . . ."

"As old age, death, and taxes on fools. I just let him in."

"Is he a Pinkerton, spyin' on us?"

Denny paused for a moment, thinking and looking over the flock of pigeons they were about to take to the cleaners, being careful with his answer. He said, "Boss, I don't know what else he could be. The Federals ain't gonna mess with somethin' small like this, and everybody in Denver law enforcement that matters is on our payroll."

Adolf Duff grinned and Smitty the charmer was back. Taking a moment to produce and light up a tailor made cigarette while he surveyed the room, he said, "That him, over by the beer keg . . . the one in the tweed suit . . . wearin' a red bow tie and eatin' a sandwich?"

McCullough snuck a look. "Yeah. He's the one."

"Delbert escort him in?"

"Right up to me an' Andrew."

"Did you search him?"

Denny hesitated, then lied. "Naw. Del told us the guy was clean, then Andrew patted him down. Nothin' found."

Smitty, who had a nose for lies because he was such an adept himself, said, "There's gonna be hell to pay if he's got anythin' but his dick in his pants . . ."

Denny's face lost its color. He'd once seen Adolf Duff—Smitty— break a man's fingers, one by one, for trying to pass loaded dice in a craps game. Then, while the man cried in pain and begged for mercy, Smitty shot the poor bastard in both elbows with a .41 caliber Iver Johnson pistol. He knew his boss was twisted. Sick and sadistic too. He said, "I don't believe there's nothin' to worry about."

Duff, watching closely, said, "I hope not, for the sake of all of us. I'm takin' the first shift at the table . . . I'll let him win a few hands . . . see how he acts. Tell Delbert I said to stick around. I'll want to see him when Buda, excuse me, Dolly starts dealin'."

"Will do boss," a relieved Denny McCullough said.

"And Denny, be sure and let her know about this ringer. Tell her to watch me for hand signals when I wanna start his losin' streak."

Denny was careful not to look around, or make eye contact with anyone, as he made for his post at the entrance.

From the other end of the suite, Frank Rogers watched them surreptitiously, munching on a roast beef sandwich and sipping a glass of draft beer. He saw the hushed conversation and the furtive looks in his direction and knew that just as he recognized them, they had put a name to his face too. *I wonder if they think I'm out to get them, or somethin' . . . maybe they think it's just a coincidence . . . yeah, and maybe they've got me pegged as another fuckin' eejit degenerate gambler. Busy spendin' someone else's money. We'll soon see I guess.*

Frank turned his attention to the others in the room, looking for players he'd last seen at the Palace Hotel, down in the Indian Territories. He spotted the fat man with the walrus mustache first thing. *He was the one who sat to my right and chewed tobacco, kept spittin' his juice in that brass spittoon he had between his feet . . . distractin' me. Fat man's a shill for damn sure.* And how many others, he wondered.

Rogers let his gaze drift around the room, taking quick scans of faces, trying to remember, seeking to identify anyone from last weeks game, looking for potential threats and possible adversaries. He was on his third sweep when someone wrapped a hand around his left elbow. Startled, he turned and found himself face-to-face with a woman in her mid-twenties, wearing a frilly low-cut pink dress.

She said, "Hello. My name is Charity Moon. I'm a friend of Matties, and I'm one of the ushers for tonight's game. Would you come with me please?"

Frank looked at her and smiled. He said, "You mean Mattie Silks? I know her."

"Many do. And yes to your question."

"Well lead on Miss Charity. Truth is, I'd follow you anywhere darlin'."

She had, he noticed, dimples in her cheeks when she smiled, and a sparkle in her eyes that promised other fun things as she took him by the hand and lead him to the poker table.

Chapter Twenty-Nine

Charity Moon situated Rogers in the furthest chair on the right. He'd be on the dealers left, and the first to get—and see—his cards. Frank thanked her with a silver dollar and said, "Maybe later, we could get together for some sport."

"Maybe is right. You look more like a plow horse than a race horse to me. I'm not sure your heart could handle it, Hon."

"Oh, it can, Darlin'. It can. Ask Mattie."

"May. Be." She said, smiled again and left.

Frank squirmed in his chair and crossed his legs, hoping to hide his arousal. *Pay attention,* he chided himself. *You gotta think with the big head,* he added, as he looked down at the tent in his pants. *We'll have plenty of time for pussy after we're done here.* When he looked up again, the fat man from Oklahoma was sitting in the last chair at the table and staring at him with eyes so intense that they could have drilled holes in a granite rock face. Frank glared back until the adversarial one lowered his face to spit, making a loud metallic ping when the gob of brown juice hit bottom. Disgusted, Frank turned away and watched as the other five players were seated.

As he was sizing up the competition, the man who called

himself Smitty at the game last week in Oklahoma, sat in the dealers chair and clapped his hands. When the talking stopped and he was sure that everyone was listening, he said, "My name is Duffy. Some call me Kid. I'll answer to either, just don't call me late for drinks at the bar. We will play stud—five or seven card—table stakes, for cash. Everyone understand?"

Silence raged.

"The ante is twenty dollars. And you," Duffy pointed to the man in the center chair who wore a black waist coat and a pair of red sleeve garters, "will call the game, and pass the button to your left." The man did so and the game began.

Frank tossed his cards on the first three hands, losing his ante and a couple of small bets. On the fourth, he drew a pair of aces and called the fat man, who he thought was bluffing because the three cards Duffy had turned up were the three of clubs, and the five and six of hearts. Frank bet. The fat man raised. Frank said, "I don't believe you've got it."

"Only one way to find out," was the answer.

Frank called. His opponent smirked and turned over the deuce and four of spades.

"Straight beats a pair," Duffy said, as he recovered the cards and the big man opposite Rogers raked in the huge pot. The loss cost Frank nearly a third of his cash. He considered quitting, but decided to carry on, play conservatively and try to figure out which one to rob when the game broke up.

The button passed to him on the fifth deal, and Frank said, "Seven card stud." That's when his luck changed and the cards started coming his way. Where earlier, he could do no right, now he could do no wrong. He was getting big pairs, trips, straights and full houses . . . even a couple of flushes. Once, he drew four Jack's and captured the biggest pot of the night. It was large. So huge in fact, that one of his competitors wound up broke, and another was down to his last few dollars. For Frank, it was poker paradise—but he knew it wouldn't last—as he watched the man who was now calling himself Kid Duffy, deal hand after hand after hand, from the bottom of the deck.

Three and a half hours later, Frank Rogers had amassed an impressive pile of winnings. He snuck a peek, and guessed that he had at least four or five times what he'd started with. But, just as he came to that conclusion, Kid Duffy stood up and said, "Would you excuse me now, and welcome the lovely Miss Helen, who'll be your new dealer."

Frank watched as the woman he'd known as Dolly down in Oklahoma City, took her seat and opened a fresh cellophane-wrapped deck of playing cards and went through the routine of fanning them out, flipping them over, shuffling, cutting, burying the top card and finally . . . dealing. She said, "Good luck to each and all of you gentlemen," as she began allocating the hand.

When Duffy stood and announced the change of dealers, Frank began gathering up his cash and stuffing it in his pockets as quietly as possible. He stopped when he thought he was being watched, leaving some small bills in a pile that he pushed around and mounded up in an attempt to make look larger. Before she dealt to him, Rogers said, "Deal me out of this one Miss Helen. I've got to make a rest stop." She nodded and passed him by. He stood up and headed in the general direction of the rest room, with the intention of escaping out the front door with his coat, stuffed full of thousands of illicit dollars.

He almost made it.

Chapter Thirty

Frank found the rest room and stood at one of the marble urinals while he looked for escape routes. Finished, he went to wash up at the row of sinks, where he was given a towel by the attendant, and Rogers tipped him a quarter. As he dried his hands, Frank looked in the mirror at the man in the white muslin coat and said, "Say pardner, what would y'all do in case of a fire up here?"

"Pray. An' try an' be first down 'de fire escape in back. Git down fo' it fall off from too many folk all tryin' use it at 'de same time."

"Well thanks," Rogers said. "Let's hope there ain't no fires then."

"Sho' 'nuff," the old man said.

"Here. This is for you," Frank added as he slipped the attendant a silver dollar.

"You ain't ast, but it's out by the lil' kitchen," the man said as he busied himself wiping down the already spotlessly clean sink.

Frank nodded his thanks to the bathroom custodian—whose eyes were glued to his in the mirror—then left the damp towel and a second silver dollar on the marble surround.

When he exited, Rogers was intercepted by Bunyan, who took him by the elbow. "Come," was all the behemoth said as he pinched the nerve in Franks arm, commanding his immediate compliance.

Frank was marched down a short hall to the rear of the suite, where Denny McCullough waited in front of a locked and bolted door. When Bunyan nodded, Denny unfastened it and Frank was ushered into the adjoining room, where the sparse furnishings and plain decor told him it was the servant's quarters. He had just stepped in there, when he sensed a presence behind him. That was only an instant before he was hit on the back of the head, and his whole world fell into the utmost darkness Frank Rogers had ever known.

When Rogers awaked, it was into a new reality . . . he was woozy, disoriented and unsure where he was. He had a world-class headache, was desperate for a drink of water, and at the same time had an urgent need to urinate. He was stripped to his shorts, gagged and bound hand and foot to a heavy oak chair. *It must weigh seventy-five pounds,* he thought, *or be bolted to the floor.* He was freezing cold, stuck in a room that was so dark, it felt like he was down in a mine. He struggled, trying to find a way to escape, but the ligatures had been tied by experts, and all he managed to do was make them tighter. It was a situation Frank Rogers had never been in before, and all he could do was wait—apprehensive and anxious, but thus far unafraid—for whatever was coming next.

The absence of light and sound was disorienting. Frank lost all sense of time. He couldn't tell if he'd been tied up for minutes, or hours . . . days even . . . and his mind started playing tricks on him. Sometimes, he thought he could hear people talking, dogs barking, or horses hooves, clip-clopping into the distance. His brain was telling him that water was running somewhere far away, or perhaps faint music, playing so soft and indistinct it was almost beyond his ability to hear. That's when the light came on.

It was bright, just inches from his face, blinding and confusing him. Somehow, at least one other person had entered the room without him being aware of it. He sat, waiting, unable to speak, when there was a swish from his right side that Rogers heard at the same instant he felt a searing pain in his abdominal region. That's where he was hit with a rubber hose by someone who knew what they were doing. It was taped shut at the business end and contained a few ounces of lead shot that made a loud *thwack* when it connected with his skin.

Frank sucked air. Tried to scream. Almost choked on the rag on his mouth. He spasmed, then shook uncontrollably for half a minute before regaining control of himself. But, before he could take a normal breath, his assailant struck again, lower and with even more force. Rogers had never experienced such intense pain. It caused him to convulse and lose control of his bladder. He soiled himself then, and felt deep, pathological fear. It was fear of the unknown, of uncertainty and an uncontrollable fear of more torture.

"That's enough, Denny," said a voice from the dark that Rogers recognized as the man he'd known as Smitty, or Kid Duff. "And take the gag out too."

Frank heard the snick of a jackknife being opened, felt rough hands cut the cloth holding the rags in his mouth. As soon as it was removed, he tried to spit at the big cop and got punched in the side of his head for the effort. It made his ear ring and left one of his back teeth sitting sideways in his mouth. Rogers was tasting blood and poking the loose molar with his tongue when Denny said, "Do that again Boyo, and I'll rip yer fookin' ears right straight off yer fookin' head."

Swallowing his fear, and eating his pain, Frank vowed to himself that if he lived through the next few hours, he'd make it his mission to kill the big mick at the first opportunity. *And I'll make it hurt . . .*

His dream of revenge was shattered by the voice of Smitty, who said, "Who are you?"

"Frank Rogers."

He was hit on the knees with the rubber hose and howled in pain for several minutes.

A match flared in the dark and Rogers saw Smitty lighting a cigarette. When he'd taken a lungful, he said, "I'm gonna ask you this just once . . . if I don't believe you, or think you're lyin' . . . I'm gonna have Denny kill yuh. You'll go out hard, and alive, in the incinerator back there behind yuh. So think good and answer true. Who are you—a Pinkerton?"

It was said with such quiet menace that Frank had no doubt as to Smitty's sincerity and it scared him so bad that his whole body went rigid. He said, "I ain't any closer to being a detective than you are. I'm wanted in several states, a couple of territories, and down in Mexico too."

"Under your name?"

"Yeah. Or Ralph Stuart."

"Any others?"

"No."

Without another word, the light went out and Frank was alone again, in the absolute dark.

Chapter Thirty-One

Hours, or days later—just like the first blackout, it was impossible for Frank to tell time in the absence of light, sound, or any kind of movement—he suddenly felt as though he was looking straight into the face of the sun when, without any warning, the high-intensity desk lamp was switched on again. It was so close to his face that it was burning his skin, while at the same time he was blinded from the flash. He sensed others were nearby, but couldn't see them. Uneasy, he waited.

Rogers heard a door open, footsteps approaching . . . then a voice . . . raspy, deep, and unknown. "Why are you here?"

"What do you mean?"

"Just what I said. Why are you here in Denver?"

"It was the first train leavin' outta Oklahoma City after I got to the station."

"What were you doin' down there?"

"Gettin' away."

Frank heard a sharp intake of breath. Raspy-voice said, "You wanna get outta here with all yer parts attached, yuh better be more forthcomin' with yer answers, or I'm gonna have Denny here, stick that fancy little knife of yours under your toenails and start poppin' them off."

Franks foot clenched and his gut fluttered. He said, "I was gettin' away from a shootout down in Texas. There's a Ranger after me."

"Where was it, and why?"

"A place called Clarendon. We was tryin' to rob the bank. They were waitin'. Ambushed us. We got shot to hell an' gone. I made for the territories an' changed my looks there."

"There's a bounty on yuh?"

"Don't know. Maybe. Prob'ly."

"You ain't doin' too good, are yuh. What makes yuh think you're a poker player?"

"I don't . . ."

"Don't what?"

"Think I'm a poker player. Truth is, I was gonna stick the place up, or roll whoever won the most money."

"Why didn't 'cha?"

"I was alone and there was too much security. When I saw Smitty, or Duffy . . . whatever his name is . . . dealin' from the bottom and the fat man shillin', I realized it was a turkey shoot and got the fuck outta there."

"How'd you know he was dealin' from the bottom?"

"Cause his thumb wasn't moving. When you stack the deck and flip out the bottom card, the mechanic has to press down with the top thumb so that the bottom one can be pulled out with the middle finger."

"Well done. Not many can discern the slight of hand it takes to do that. If you make it through the next day or so while we check on yuh, you may even have a future with us. We'll see."

The raspy voice didn't speak again. Frank heard footsteps receding into the darkness, then the door slammed and the light went out as abrupt and unexpectedly as it came on, leaving him in an utter, absolute, and total absence of light. Once again, he was alone. The difference now however, was that he was exhausted, cold and losing hope. He thought about Smitty's threat of death by immolation and shivered; for the first time in his life Frank Rogers was helpless . . . and he was scared . . . all the way down to the marrow of his bones.

* * *

In Ft. Worth, Texas, Boyd Pirtle was completing his duties as Judge Hightower's henchman and Lord High Executioner.

After the three hanged men were pronounced dead by the coroner, the undertaker and his assistant cut them down and loaded the bodies into a buckboard with the nooses and a foot of rope still wound left around their necks. They were covered with a tarp and taken to the pauper's graveyard, where the indigent were buried in unmarked plots. The corpses of Edrington, Ethel and Dura were wrapped in cheap canvas, unceremoniously dumped in the three open graves, and covered with dirt by the only drunk who showed up to finish the job.

As Boyd was paying the sweating man off with three Columbian Exposition commemorative half-dollars, he said, "I 'preciate you keepin' your word and finishin' what you started."

"You're welcome. I'm just glad to have some honest work, and not be one of them unfortunates," the man said with a point of his chin at the mounds of dirt he'd just spaded.

Pirtle just shook his head and climbed up on the buckboard seat, alongside the undertaker and his assistant, for the four mile ride back to Ft. Worth. The drunk tossed the short-handed shovel in the wagon bed and hopped up on the buckboard. He rode for a while, looking back at the burial grounds, with his legs dangling over the wagon tracks.

Somewhere on the way to town, he silently took his leave of

them, and was swallowed up in the vastness of the land. Lost in thoughts of his own, Pirtle didn't even notice when the boozer departed . . . he was just gone when they made the city limits and the lights of civilization.

Chapter Thirty-Two

The crowd that began gathering in the courtyard of the judicial building a couple of hours before dawn expected to be treated to a public spectacle. They came to see the hangings, but were disappointed to learn that the event had already taken place, when Thorvold and his construction crew arrived in the gray light at six a.m. to dismantle the gallows they'd finished building only the day before.

Boyd Pirtle, who'd been able to grab just a couple of hours of sleep, was operating on personal grit and the two cups of coffee he'd pumped down his throat while he shaved and got dressed for a ten o'clock meeting with Judge Hightower. Pirtle was going there on Hightower's orders, to give an informal oral report of the executions, and be formally discharged from his court duty.

Walking into the pink sandstone building for what he hoped would be the last time Pirtle found himself thinking about the hanged men. *Can't say they didn't earn their punishment, but hanging's a sorry way to go. There's just something demeaning about it . . . but I guess that's the point . . . to be executed in that way is shameful and humiliating, and meant as a deterrent. But is it? If deterrence worked, there wouldn't ever be any executions, because everyone would be too frightened of the potential consequences of their crime. And what about those who have no moral core—the insane, the savage and amoral among us—the ones who just plain enjoy hurting and killing their fellow human beings? They're sure as hell not deterred by consequences . . .*

Pirtle was so lost in his own thoughts he didn't realize he was at the door to Hightower's chambers until he heard the Judge speak. "Come in Boyd, come in. You look like you have a problem. Can I help?"

"No, Judge. Nothin's amiss. Everythin' went like clockwork and the three felons are hanged, dead and buried. The carpenters are tearin' down the scaffold as we're talkin'. The foreman said they'd be done by dinnertime or a little after, and all I need now is to get outta here so I can track down the last of the gang."

"You mean Frank Rogers?"

"Yeah. And there's a couple of Mesicans too, although I reckon they're south of the border by now."

"No doubt, but they'll resurface at some point. The outlaw kind generally does. But, I want to thank you for your help and your willingness to carry out such an odious task."

"That's what I was thinkin' about when I came in."

"How disagreeable the task you'd been given to do?"

"Not my part of it. I have always stood for the law, no matter what the job, and I always will. No, what I was concerned with was the nature of hanging itself, the shame and disgrace of it, and wondering if the threat of being hanged prevents crime from ever happening, or if it makes any difference at all?"

Judge Hightower smiled and said, "That my Ranger friend, is the great conundrum of the law . . . and law enforcement . . . that we have been wrestling with ever since old King Hammurabi first laid it down in writing nearly four millennia ago. Do we, as a society, seek to prevent crime, or are we wanting to extract revenge, or reparation, or is it restitution we desire the most? What is justice? How and where do we find it? Is it the same for all of us? I've sought justice all my life without quite knowing how to find it, and so I hold fast to the law as written, do my best to adjudicate it as fair, honest and impartially as possible, while always keeping in mind the notion that somewhere down the line I'll be explaining how and why I did the things I did, as I stand naked before God Almighty, pleading for entry into paradise."

Pirtle said, "Never thought of it like that."

Judge Hightower took two cigars from the wooden humidor on the corner of his massive desk, clipped both and handed one to the Ranger. As they lit up the Judge said, "We who uphold and carry out the law bear great responsibility . . . the power of life and death over all those we come into contact with. Never forget it. I'll also send a letter of commendation for you to Captain Newton down in Austin. You're free to go Boyd. Many thanks, and all success to you."

"You as well, sir," Pirtle said, as he took his leave of the Judges chambers, the courthouse, and the city of Ft. Worth, Texas, ready and eager to resume the hunt for the renegade killer Frank Rogers.

Chapter Thirty-Three

Frank Rogers was losing his mind in the overwhelming dark. His brain was playing tricks on him, conjuring up images from his subconscious. He was imagining things to fill the big blank space he was experiencing from sensory deprivation, and the utter absence of light. Time was supplanted by pain, anger by fear, and thought by hallucination. Phantasmal figures materialized in front of him . . . fanged beasts with slavering jaws lunged out of the dark, their sharp yellow teeth snapping together in front of his face.

At first, Frank saw monsters, then men he had killed. They came for him out of the graves they moldered in . . . men without eyes or lips. Dead men with rotting flesh and skeletal fingers, corpses who wanted to tear him asunder, to rip and claw and defile his flesh and send him to Hell, where more of their kin waited, eager to settle accounts. Last—and sorriest—were the women he'd abandoned, starving and wretched, holding the children he'd fathered and left. Then, he saw his sister. She was the fiercest of them all, the most formidable and the most frightening. Clothed in incandescent white robes of fire, with bolts of blue and white lightning that sizzled and snapped and crackled about her hands and arms and feet, his twin terrified him. As she approached, he was helpless. It was the moment Rogers saw the nest of rattlesnakes in her hair. They writhed and lunged at him, with poison dripping from their fangs. When Ella stopped to leer and hiss at him, the snakes detached from her head and crawled down her face. They wound around her neck and slithered across her shoulders, under her bodice and between her breasts. Frank could see them undulating about her torso, sliding between her thighs, then dropping down with a thump that froze him. They writhed across the floor, getting closer, growing larger, and more horrifying with each undulation. Frank Rogers was crazed with fear and fighting to tear away the ropes that held him before the demonic reptiles got close enough to bite. He was howling like a wolf when the lights came on.

He stopped when someone threw a bucket of water on him.

Gasping, spitting and sucking for air, Rogers came back to reality, slow and shaky. At first he thought it was another nightmare, but regained a bit of his senses when he recognized the blue-eyed copper he'd seen at the door to the card-room—*Andrew*, Rogers thought, *that's his name. Andrew.* He saw that Andrew was carrying a knife in his left hand. It was all Frank could focus on; the shine and glitter of honed steel and bone handle; it looked razor-sharp and ready. Rogers started to shake all over. It was as if his body was hooked to the electrical circuits that powered the incandescent bulbs illuminating the room. Teeth chattering, he said, "Are you come to kill me then?"

"Meself? Oh. No. No Boyo. I come to cut yer loose and clean ya up. 'Twill hurt like a bloody bastard though, when I get the ties off." Andrew was careful, as he sliced through Frank's ligatures, and drew blood only a few times when he cut the tightest of the knots. That was where Rogers had forced the hemp deep into his flesh as he fought to get free. When the ropes came off and the blood returned, Frank Rogers felt as if every bone in his body was being tapped with tiny silver hammers. It was the most exquisite of all his tortures, and among the most painful.

As the restraints came off, his senses returned little by little as his pain diminished, and his nightmares faded. Frank realized that he was covered in his own waste. He was bloody and bruised from his pubis to his Adam's apple. Every square inch of his body was sore and he was dying of thirst. "Water," he said, but his throat was so raw and dry from the hours and hours of screaming, that it came out like the croak of an angry duck.

Somehow, Andrew was able to interpret the noise, and produced a wet towel that he put between Frank's teeth. "Just let the water seep into your mouth nice and slow. When your throat feels a bit better, you can have a glassfull. Go easy or you'll puke yer guts out."

Frank nodded, did as he was told and felt his old self start to come back with each drop of water he swallowed. His self-confidence had been eroded and his psyche damaged when he was alone and helpless and terrified in the dark, but his survival instincts—together with his intelligence and natural cunning—were reasserting themselves with every breath he took. He began looking for clothes, weapons and a means of escape before he was able to stand on his own feet.

Andrew Coker must have noticed the change in Rogers demeanor, because he said, "Don'a try it, Boyo. You're almost out of the woods, but not quite."

"Meaning what?"

"We're leavin' town. I'm here to get ya cleaned up, on yer feet and dressed. Then we're goin' to walk down to Union Station an' catch an eastbound train."

Frank saw a pair of older, heavyset women, pouring hot water into a portable tin bathtub and waving him over. He looked at

Andrew, and said, "Where am I? And how long have I been here?"

"You're in a sub-basement of the Oxford Hotel, and you've been here for a bit over four and a half days. It's Tuesday by the way, four o'clock in the afternoon."

"We ain't goin' to Oklahoma, are we . . . I don't want to go there."

"No. We're goin' to St. Louis. I'll fill yerself in on the train, but ya gotta get a move on. It's leavin' at six o'clock, with or without us and I for damn sure don't wanna be answerin' to Adolph if we ain't on it."

"Who's Adolph," Frank said, as he stepped out of his foul skivvies and into the warm soapy bath, where two of the Irish cleaning ladies he'd last seen at Maddie Silks place began tending to him.

"Adolph Duff," Andrew said. "The guy who runs some of our outfit. The Boss. He's the one who decided to let yerself live when the others wanted to kill ya."

Chapter Thirty-Four

Boyd Pirtle went from Judge Hightower's chamber to the studio of a local portrait artist and spent the rest of the day with her, sketching a likeness of Frank Rogers. Pirtle, who had a good memory for details and faces, was pretty sure by the end of the afternoon, that he had a near-photographic representation of the outlaw. He thanked the woman for her patience and attentiveness to his almost ceaseless and minute changes, and told her that he felt the portrait was as accurate as they could make it.

She laughed and said, "*De nada, señor, de nada,*" and refused to accept payment for her work, claiming that it was every citizen's duty to assist law enforcement officers, however and whenever they could.

"Well," Pirtle said as he folded the ink drawing and secreted it inside the sweatband of his Stetson, "we could sure use more like yourself." She smiled, and bid him a good afternoon. Pirtle tipped his hat in response, and took a short walk and trolley ride downtown to his hotel, where he ate an early supper and checked out. He telegraphed Captain Newton in Austin of his plans, made his way to the train station and hopped aboard the next mail car headed north to Oklahoma City. He was acting on logic, plus a hunch, that it was the place Frank Rogers would've gone to . . . and the spot where he'd be found.

Arriving a bit after midnight, Pirtle napped until dawn on one of the hard station benches, using his gunbelt and coat for a pillow. At five in the morning the place started to come alive, and he awoke, aching, rumpled and tired . . . but eager to start hunting for *That spawn of the Devil,* the outlaw and murderer, Frank Rogers.

Ten days later—although hints and rumors were rife, and an Oklahoma City Marshal had made him privy to the unsolved, execution-style murder and robbery of a pawn shop owner and his assistant that Pirtle thought, *Sounds just like somethin' that evil bastard would do*—Boyd Pirtle was no closer to capturing Frank Rogers than he was the day of the Clarendon bank robbery. When the telegram came that night, it was a frustrated and angry Special Agent who replied, *On my way now,* to Captain Newton in Austin. He had other work to do.

* * *

In Denver, Colorado, a dazed Frank Rogers was being shanghaied aboard an AT&SF passenger train by a tough and unrelenting guard named Andrew Coker. Weak from four and a half days of starvation, sensory deprivation and being beaten, almost to the point of organ failure, Rogers was feeling closer to death than life. By rights, he should have been hospitalized—but he was young and tough, strong-willed and vindictive—and he craved revenge. It was a family trait. *"Never, never allow a trespass against any of us to go unpunished,"* had been drummed into his head from his earliest childhood. His father always told him that, *"Anyone who does injury to a Mormon shall atone with their own precious blood."* As he was helped down the platform, into the Pullman and half-dragged, half-carried to his seat, Frank Rogers made a silent vow to draw the blood of Denny McCullough and watch him die. But he had to recover first.

Frank Rogers' return to health began less than an hour later in the dining car. He began to eat, and was able to hold down some poached eggs, toast and tea with cream and sugar. As he ate, his color and strength improved, followed by heightened curiosity. Lighting an after-dinner cigarette he bummed from Andrew, Rogers said, "What can you tell me?"

"About what"

"Everything. Why'd you all jump me like that . . . where's my money, 'n guns, and clothes? Where the fuck are we goin' right now?" As the words gushed out, Frank's agitation rose with each word, and his anger with every question.

Andrew smoked, watched Frank and waited for him to run down. When he did, Andrew said, "Your story checked out. Otherwise, Denny would've put yez in the furnace. Just like Adolph said."

"So that wasn't just scare tactics."

"No. Been done before."

"What about the rest of my questions. And how'd you check me out?"

"We figured yerself for a Pinkerton or Burns man. We had to be sure ya wasn't some kind of spy—like when they infiltrated the Mollie McGuires, up in Pennsylvania, back in the eighties."

"I don't know what you're talkin' about."

"Long story," Andrew said, as he put his cigarette out, then continued. "The Mollies were disruptin' and interferin' and vandalizin' the workin's of the coal mines—tryin' to unionize the miners. They were figurin' that if they cost the owners enough, they'd give in to the union and pay more. They was a tight knit bunch, the Mollies, tough bog-diggin' Irishmen and secretive as all hell. When the owners couldn't stop the destruction, they sent in a Judas—a Pinkerton man and a mick himself—who gained their trust and informed on 'em, then testified at their trial. The bastard watched 'em all hang."

"Informers are the downfall of an independent Ireland."

"That they are Boyo."

"And my other questions," Frank said as he drained another glass of water and signaled the waiter for a fresh pot of coffee. He'd had enough tea.

Chapter Thirty-Five

Andrew Coker lit another tailor-made cigarette and looked out at the wide open prairie, where grasses and spring flowers grew from Colorado to Canada, and where, once—not so long ago—buffalo herds roamed, that were so vast they stretched from horizon to horizon, and took days to pass by a single point.

Frank Rogers, watching his keeper for a tell, saw him studying the landscape and said, "They are surely the Great Plains of God."

Andrew refocused on Rogers. "Yes. Yes they are. I was just imaginin' what they looked like when the great buffalo herds still existed."

"Then it would take us ten, twenty, or even thirty times as long to get where we're goin' . . ."

Andrew smiled. "Nicely done. Smooth. You're gonna fit right in, once we get you trained."

Rogers just stared and said nothing. He waited.

"You and I are going on to St Louis. Adolph and the others will stop in Kansas City and run a few games, pluck a few pigeons . . . maybe even shear some sheep. Then they'll come on east and meet up with us."

Rogers helped himself to another one of Coker's cigarettes. He lit it, sucked in smoke and said as he exhaled, "I'm a common man, with only a basic education and a simple understandin' of terms. What the fuck d'you mean about *games, pigeon-pluckin'* and *lamb-shearin'?*"

Andrew chuckled, coughed on some smoke and pocketed the box of French cigarettes he'd put on the table. "Those are the terms," he said, "for what we do. Another way to put it is, we part certain suckers from their money. Pigeons, lambs and geese are some of the terms we use to describe those we take money from."

"With the crooked card games."

"Oh, hell . . . that's just a part of what we do . . . what we are, and to tell yuh the truth, it's not where most of the dough comes from."

The food helped. Rogers was beginning to feel better, but he was still suffering from the repeated beatings and other tortures he'd absorbed. He winced with pain as he reached for his coffee, and said, "I'm always interested in money. The more the merrier, and the faster the better."

Andrew Coker poured more coffee for himself. He took a sip and reflected for a moment, then said, "We all want the same thing, Boyo. We wanna be rich, and we don'a want to be old folk before we get it. The difference is how. I know you've been a tough guy . . . shootin' up towns and robbin' banks . . . killin' people. Your problem is, you lack skill and style. You charge in, like a bull in a china shop. You wind up breakin' more than yuh steal."

Rogers inhaled, "Are you sayin' I'm stupid?"

"No. Not in the least. Yuh just don't know any better is all. When the Chief checked on yez, we were all impressed by what a wide swath yerself's been cuttin'. None of us has any doubts about yer dedication to criminality. It's one a the things that kept Blonger from havin' Denny turn yer lights out."

"Who's we? And what Chief . . . Blonger? Blonger what? I don't get it."

Andrew Coker put down his cup. "That's because yerself's more or less undisciplined. I was the same way until I met Adolph, Lou Blonger and the others. See, we're organized for the purpose of takin' money from others. And we do it in big ways. The Chief is the head of the Denver Police Department."

"No lie . . . The Police Chief?"

"Yep. The one and only."

"Organized for crime," Rogers said, "I want the rest of the story, and another one a them smokes."

"Glad to oblige, but it's gonna take some time. Do ya think yez can walk . . ."

"I believe so. Why?"

"Because," Andrew said as he stood up, and stretched out the pain in his lower back, "the seats are a helluva lot more comfortable in the parlor car and I have much to tell yez."

Rogers made the journey on unsteady legs by holding on to the seatbacks as they shuffled down the aisles of two Pullmans. His worst moment came on the platforms between cars, when Andrew had to keep him from falling as the train rocked and swayed its way east at a steady sixty miles per hour. By the time he plopped down in one of the padded easy chairs the club car provided, Franks face was coated in sweat and every nerve cell in his body screamed for relief. The pain was harrowing, but it kept him fully engaged and focused on every word Andrew Coker spoke. They were momentous and they were life-changing. Rogers was about to be wedded to organized crime, and transformed from a crude thug to one of the most able grifters to ever come prancing into the lives of ordinary, honest people. Because, as Coker was about to lay out for him, the gang of bunko-artists he was being pressed into, owned almost all of the police, prosecutors, judges and politicians in Denver. And from there they'd branched out into Kansas, Missouri, Georgia, Florida, New Orleans and Galveston,

Texas. There was no person of wealth who was safe from the schemes of the grifters of the Blonger-Duff gang, and the gang was protected from prosecution.

* * *

As the year 1897 rolled on, the new President, William McKinley, promised prosperity and a full dinner bucket for all; the yellow journal sensationalist newspapers of William Randolph Hearst and Joseph Pulitzer were beating the drums for war with Spain; and jingoism was sweeping across America.

Frank Rogers, aka Ralph Stuart, whose real name was Chester Stringfellow, embarked on a forced two and a-half year odyssey through several midwest and southern states, learning from the masters, the craft of swindling honest—but greedy—folks out of their money.

Texas Ranger Special Agent Boyd Pirtle was always on the move in the Lone Star State he loved and served . . . from the Red River in the north, to the Rio Grande in the far southwest, wherever the biggest crimes happened and the baddest outlaws operated, Pirtle was there to defend justice, represent the law, and speak for the dead. But he was forever on the lookout for any sign of the outlaw Frank Rogers . . . who seemed to have disappeared from the earth.

In Cleburne, Texas, Ella Stringfellow kept living her life as she always had, keeping to herself in her big lonely house, seeking any kind of news of her twin, teaching school and working part-time at the library. She continued to tutor and read with a boy named Skipper, whenever he could get a break from one of his many jobs, and together they watched the antics of a fast-growing kitten named Duke, who was the unholy terror of any small creature that crept, crawled, wriggled, or flew into his presence.

It was a quiet period for all of them—those last years of the nineteenth century—as the Old West eased into the pages of history and became the stuff of legend. Neither Ella, Pirtle or Frank Rogers had any inkling of the momentous changes coming with the new century, but the modern age, and all of their lives, was about to intersect in ways that none of them could have imagined.

The Twentieth Century would bring earth-shaking advances in industry, medicine, technology and science, plus stupendous changes in society and the power and scope and size of governments. Nations were going to be born, empires crumble, and colonialism disappear as wars were fought on a world-wide basis, where tens of millions would die from the malfeasance of men and the perfidy of their plans. It would become the age when mankind achieved the unthinkable . . . the ability to slaughter every living being on the planet. The Old West would evermore be revered as the last age of innocence.

Chapter Thirty-Six
1901

The first year of the new century began with a fortuitous bang in America, when a massive underground lake of oil was discovered in Beaumont, Texas at a place called Spindletop. The first well—known as the Lucas Gusher—spewed 100,000 barrels of oil per day, for nine days, before it could be brought under control. Its discovery ushered in the oil age, and made the United States the world's leading oil producer. A bit less than two weeks later, Queen Victoria, England's reigning monarch for more than sixty years, died and was succeeded by King Edward VII, thus ending the Victorian age of empire, when Great Britain colonized the world and bestrode it like a colossus. Back in America, an axe-wielding woman named Carrie Nation began publicly smashing up saloons. Her antics brought all of America's attention to the scourge of alcoholism and helped kick off the Prohibition Movement. On the third of March, William McKinley, the twenty-fifth President of the United States of America, was sworn in to his second term of office. The former Police Commissioner of New York City and the leader of an all-volunteer group of horse cavalry known as the Rough Riders during the War of 1898—Theodore Roosevelt—was sworn in as the Vice President. In early

May, a boiler explosion at a candle factory in Jacksonville, Florida set off a conflagration that burned more than 1700 buildings to the ground and decimated the city.

In Cleburne, Texas a woman named Ella Stringfellow was determined to find her only brother, Chester. He was her twin, who'd vanished two days after their father was shot and killed by an unknown assailant in the fall of 1881. There'd not been a single word of his whereabouts—no news of his life or death in all of the intervening years—until the checks started coming. They were sporadic, the amounts varied and she never knew if, or when, the next one would show up. The monies were always sent to the same bank in Ft. Worth, always in her name and the remitter was always Chester Stringfellow. Ella had no idea whether or not the funds were actually from her brother, and she left every cent in a savings account at the same bank. It amounted to a large nest egg.

In an attempt to solve the mystery, Ella resorted to placing a classified ad in the personals section of the Ft. Worth newspaper . . . seeking information and offering a reward for help finding the long-lost twin brother. The simple plea ran on the last day of the month for a couple of years without results, until late in May, when a handsome, wiry and tough Special Agent with the Texas Rangers came to her door. He said his name was Boyd Pirtle and that he was hunting for a notorious outlaw named Frank Rogers—a man who'd robbed, raped, pillaged and murdered his way across four states and some of old Mexico—who'd disappeared back in the summer of 1897 after a failed bank robbery. When Pirtle showed Ella Stringfellow an artist's pen and ink drawing of the rough-cut bad man, it was a near-perfect likeness of her twin, and left no doubt about his identity. Frank Rogers and Chester Stringfellow were one and the same person. The news touched, and dismayed the young woman, who, it appeared, had a hard time believing that her own flesh and blood had sunk so low, and become so wonton.

As he left Cleburne, Pirtle assured Ella Stringfellow that he'd let her know when he captured Frank Rogers, dead or alive.

Frank Rogers himself, was five states away at that moment, down in south Florida, where he'd served his apprenticeship with some of the greatest swindlers who ever lived. Now, Rogers was a rising star in the Blonger-Duff gang . . . and the organized crime groups most outstanding new talent. He was *Creative, ruthless as a hungry badger and bold as a Baghdad thief,* in the words of Lou Blonger, the patriarch and founder of the gang. He'd been cheating folks for decades, and never spent one single day in jail. Frank Rogers had emerged from his chrysalis in refined crime, as polished as the scrying stone Joseph Smith had used to discover the golden breastplate and magic spectacles.

Now, Rogers was on the move. One of the spotters up in Colorado had befriended a mark who; *Inherited more money than he knows what to do with . . . owns half the City of Philadelphia . . . and got about as much sense as a common housefly. He's a friend of the General who owns the D&RG railroad and started Colorado Springs. Get here quick,* the telegram said, *I'm not the only one who knows about him, but at the moment, I have the most control. He's in love and looking to buy a gold mine. Hurry, Sugar.*

Frank Rogers smiled, packed his bags and took the next train out of town. The mountains were calling, and he was looking forward to fresh air, cool nights and harvesting what was sure to be a monumental payout. Charity Moon had never let him down. Not ever.

Chapter Thirty-Seven

It's always hot in Texas in the summertime. It's so searing in fact, that Phil Sheridan, the renowned Civil War general and Indian fighter once quipped: *If I owned Texas and Hell, I would rent out Texas and live in Hell . . .* But that was before the summer of 1901.

The heat wave began early in June, two weeks after Boyd Pirtle tipped his hat to Ella Stringfellow on Featherston Lane and drove away in a rented buggy with red wheels. Day after day, the sun rose up into a clear and cloudless blue sky and began baking the juice out of every living thing it touched. Rain became a distant memory, and the streams dried up, then the ponds and lakes, the reservoirs and the wells. Trees and grasses wilted and went brown, curled up and died from lack of water as the soil baked and became a hard scabby crust, just before it cracked and split, and turned to powder. Farm animals, wild creatures and people all began to suffer and die as the heat persisted, no moisture came, and the temperatures stayed in the nineties and hundreds day after day, week after week, and month after month in an area that went along the Colorado-Kansas border north into Canada, south into Mexico, and all the way east to the Atlantic Ocean. It was the greatest heat wave ever recorded. Before it was over, it killed more than nine thousand people—the aged, the infirm and the very young—they were all taken. Death didn't discriminate.

Ella Stringfellow was at her wits end with the scorching hot days and nights from which there was no escape. Her lawns, flowers and vegetable gardens were all casualties of the unrelenting and unsparing solar furnace in the center of the summer sky. She was hot and sweaty, itching and uncomfortable, grouchy and bad tempered from the time she got up until she went to bed . . . where she was too hot to sleep. The nights and days seemed to be endless and alike, with no relief in sight.

Ella found herself wondering about her brother, but whenever she did, it brought her thoughts quickly back to the Ranger who'd come in May with the news of the outlaw and murderous bandit named Frank Rogers; Chester's sinister other self. *Like Jekyll and Hyde,* she thought, *but Hyde is the dominant one . . .* Then she wondered where Texas Ranger Special Agent Boyd Pirtle was at that moment, what he was doing . . . and if he ever thought about her. She smiled to herself and went to the kitchen to pump some well water onto a rag to cool her face and neck.

* * *

After Pirtle left Cleburne, he'd visited the Stockman's Bank in Ft. Worth, then gone to Austin, Texas, where he briefed Captain Wiley Newton about the information he'd gleaned from his visits to Ella Stringfellow and Oliver Witherspoon that confirmed, almost beyond a doubt, that Frank Rogers was likely in the Pikes Peak Area, somewhere in Colorado Springs.

The second half of Pirtle's debriefing had graver impact on the stalwart Ranger Commander, because it had far greater implications for everyone. The security of the whole country might be at risk. Captain Newton listened to each and every one of his Special Agent's words with the gravitas of St. Peter hearing a penitent at the Pearly Gates, when Pirtle recited the known facts, plus Ella Stringfellow's comments about her father—a Mormon Bishop and high-ranking officer of the ultra-secret LDS vigilance group known as the Danites—and his role in the appointments of U.S. Marshals and their deputies all over the west, the Captain was incredulous. But his disbelief was overcome by Pirtle's notebook, which had names, dates, places and real estate transactions he'd gleaned from the copies Ella had made of her father's secret files.

"Where are those documents now," Captain Newton said, as he laid his knife and fork at the back of his plate with military precision and dropped his napkin on top.

Pirtle speared the last bit of well-done steak and chewed. He swallowed and said, "She told me that a few days after her father was murdered, a couple of high-rankin' members of the LDS church with seats on the Council of Elders—the ones who make the church doctrine—showed up with a U.S. Marshal and took everythin' in her father's office."

"Furniture too?"

"No. They left his desk and chair, a stackin' bookcase and a double student lamp. But they grabbed every scrap of paper, includin' his collection of huntin' and fishin' books, which she complained about. They brought a dray wagon, some husky young workmen and took it all . . . lock, stock and barrel."

"So if she hadn't made those copies . . ."

"We wouldn't know one damn thing about this plot by the Mormons to insulate, protect and propagate themselves and their beliefs throughout the country."

"Sweet sufferin' Jesus . . . as if we didn't have enough to do . . ."

Pirtle pushed his plate away. "Thanks Wiley, for buyin' our supper. I'm aimin' to get outta here by the end of the week, head up to Colorado. I'd like to take Will Posey with me. He deserves to be in on it when I get Frank Rogers."

Captain Wiley Newton twisted in his chair and shoved it back from the table. He said, "You still have your room at Mrs. Orr's boardin' house?"

"Sure. She don't charge me, don't mind my extended and frequent absences neither. I give her money from time to time anyway. But the truth is, she likes havin' a Ranger for a tenant. I believe it helps her keep the peace."

"Okay. Here's what I want yuh to do. Go home. Get cleaned up and sleep in a real bed for a change. Be ready by ten o'clock tomorrow morning. I'll pick you up. Wear your best . . . we're goin' to the Governor's Office."

Chapter Thirty-Eight

Texas Ranger Special Agent Boyd Pirtle was sitting in a white wicker chair on Mrs. Orr's porch when a barouche, pulled by a pair of chestnut mares and driven by Will Posey, stopped alongside the cannonball gate of the iron picket fence that surrounded the yard.

Pirtle stood, resplendent in a black frock coat and matching pants, boiled and starched white shirt with a long black tie, a silver and turquoise mounted leather belt and black leather boots, polished to a mirror shine. As always, his .44 caliber Colt pistol was holstered at his hip, but now it sported aged ivory grips instead of the usual walnut ones. With his high-crowned, curled edge black Stetson and the heavy black moustache on a tanned and seamed face, he made an imposing figure striding down the walk with his Ranger badge shining in the sun.

From his perch on the drivers seat Will Posey said, "Hot damn, Mr. Pirtle, if I was a law-breaker, I'd throw down my guns and surrender, just by lookin' at'cha."

Pirtle flashed his lop-sided grin as he shut the front gate. "It ain't every day I am summoned by the Governor. How's your leg doin' these days?"

"Fair to middlin' most of the time. Gets pesky when cold

weather sets in."

"Healed bones'll do that," Pirtle said as he climbed into the carriage and sat beside Captain Newton, who'd moved over to make room. "Consider it a reminder when the rheumatiz flares up, to say thanks that yuh still got your leg . . . can still walk about like a man . . . instead a havin' to gimp around on crutches like all the old vets, God bless 'em."

Posey didn't reply, just chucked the reins on the horses rumps, setting them off for the Capitol Building and the Governor's Office.

As Pirtle sat down, Captain Newton said, "Mornin,' Boyd. Y'all are handsomely dressed, for a fact."

"It's the only clothes I have, other than my every day ones. I ain't worn 'em since I buried Genevieve."

"How long's it been?"

"Seven years as of last March."

"Didn't mean to make yuh uncomfortable Boyd . . ."

"It's okay Wiley . . . I'm over it . . . just don't talk about it all that much. I left a lot behind when I sold our house a couple years after she died."

"How long you been roomin' at Mrs. Orr's ?"

Pirtle watched the houses passing by as Will Posey drove the mares at a steady trot. After several moments, he said, "Almost five years. Didn't realize it'd been quite so long."

"Well it ain't like you don't have nothin' to do. I've kept'cha on a constant run the whole time."

"It's crime and criminals that keep me goin', otherwise I'd prob'ly spend too much time in a saloon somewheres, feelin' sorry for myself. And speakin' of . . . just where did this fancy carriage come from? Makes me feel like I done somethin' wrong to even be ridin' in it."

Captain Newton laughed and said, "Don't worry Boyd. The

Governor sent it over special, to bring us to his office. It belongs to the State of Texas and it's for ceremonial use only."

"Like inaugural parades and such?"

"Yeah. And whenever dignitaries of some kind or another are in town for a visit."

He was about to say something else when Will Posey turned and said, "We're almost there, Cap'n. You want me to go around back?"

"No. Pull up front, so Boyd and I can go in the front door."

"Like dignitaries," Pirtle said with his trademark crooked grin.

A few minutes later and still chuckling, the two senior Rangers entered the building, signed in and were escorted to the Governor's Office, where they waited in the antechamber with a pair of armed guards for Governor Hoyt Slater to receive them.

A tedious fifteen minutes went by, in which Pirtle examined the western paintings that adorned the room, and Captain Newton conferred in hush tones with the pair of Rangers at the door. Then at last the door to the inner office opened and a harried young man in a rumpled seersucker suit came out with a large sheaf of unbound documents in his hands. He said, "Thanks for your patience gentlemen. My name is Milton. I'm Governor Slater's assistant, and it'll be just a few more minutes I'm afraid. He's on the telephone with Señor Porfirio Diaz, the President of Mexico."

Pirtle, standing alongside Captain Newton at that moment, heard him say under his breath, "Diaz, is the great defiler of Mexico and the corrupter of all he touches." He didn't acknowledge the *sotto voce* comment, and watched, as Milton deposited the pile of papers on his desk and hurried back into the inner sanctum with the top man in Texas.

When Pirtle looked at his boss and raised his eyebrows in a *'What the . . .'* expression, Wiley Newton just shrugged. It took another twenty minutes of standing around before they were ushered into the Governor's Office.

Chapter Thirty-Nine

Boyd Pirtle was in for a shock when he was introduced to Governor Slater. The Ranger had braced himself for a stuffy, stiff and uncomfortable meeting with a man born of the aristocratic and patrician classes Pirtle detested. He was disabused of the notion in seconds.

When Milton opened the door and led the Rangers into the Governors private office, a coatless Hoyt Slater stood up from the executive desk where he was working through a pile of folders and said, "Hello, Wiley. It's good to see you again. And you, must be the dedicated Special Agent I've been getting such glowing reports about. Hoyt Slater. I'm pleased to meetcha," as he stuck his hand out.

"Boyd Pirtle, Sir."

The Governor came out from behind his desk and guided them to a sitting area at the far end of the office. As they took positions around a low central table he said, "Milton, send the steward up with coffee."

After the young man left the room and closed the doors behind him, the Governor said, "Okay Wiley, what's so important that I had to get *El Presidente* off the phone."

"It's complicated, Sir. I'm gonna have Boyd go through it all. He's the one who sussed it out. But yuh better get ready, 'cause it's gonna readjust some of your thinkin' and it's gonna require action. And the sooner the better."

Just as Pirtle was about to speak, there was a soft knock at the door, and Milton, followed by a white-coated steward carrying a large silver tray bearing cups and a coffee service for four came in the room. "Please leave it on the table Polonius," the Governor said. "We'll serve ourselves. Milton, kindly stay and take notes."

Governor Slater himself, assisted by Captain Newton, poured coffee for them while Pirtle arranged his notes and began his narrative, accompanied by the furious scratching of Milton's pen.

It took a bit less than two hours to lay it all out. Pirtle began with the tip from Juan Medina, the El Paso, Texas Ranger who alerted them to the pending robbery in Clarendon by the Frank Rogers Gang, followed by the shootout, the escape and the three hangings in Ft. Worth. He didn't embellish, aggrandize, or spare any details of his fruitless search to find Frank Rogers. Pirtle recited everything and the Governor listened patiently.

When he began detailing about his wild hunch after seeing Ella Stringfellow's personal advertisement in the Ft. Worth newspaper, the Governor interrupted Pirtle's account. "Do I have this right? You went to interview that woman based only on a guess?"

"Yes Sir. I did."

"Wasn't that pretty presumptive of you . . . a potential waste of time and money?"

"Sure. No question. But I had no other option. I'd exhausted every other lead. The case was gettin' colder by the day, and I promised our dead lawmen that I'd never stop lookin' until I was either dead, or had caught the murderous bastard, dead or alive."

Governor Slater put his cup down. "I admire your dedication and tenacity, but this doesn't come up to the level of my involvement . . . not even close."

Wiley Newton, who'd been silent up to that moment, said, "No Governor. It don't. I wouldn't be here if that was all. It's this next piece that concerns all three of us. Boyd gleaned it out by listenin', lettin' the woman speak and takin' good notes. We can't handle this next part by ourselves. It's gonna take you . . . and the Federal Government to straighten it out."

"I'm listening," the Governor said, but his frown and crossed arms betrayed his skepticism.

Pirtle began by saying, "Governor, you're only the third person after myself and Captain Newton who's been made aware of the situation I'm about to disclose. It's a third-hand account . . . but I am certain of its truthfulness, based on the woman's demeanor as I interviewed her, the extensive notes she took—and which I've accurately reproduced—that give confirmin' names, dates, places and amounts. The records are meticulous, the execution flawless and the plot diabolical. It is nothin' less than a threat to our union, our democracy and our way of life. In my humble opinion it represents the openin' moves of a bloodless *coup d'etat* to replace our Constitutional Republic with a Theocracy run by the LDS church."

"You mean the Mormons."

"Yessir. I do."

"Were you in the late war, Pirtle?"

"Spanish-American, no. I was at Chickamauga with General Hood."

"You must have been young."

"Seventeen."

"One last question," the Governor said. "Were you pardoned?"

"Yessir. I was at Richmond and Appomattox, surrendered with General Lee to Union General Chamberlain. There I took the oath of allegiance and was pardoned."

"As did I," Hoyt Slater said, "at Meridian, Mississippi."

Pirtle said, "I don't like talkin' about it. Generally I don't."

"I understand. The reason I asked was to make certain you're committed to *e pluribus unum* and not some Lost Cause."

"*One from many,* is the motto of the United States of America. It's something I took to heart all those years ago in Virginia, when I raised my right hand, swore my loyalty and stepped forward."

"The floor is yours, Mr. Pirtle. I'm all eyes and ears."

Chapter Forty

Pirtle laid his first piece of evidence on the table for all to see—the ink drawing he'd made with the Hispanic artist in Ft. Worth. "This," he said, as he folded it out on the table, "Is the outlaw Frank Rogers. The Stringfellow woman positively identified him as her twin brother, Chester. He disappeared two days after their father, Carl, was gunned down in the street in front of his house in November of 1882. His killer has never been found. I intend lookin' into that as this investigation proceeds. He, Carl Stringfellow, was a Mormon Bishop, a founding member of the Council of Elders and the equivalent of a Commanding General in the secret Mormon vigilance group called the Danites.

The Governor said, "The Mormons have denied them for at least fifty years."

"Yes, and they disavowed plural marriage too, but Ella Stringfellow disclosed that there's at least two colonies of Fundamentalist Mormons carrying on with the practice down in Mexico. She hinted at the possibility of others, unofficially sanctioned by the church, here in the US."

"What do you mean by that?"

"The Elders know about it, but choose not to do anythin' to

stop them. The Fundamentalists openly defy the stated, public policy of the LDS church—without which Utah would never have been admitted as a state—and nothin' happens. It's only a small part of a far larger plan, in my opinion, that Miss Stringfellow enlightened me about."

Pirtle then laid out Bishop Stringfellow's scheme, step-by-step, and deal-by-deal, showing how the LDS Elder had traded properties all over the west for appointments throughout the U. S. Marshals Service. It took about two hours, but when the Ranger Special Agent concluded, the Governor looked ill at ease, and sat with a stunned expression on his face. The silence was deafening.

The quiet lasted for an age, while Governor Slater composed himself. At last he drew in a lungful of air and said, "This information is twenty years old. Is it even relevant now?"

"Yes," Wiley Newton said, "now more than ever, for several reasons. First, they've had all that time to improve and expand their strategy and recruit and train more Danite soldiers. They've been operatin' in total secrecy. This may only be the tip of the iceberg . . . we haven't any idea how they've adapted and modified their original plans, or what they're up to now. Last of all, Utah achieved statehood four years ago, which means that they now have Senators and Congressmen in Washington, D.C., where they trade favors and influence like old men swap war stories. They all get elected as honest and poor men, but every damned one of 'em retires rich. You may say whatever you want about 'em, but the Mormons are smart, devout, and hard workin'. With a plan this nefarious, in place for this long, there's no tellin' how far they've got with it, but you can bet your bottom dollar—it won't only be surprisin'—it's gonna be hard as hell to stop."

The Governor looked like he'd been gut-shot. He said, "You're right. I agree. The problem is, what do we do about it now?"

For the first time since they'd convened in the late morning,

Milton spoke up. He said, "Sir, it might be time to get the State Attorney General in here, and the Leaders of the Texas House and Senate as well, for advice and consent."

"It's a good thought, and under normal circumstances, I would do just that, but these are not ordinary events. I want to keep this information close . . . the less who know about it right now, the better. I'm counting on discretion from all three of you, and Milton, I want all of your notes kept under lock and key at all times. And kindly send Polonius up here with sandwiches and drinks. We're going to be here for a while."

"Yes, Governor," Milton said, as he put his portfolio of handwritten records on the executive desk and left the room.

The afternoon passed with the four men shucking off their heavy coats and ties and working in rolled-up shirtsleeves as they formed plans to try and verify as much of the Stringfellow information as possible. And after a short intense debate with Governor Slater as the arbiter and final decision-maker, they decided to start in Texas. Boyd Pirtle would do the investigating, with the full authority of the Governor's office behind him. Wiley Newton and Milton would act as facilitators for him, with the Ranger Commander allocating men and materials as needed, and Milton obtaining any legal documents, and providing a fast, secure conduit to the Governor, while at the same giving him deniability if he should need it. To Pirtle's great disappointment, Colorado Springs and Frank Rogers would have to wait.

As they went through the details, refining some, modifying others and erasing a few altogether, Pirtle said, "This is gonna involve a great amount of travel."

"There's no doubt about it," Governor Slater answered. "Will that be a problem?"

"No Sir, it isn't. But I'm tired of ridin' around in baggage cars, and sittin' on sacks of mail. It's only a step above ridin' the rails like a vagabond. And it's uncomfortable and dirty. I get where I'm goin', lookin' like a derelict."

"I think I can take care of that," Milton said "I could issue him an all-access, all railroads pass when I write his other credentials. With your permission Sir."

"Good idea," Governor Slater said. "Make it happen. Wiley, any other thoughts?"

"I'm wonderin' if we oughta send an escort with Boyd . . . someone to watch his back?"

"The thought crossed my mind too," Governor Slater said. "Mr. Pirtle?"

"Probably a good idea, but I'd like to think it over tonight, weigh the pros and cons . . . if we do, I want to take Will Posey. He's the best shot I've ever seen with a rifle, pistol, or shotgun."

"Isn't he the disabled Ranger? The one with the pronounced limp?"

"Yes, Governor, he is. But I'd bet my life on him," Pirtle said.

"Well then, you are," the Governor said, "because I'm pulling rank. This isn't the Wild West any longer. You're getting a bodyguard."

Two days later, Boyd Pirtle and Will Posey climbed aboard a Southern Pacific passenger train headed for west Texas, and straight into the teeth of the worst heat wave ever recorded.

Chapter Forty-One

Skipper didn't show up to read with Ella for the third consecutive time in late July. They met every Tuesday and Thursday without fail, at four in the afternoon. It was the only break the poor kid got from a brutal work schedule that would likely have crushed many an adult and for that reason alone, she was pretty sure his absence wasn't on purpose. She'd grown fond of the young boy over the past four years, and was delighted to find that he had a lively and quick mind which soaked up knowledge like a sponge. She enjoyed tutoring him. He was smart as a slap in the face, enjoyed learning and thirsted for an education. His absence was unprecedented. Ella was worried about him, and decided to take action.

Two summers earlier, Ella Stringfellow had joined the national craze and treated herself to a brand-new Columbia standard bicycle with polished wooden rims, tuned metal spokes and rubber tires on twenty-four inch wheels. It had a tubular steel frame, cable brakes with cork handlebar grips, varnished wood fenders, a bell, a woven wicker basket in front, a battery operated headlamp and a padded horsehide seat with a small leather bag of tools strapped underneath. It was her pride and joy. She kept it in the front hallway of her house and rode it everywhere: shopping, church and school. Now, she was going to take it on a mercy mission.

Early Friday morning Ella put on her riding clothes and a flat-brimmed straw hat with a purple satin ribbon, packed some snacks and a jug of water, and set out for the other side of town. Thirty minutes later—after a wrong turn that got her lost for a bit, and being chased on two different occasions by stray dogs—she pedaled down an unnamed dusty wagon track to a small run-down and weather-beaten adobe house. She could see two little girls, playing with a ball made of rags in the shade of the front porch. In front of them, some household items were thrown on top of a large pile of wood crates and boxes in the yard.

The girls were so intent on their game of catch, that they didn't notice Ella, standing there beside her bicycle, until she spoke. "Hello young ladies. Are you having a good game of catch?"

Startled by the sudden appearance of an adult, the smaller girl missed the ball, which rolled off the porch and out into the dusty, weed-infested expanse that passed for a front lawn. She burst into tears and hid behind her bigger playmate. Neither of the girls said anything, they just clung to each other and stared. Ella could see that both of them were painfully under-nourished—skinny as toothpicks—barefooted and wearing shifts made from old flour sacks. But they were clean, bright-eyed and well cared for . . . just dirt poor. Ella tried again. As she leaned her bicycle against the porch and retrieved the rag ball, she said, "My name is Miss Ella. What are your names," as she put the ball back on the porch in front of them, and stepped back.

The bigger of the two girls said, "I'm Carole, and this is my sister, Evelyn."

"Evelyn Ruth," came a second tiny voice between hiccups.

"Carole, Evelyn Ruth, I'm pleased to make your acquaintances."

"You don't have to say Evelyn Ruth, just Evelyn is okay . . . she only says that when she's being prissy."

"Am not."

Not wanting the girls to get into an argument, Ella said, "I'm wondering if you could help me . . . I'm looking for Skipper. Do you know him? I thought he lived here."

"He's our brother. But he's not here. He and Mother went to take care of Daddy."

At her sister's mention of their father, Evelyn began to cry, while her big sister held her close and rocked her back and forth.

Ella said, "Skipper told me his father had been sick . . ."

"He died," Carole said, as she too began to weep.

Ella sat down on the edge of the shabby porch and wrapped her arms around the pair of sad little girls and comforted them as they grieved. They clung together like that for a long time and wept.

The sun was risen high enough in a relentlessly blue sky to have driven the morning coolness into memory by the time the girls had cried themselves dry. In an attempt to cheer them, Ella asked if they'd like to have some snacks and water. Moments later, Carole and Evelyn were both biting into juicy Texas peaches, picked the day before by Ella, from the tree behind her house. "My goodness, you girls must really like peaches," she said as she unscrewed the lid on a quart Mason jar of water and took a sip. "Now, how do you feel about a couple of oatmeal cookies and a drink of well water?" The three of them were chatting and devouring a ham sandwich together when a well-used buckboard, pulled by a decrepit old, spavined black mule named Burt, whose best days were at least a decade behind it, appeared at the other end of the lane. Up on the seat with the reins in his hands, Ella could see Skipper. Next to him, her face a mixture of privation, sorrow and bewilderment, was his mother, Mimi Lynn James.

Chapter Forty-Two

Ella watched the wagon approach and stood up when Skipper said, "Whoa," to the ancient mule alongside the pile of old crates and boxes. Skipper set the brake lever with his foot—as if he were a bigger, older man instead of a thirteen year-old boy—wrapped the leather traces around it, then rose to his feet and said, "Hello, Miss Ella. Would you just give me a moment here? This is my Ma."

"Hello Skipper. Mrs. James, I'm happy to meet you at last, but I feel like I've known you longer . . . Skipper's told me a lot about you."

"Did'ja come here to see how the poor folks do it," the stout woman in the threadbare black dress said as her son assisted her down to the ground.

Ella couldn't help but notice that the woman was about the same age as her, but three children, worry, and grinding poverty had all taken their toll. She looked much older than she was. Choosing her words with care, Ella said, "No ma'am, I did not. I came to check on Skipper—it's not like him to miss out on any of our reading sessions—but after spending a little time with Carole and Evelyn, I'd like to offer my condolences to you all. I'm sorry for your loss."

"Well, as you can see, Calvin weren't much of a provider, but he was a damned good planner. Yessiree, Lily Longtree. All he ever done was make plans . . . Mister Gunnadoo. That's what I called him. Get a job, I sez to 'im. 'Ats what I'm gunnado, he sez. Only he never done it. Now whatamIgonnado . . . three chilrens, no money and now no home, neither.'"

It was apparent to Ella that Mimi James's circumstances were crushing the woman. She made her way to the porch and sat down with a thump that was so violent, it made Ella cringe. Then the woman buried her face in her hands and sobbed, as she moved back and forth, with her whole body quivering. As she rocked, she made a high keening sound that came from somewhere down in her soul. It was an honest lamentation for the dead . . . and perhaps the living too, as she tried to deal with her misery. Carole and Evelyn stood on each side of their mother, trying to comfort her, as Ella had consoled them, only a short time earlier. In the yard, Skipper began loading wooden boxes and crates onto the buckboard, with tears streaming down his face. Ella Stringfellow, feeling callous and out of place in the midst of so much suffering and destitution—dressed in her fancy attire and riding her expensive bicycle—moved to help the boy.

After the first few boxes, Ella said, "I'm taller, why don't you get up on the wagon and stack, and I'll hand stuff up."

"Okay, Miss Ella," Skipper said as he wiped his nose on his sleeve. "There ain't much and I ain't sure where we're even goin' with it, and heck, I ain't even sure old Burt can pull the load, broke down as he is."

"Well, let's do one thing at a time and get the most important stuff. What's going on here? Why are you moving?"

Skipper took a wooden box that was stamped "Seattle Fish Co" on one end, and stacked it on top of a steamer trunk with a caved in side, and next to a galvanized wash tub stuffed with bedding, before he answered. Then he said, "Truth is Miss Ella, that even with all my jobs, I can't make enough to feed us and pay the rent. The rancher who owns the shack told us to clear out. He's gonna put his foreman in here as soon as we're gone. The only reason he ain't done it before now is 'cuz he knew Pa had the consumption . . . and he was nice enough to wait until Pa died before he kicked us out. We knew it was comin', just didn't know it'd be so soon."

"What's your momma's name Skipper?"

"Mimi. It's Mimi, Miss Ella."

"I'm going to send your sisters over here with you."

Ella handed several more boxes up to Skipper in quick succession, then made her way to the porch, where the two girls sat on either side of their mother. "Girls, would you go help Skipper for a bit? I need to speak with your mommy."

"Mrs. James, my name is . . ."

"I know who you are—you're all Skipper talks about—*Miss Ella this and Miss Ella that.* You're the one he left the cat with, the one I told him to drown."

"Yes I am. Skipper named him Duke, on account of his black and white fur, like he's all dressed up for a costume ball."

"I remember. It wasn't my finest day. I regret sayin' that, and tellin' him that . . . but life's hard . . . and it ain't gonna get no easier. Best all three of 'em learn it sooner, instead a later."

"No apology's necessary. I shouldn't have come here looking like Astor's pet goat. I wasn't using my head either. I hope you'll overlook my thoughtlessness."

"I will and I do. But now that my breakdown and hissey-fit's over with, I gotta figure out what to do next."

Ella looked at the buckboard, where the three youngsters . . . through no fault of their own . . . already had the twin strikes of poverty and ignorance against them. She watched, as they sweated and toiled together . . . and decided. She took a deep breath and said, "Do you think you'd be interested in a position as a live-in housekeeper and cook? I teach school and work part-time at the library. I can't pay much in the way of cash, but I can provide food, and shelter, and tutor all three kids. It's a long story, but I've got this big house I inherited twenty years ago when my father died."

It turned out to be an inspired suggestion—and the rarest of arrangements—because everyone involved benefited. By that Friday evening, Mimi James was moved into Mrs. Ince's old apartment, Skipper had his very own bedroom down the hall, and the two little girls named Carole and Evelyn were fast asleep in a room set aside just for them, inside their mother's apartment.

As far as Mimi was concerned, she'd awakened in Hell that morning . . . marched through Purgatory all day; buried her tubercular-ridden husband, Calvin 'Gunnado' James; moved all of her worldly possessions out into the elements under a blazing hot sun not knowing where—or how—she and her babies would survive; then was rescued by an angel and taken to Heaven . . . where she was now living in the most beautiful house she'd ever put her eyes on. She felt happy—and secure—for the first time since her father had sold her. He got a case of rotgut whiskey and two yearling colts as payment for his daughter when the tribe was camped on the Arkansas River in the summer of 1880, while the last of her people, the Southern Ute Nation, was being driven onto the reservation. She was thirteen years old at the time, and ever since, had been doing the bidding of Calvin 'Gunnado' James . . . submitting to his every whim . . . and shackled in servitude. *No more,* she thought, as she unbound her hair, still as black and shiny as a raven's wing, in preparation for bed that first night on Featherston Lane. *No goddamned more.*

Every morning for the rest of her life, Mimi Lynn James said a short prayer of thanks to the Great Spirit for her deliverance, using her Southern Ute tribal name . . . Rising Fawn.

Chapter Forty-Three

Frank Rogers was a true wolf in sheep's clothing. He'd honed and perfected the false persona he'd first invented back in Oklahoma City so well, he himself almost believed that the mild-mannered gent in the mirror was real. With his hair parted down the middle, his stylish mutton-chop whiskers, the precise, carefully groomed moustache and his round gold-rimmed spectacles, all of which, when combined with his cultured speech, stylish clothes and manicured nails, made Rogers look exactly like the lawyer, banker or Wall Street speculator he pretended to be. But under the disguise lurked the same murderous, amoral savage who'd always dwelt there. Only the veneer was different. The man was evil, right down to the bone.

Rogers worked on his card-manipulation skills for all five days of his rail trip from Florida to Colorado. He'd never be an adept like Dolly or Smitty, but his bottom-dealing and deck-stacking talents were good enough to win him a couple of hundred dollars in a low-stakes game the first few hours in the Club Car. By the time the train pulled into Atlanta—where he transferred lines and headed west—he was up nearly four hundred and fifty dollars without any of the other players being aware that Frank was cheating them. He was glad for the diversion, it helped him not think about the heat, which was devastating, and it gave him a little extra money to walk around with. He spent some of it during the overnight stop in Atlanta on a fancy hotel, a steak dinner and some female companionship for a few hours of fun and games between the sheets. It was a well-sated Frank Rogers who sent telegrams to Charity Moon and Adolph "Kid" Duff the next morning, letting them know that he'd arrive in Denver by the weekend.

When he stepped onto the platform in Denver on Saturday afternoon, Delbert McKnight—who Rogers would forever think of as 'Bunyan'—was waiting for him. He touched his hand to the brim of the black derby he was wearing and said, "Mr. Rogers, you are lookin' well, and prosperous too."

Frank Rogers, resplendent in a white linen suit, and appearing to be every inch the genteel southern lawyer he was pretending to be, eyed Bunyan, wearing blue-striped engineers overalls, a denim shirt with the sleeves rolled up to his melon-sized biceps and a red sweat bandana tied around his neck, "And you, Del, appear to be bigger, stronger and more fearsome than last I saw you down south."

The big man grinned and said, "Aye, that was a donnybrook to be remembered . . . me, yourself an' Andrew Coker against all them Florida crackers . . . wonder if they ever got the place put right."

"No. They were broke—and broken—by the time we got done with 'em. The place was burnt to the ground two weeks later."

"Dumb fookers."

"I think they were more naive than dumb. They just couldn't believe we could steal a whole peanut processing plant with a pen."

"Thought they was helpin' to cheat a big yankee bank outta all that money. I gotta laugh every time I thinks of it."

"It was a good score," Rogers said as they made their way down the platform to where a couple of porters were stacking baggage.

Frank pointed to a hefty brown alligator hide valise and said, "That one."

"What else," Bunyan said as he grabbed the suitcase and put it on the ground beside him.

"That's all, other than this here," Rogers said, and patted the brown leather briefcase he carried everywhere. "The rest of my things went on down to Colorado Springs, to the Antlers Hotel."

Without another word, the big man picked up Frank's luggage and set off through Union Station. Thirty minutes later, Rogers was ushered into the back room of a popular bar and watering hole on Broadway, a little bit south of downtown. Sitting at the table playing cards and drinking beer was Lou Blonger, Adolf Duff, a man in a Denver Police Uniform that had three silver stars on each side of his unbuttoned shirt collar, Helen Strong—or Dolly—as Rogers called her, Andrew Coker and Denny McCullough. Frank's eyes squinted an imperceptible amount when he saw his nemesis and sworn enemy, but he kept his burning desire for revenge to himself. He meant to keep his promise to do away with McCullough, but reminded himself that it had to be undetectable . . . *Not here, not now, not yet,* he thought as he smiled and nodded a silent greeting to the room.

Duff said, "The prodigy returns to the nest. Welcome back. Grab a beer, have a seat and join the game."

Rogers smiled, laughed and said, "Don't know about the prodigy stuff. I feel more like a coyote in the middle of a roomful of Alsatian Mastiffs."

His gibe earned him a laugh from the assembly, followed by Duff, who said, "Oh, so you're callin' us dogs are yuh?"

"Yep," Rogers said with a grin, adding, "big fucking dogs with sharp teeth and bad attitudes . . . especially that one over there," pointing with his chin at the police chief.

"He ain't here," Denny McCullough said, "and he ain't nivver gonna be here neither, Boyo. Don't you ever forget it."

The look Frank Rogers shot at him could have knocked a hole in the wall as he remembered, *Not here. Not now. Not Yet.*

Lou Blonger, speaking in the raspy voice Rogers remembered from his torture in the utter dark of the Oxford Hotel sub-basement, said, "Oh, shut the fuck up Denny. And you," he pointed at Frank Rogers, "sit your coyote ass down and join the fun."

Chapter Forty-Four

Two hours later, Rogers realized he'd made about a two-hundred and forty dollar contribution to Chief Whasisnames retirement fund, as he watched Dolly deal him hand after winning hand from the bottom and middle of the cards. Frank marveled at the level of her skills as she effortlessly manipulated the deck. *And the greedy old bastard don't even know . . . he really believes he's a world-class poker stud . . . when the truth is, he's a patsy, and a crooked-assed copper gettin' paid off.*

The game broke up a little while after that, when The Chief raked in an extra cash-heavy pot and announced he was sorry, but he had an important meeting downtown and he'd have to go. "Thanks all. Let's do it again next week," he said as he gave Dolly a twenty dollar tip, put on his hat and strolled out of the room.

And he's a tinhorn too, Frank thought, as he watched Blonger offer to buy everyone a drink at the bar outside, leaving himself and Adolph Duff alone at the table.

When he heard the door close, and the last of the players leave the room, Duff came right to the point. "Tell me," he said as he pulled a silver cigar case from his pocket, selected a fat black Colorado Claro, clipped the tip, then lit it with a wooden kitchen match and puffed, "what you're planning, and how you plan on doing it. My understanding is that you and Charity Moon have something cooking down in The Springs."

"Yeah," Rogers said, "we do. Charity has a rich young cluck from Philadelphia on the hook that she spotted in the casino that a Count from Austria—Pourtales is his name—built at a place called the Broadmoor. It's down in a canyon a little bit south of town. He, the Count, had a dairy farm down there, and he's been tryin' to sell luxury building lots on the property without much success. I guess he figured that a casino would attract the kind of rich swells he needed to buy property and build fancy houses down there. The Count pulled out when . . ."

"I don't care about the history lesson. What's it got to do with us and our outfit? Where's the payoff?"

"I'm gettin' to it Boss. Bear with me. It'll all make sense in a bit."

"Well bring it on, fer chrissake, before I die of aggravation."

Rogers looked at Duff for a long few moments without saying a word, until Adolph dropped his gaze. The implication was clear. Duff was a manipulator who used suasion to get his way, but Rogers was an apex predator who wouldn't hesitate to kill. After he re-established who was who, or what, Frank continued as if he'd never been interrupted. "So, the Count took his whippin' and sold out after the gold strike up in Cripple Creek. But it's who he unloaded it to that's important."

"Why," Duff said.

"Because that's where the Philadelphia connection comes in. See, a Civil War General, a Union General named William Palmer is the one who founded Colorado Springs."

"Everybody knows that."

"Sure, but he comes from the richest part of The City of Brotherly Love . . . an' he convinced others in the high hat crowd to join him, and prove themselves by makin' their own fortunes out in the west. Two of 'em, named Penrose and Tutt did, up in the minin' district on the backside of Pikes Peak. They're some of the investors who bought out old Count Pourtales and now there's all kinds of talk about buildin' a world class hotel next to the lake and casino. I don't know if it'll ever happen or not, and I don't care, 'cause the result is that those rich fucks back east are flockin' to the Springs like crows to a cornfield. The place is sloshin' knee-deep in money . . ."

"And it's attracting more of it. I see. But what's your plan? Who's the mark?"

"His name is Mapleton Sherryl Jones. "Mapes" to his fraternity brothers at Harvard and other close friends and associates. He's a polo player, a playboy, a lush and he stands to inherit a trainload of money. He's an only child whose family dotes on him, and, like others of his class, he's determined to make another fortune on his own. He's lookin' to buy a gold mine. We aim to help."

"That's a lot of information. Where'd you get it from?"

Rogers grinned, took out a tailor-made cigarette, lit up and said, "Pillow talk with Charity Moon. The surest and most infallible of all sources."

"How well I know," Duff said. He puffed on his stogie a few times while he thought about everything Rogers had told him Then, he leaned back in his chair and blew a large, perfect smoke ring which hovered in the air between them, as if it were a target for his next words to hit. "So, it's a long con . . ."

"Yeah."

"How much time, and what kinda stake money are we talkin' about . . . an' now that I'm thinkin' on it . . . will it be a stock trade or a real estate deal?"

Rogers stood and stretched, paced to the door and back trying to work off some of his nervous energy, then sat down again, with his arms on the top rail of a backwards-facing chair before he answered. "It's gonna take the rest of the summer. These kind of marks are always on alert for somebody tryin' to get between, theirselves and the family fortune."

"Yuh don't hafta tell me that, junior. I taught you, remember," Duff said, attempting to reestablish his dominance.

Rogers thought about putting the stink-eye on him again, but decided against it—he'd need help pulling this one off—so, on second thought, he said, "I'll never forget it," and felt a small shiver go down his backside as he remembered his nightmarish torture in the bowels of the Oxford Hotel. He sat down, stubbed out his smoke and began organizing all the plans in his head.

"And have you thought about how many others you're gonna need . . . and what kinda splits we're gonna be givin' up?"

"Yeah. I have. A lot. For the last five days on the train, all I've been doin' is thinkin' about this one. Done right, it'll be the biggest job we've ever pulled . . . but some things I just don't know yet and I won't be able to tell until I get down there and find out . . ."

"Yer goin' in blind?" Duff said as he relit the dead cigar he'd been holding between the first two fingers of his left hand.

Rogers watched the match flare, heard the scratch as it was sparked into life and smelled the sulphur that gave it animation, just before it was shaken to death. "No. I ain't no ignorant fool . . . I been readin' up on the family . . . and Charity Moon's been givin' me a lot of information also. Right now, the plan is for me to come in as a lawyer, representin' a wealthy widow down in Florida who inherited a mine she don't need, don't want and can't wait to get rid of, so she can go back to Europe."

Duff said, "Make it New York, with a satellite office in Denver. That way we can cover yuh. Get rid of those tropical suits, clean up your language . . . if you're gonna be a lawyer, yuh gotta talk, act and dress the part . . . and for fuck sakes, when it comes time to gut this golden goose, do everything up here: contracts, deeds, statements, checks and stock certificates. Denver. Only. Got it?"

"Yes, Boss."

"Anythin' goes wrong, you're screwed down there in the Springs. The Marshal, Sheriff, District Attorney, Mayor, Police Chief . . . they're all straight-arrow boy scouts who'll slap yuh in stir faster than you can cry '*NOT GUILTY*' . . . and you'll find yourself breakin' rocks down at the State Pen in Canon City."

"Yeah Adolph. I'm listenin', and thinkin' about all the things that could go wrong . . . and I'm gonna be as careful as if I was stackin' warm jars of nitroglycerine, because this one could be worth a million dollars . . . maybe even more. No way am I gonna let it get messed up."

Duff looked at Rogers through eyes that were squeezed down to slits to keep the smoke out of them. He took a last puff, laid the butt in the ashtray and said, "Well, you're the one who's gonna be fuckin' this tiger . . . I'm just holdin' his tail for yuh . . . and it's your ass that's on the line. Whatever yuh do, stay in touch—call me on the telephone, no names, in code only—whenever ya need anythin', and I'm gonna send Del McKnight in a day or two, so he can run interference for yuh . . ."

And spy on me, Rogers thought, as Duff continued " . . . He's great at blendin' into the background and makin' friends. And he's the one yuh want helpin' if it comes down to a fight."

"All well and good," Rogers said, "I may use him to relay messages. How do I get in touch with him?"

"He'll find you, and it won't blow your legend neither. He's done this kinda work before and he's goddamned good at it."

Rogers stood and said, "I defer, as always to yourself and your superior knowledge and skill. I'm at The Brown Palace tonight, leavin' first thing tomorrow and I'll be at The Antlers in Colorado Springs."

Adolph looked at his star pupil for several long heartbeats, then said, "One last word to the wise . . . don't forget—for even one second—who's in charge around here. Don't get cute, don't even think about tryin' to shortchange us, 'cause you won't live long enough to spend it. I got resources you don't know about, cards we ain't never played. Understand?"

"Perfectly. I'll be in touch," Frank said as he made his way out, wondering, if Adolph was bluffing, or if he knew that Rogers had always cheated . . . never gave an honest cut . . . *And I ain't startin' now.*

Chapter Forty-Five

Things were going well at the Stringfellow house on Featherston Lane in Cleburne, Texas. Other than the heat, which continued to oppress everyone, day after day with monotonous regularity, and the occasional nasty remark from one particular neighbor about 'Savages being allowed to live among the civilized folk', life was pleasant and agreeable.

By late July, Ella Stringfellow and Mimi James had become the best of friends who connected on so many levels, it was as if they had grown up together. The household itself was running in a quiet and efficient manner, thanks to everyone pitching in and helping without having to be asked, and strife was—for the time being at least—nonexistent. Mimi took over the kitchen and made it her domain before the first week of her residency was over, and Carole and Evelyn became her willing assistants in all the normal household chores. Skipper and Ella both had outside jobs which brought in cash . . . but the truth was . . . Ella had no need to work. It was one of her closest-held secrets, and it had to do with her father, the Bishop.

One of the tenets of Mormondom has to do with self-sufficiency: always be prepared for the unexpected, and ready for an emergency. All Mormon families, for example, are expected to keep and maintain a two-year supply of food on hand. As a devout and early member of the LDS church, Bishop Stringfellow not only took that to heart, he took it to extremes . . . and his daughter Ella knew it.

When her father was mysteriously gunned down by an unknown assailant, Ella Stringfellow went straight to work ransacking his office. With the help of her longtime governess and companion Abigale Ince—who could neither read nor write—Ella checked every file, deed and receipt in the room. She was looking for a second set of records, the secret journal her father kept, that detailed all of the properties he'd skimmed off from the church and put into the *Stringfellow Land Development Co.* name. She'd seen it once, when she went into his office to tell him goodnight, and he was called to the privy by a sudden distress of the bowels.

Ella found the ledger, only after several hours of searching, along with a bonus: the keys to a medium-sized fireproof safe hidden in the barn, out back of the house. When opened, it contained several thousand dollars in gold coin . . . a fact Ella kept to herself . . . which became another of her many secrets. With the account book in hand, she was able to find and remove the files and deeds pertaining to all those stolen income producing properties which Ella and Mrs. Ince put into crates that they hid under the hay in the same horse barn. After a couple of days of nonstop work, Ella and Mrs. Ince finished rearranging everything so that it looked untouched, just as a pair of Mormon Elders and a US Marshal from LDS Headquarters in Salt Lake City, Utah showed up with a dray wagon and some laborers. They confiscated everything in her father's office, claiming that it was all property of the LDS Church.

One of them, who introduced himself as a Bishop Arnold, was dismayed to learn that the house on Featherston Lane had passed in an irrevocable trust to Ella and Chester immediately upon their father's death, and there was nothing he could do about it. He did, however, say to her as he was leaving, "But don't you worry none Honey, because I'll be sending a nice, hard-working Mormon man down here to court you and take your hand in marriage. Pretty little thing like you oughta be having babies by now." The prophet told us that there's millions of souls waiting to come to earth, so we should have as many children as possible. It's your duty as a Mormon woman."

The woman child of sixteen years looked at him wordlessly, the uninvited, invasive and overbearing man in her home, and thought, *That will be the day when Hell freezes over, you lecherous old bastard,* and vowed to herself that she would always make her own choices. Always.

And so she had. By mid-summer of aught-one, Ella Stringfellow was in her thirties and appeared content with her life in general. She had a large, well-maintained house, good health and a respectable job with a modest income. She even had company and help around the place now that Mimi and her three children were living in some of the upstairs rooms. Her biggest concerns were still her missing brother, the money that showed up now and then—supposedly sent by Chester—and Boyd Pirtle, the Special Agent for the Texas Rangers that she couldn't seem to stop thinking about.

Ella and Mimi James were drinking coffee together and chatting about the hottest summer anyone could remember, early one morning in the first week of August. Carole and Evelyn were upstairs getting dressed, and Skipper had left before daylight for a barn-raising job. Duke the cat, having enjoyed a bowl of chicken scraps Mimi cut up for him, was busy licking his paws and washing his face up on his favorite lounging spot in the bay window in preparation for a nap, after a long hard night of prowling. Just as Mimi was about to pour coffee again, there was someone at the door knocking, and everything changed.

Ella never was able to decide afterward, if it was coincidence, or fate, that brought the first of Boyd Pirtle's Special Delivery letters to her, just as she was thinking about him.

Chapter Forty-Six

After signing for the fat envelope with a nervous hand, Ella called out and said, "Mimi, excuse me for a moment. I have to take care of this . . . I think it's something about old business of my father's . . . I shouldn't be too long."

"That's all right. I've things to do in the kitchen and breakfast to make for a certain pair of young ladies, if they don't sleep all day."

Ella heard giggles behind her as Carole and Evelyn raced down the back stairs to the kitchen. She went into the library, as she called her father's old office, closed the door and sat down at the big desk, then opened the letter with hands that had started to perspire.

The letter was dated five days earlier and bore an R.P.O.— Railroad Postal Office—cancellation.

Dear Miss Stringfellow, it began, *I regret that such a number of weeks, months even, have passed since I last communicated with you about the status of the inquiry into the whereabouts of Frank Rogers, aka Chester Stringfellow, your brother. As I stated in my previous telegram, he appeared to be in Colorado, and I have reason to believe he is still there. Mr. Witherspoon in Ft. Worth has confirmed that he has received additional funds in your name from Colorado, remitted by Chester S., as I'm sure you're aware. I assure you that I have every intention of going after him at the earliest possible date. The reason I have not already done so, (this information is confidential . . . I'm trusting you to keep it that way because lives, including mine, are at stake.) The reason I'm not already up there, is because Governor Slater has tasked me with confirming specific information about certain Federal Officers, before he goes to higher authority—President McKinley—with it. The mission requires extensive traveling, I've been in Amarillo, Lubbock, Abilene, and El Paso so far, with Houston and San Antonio to be visited next. I can confirm to you that the information given me by a certain patriotic citizen has, thus far, proven to be reliable and fully correct. Where it will lead next, I cannot say, but I will follow all trails to the end. I expect to conclude my part of this investigation and make a report to the governor by the end of August, after which I will head straight up to Colorado in pursuit of Frank Rogers. As always, I will keep you informed. I will also keep my promise to you, whenever I find him. I remain, as ever, your obedient servant, Boyd Avery Pirtle, S.A. Texas Ranger HQ, Austin, Texas.*

Ella read the letter several times, parsing out each word, dissecting every sentence for unstated, hidden meanings and marveling at the quality of his penmanship. *Somewhere or other, it appears to me that Mr. Pirtle has received some educating . . . I wonder what other surprises he harbors,* she thought, as she reinserted the missive into its envelope and stuck it in the top desk drawer with some other papers, before going to rejoin the others in the kitchen.

"Everything all right," Mimi asked when Ella came in the door.

"Positively. I thought at first it was some old business of my father's," Ella answered as she went over to the big Home Comfort iron and nickel cook stove and poured coffee for herself, then joined Mimi and the two girls at the table, "but it turned out to be a report from the Ranger who's searching for my brother."

"The outlaw?"

"So it appears. I haven't seen him in twenty years. How's the pancakes girls?"

"Very good Miss Ella," Carole said, with her mouth full of hotcake and egg.

"Shouldn't talk with your mouth full," her sister scolded.

"That's enough, you two. Finish your food and go wash your dishes while I talk to Miss Ella."

The girls took their plates and forks over to the sink, where a pan of warm soapy water and a pan of rinse water prepared by their mother was waiting. Mimi said, "Carole, you dry. Evelyn, you wash." To Ella she said, "Would you mind takin' them to the library with you for a couple of hours?"

"Not at all. Do you want me to keep them all afternoon?"

"No. I'll come and get them after I'm done."

"With ..."

The lack of chatter, or any noise, from the other end of the kitchen let them know that Evelyn and Carole were all ears. Their mother said, "You ladies go upstairs and brush your teeth, put on your Sunday dresses and shoes. You're goin' to the library with Miss Ella."

After the two girls scampered up the stairs again, Mimi said,

"It's time I took care of that damned old mule."

"Burt?"

"Yeah."

"What's the matter with him? I thought he was doing just fine, out there in the old barn," Ella said, as she sipped from her coffee.

Mimi looked over at the window, where Duke was fast asleep on his side with one paw over his face and his tail hanging over the edge. She smiled for an instant, seeing his ridiculous position, then said, "I'm sendin' him to the knackers. I don't want to feed and doctor the animal no more. He almost didn't make it all the way over here with the buckboard last month. I was afraid he was gonna lay down an' die in the street."

"Are you sure about this," Ella asked.

"Yeah. He's goin' . . . just didn't want to do it in front of the girls."

"I understand. What happened to your tough old world attitude?"

"You've convinced me that there's better ways."

"It's good with me if you decide to change your mind too."

"I won't."

Two hours later, while Ella was reading *Aesop's Fables* to Carole and Evelyn at the library, Schultz the Knacker came up to the house on Featherston Lane with a heavy-duty flatbed wagon pulled by two huge Belgian draft horses, and driven by his son Max. Mimi had directed them to the barn behind the house, where she waited, talking in a low voice to the doomed animal, scratching behind his ears and feeding him apples from her apron. When she heard the creaking of the giant wagon and the jingle of trace chains, she gave the old mule a chunk of brown sugar she'd been saving, patted him on the neck and whispered, "Good-bye Burt," in his ear, just as Schultz and son pulled to a stop at the edge of the corral.

Shultz himself climbed down, while his son waited impassively with the reins in his huge hands. He was a large man Mimi noted, with big heavy muscles and wide shoulders. *Built for brute work,* she thought.

"Madam," Schultz said as he tipped his hat to her. "This is the animal?"

"Yes."

"Well, there ain't much left of him."

"That's why I called you."

Schultz grinned. "Fair enough. I pay for him, one dollar and fifty cent."

"Make it two dollars and I'll throw in his harness and collar."

"Hames too?"

"Sure."

"Done," Schultz said. He motioned to his son, who set the brakes and climbed down with a ten pound sledge hammer in one brawny hand. While Max pulled a steel ramp out from the rear of the dray, Schultz pulled a purse from the bib of his overalls and counted out twenty silver dimes, one at a time, and laid them on Mimi James's outstretched palm.

"The harness and things are right over there, just inside the door," Mimi pointed at the barn. She turned and walked away as Max set up the cross tree and a block and tackle attached to the front of the wagon bed, while Schultz laid a rope halter over Burt's head, then lead him out of the corral and over to the end of the ramp.

Mimi was at the porch steps, trying for the back door when she heard the grunt, the crunch as hammer hit bone, and the thump as the body fell to the ground. She brushed her eyes and didn't look back.

Chapter Forty-Seven

Rogers was checked into the Antlers Hotel, across from the Denver & Rio Grande Railroad Station in downtown Colorado Springs. He'd registered as *Franklin D. Rogers, Esq., Attorney at Law*, representing the firm of Duffy, Blocker, Gouge & Howe, with offices in New York, San Francisco, and Denver. Their advertised specialty was *Mining Acquisitions, Operations, Disposals.* It said so on the business cards Frank had printed up and was passing out wherever he went, and it didn't take long before he started getting inquiries about his services.

Frank Rogers was having no trouble blending in with the Colorado Springs high society snobs whose patrician beliefs assured them of their God-given right to the moral superiority they wore like cloaks, which hid their commonplace sins of hypocrisy, corruption and debauchery. Rogers found it hilarious that their elitism allowed them the pretence of piety and virtue. While they publicly tut-tutted and tsk-tsked the rough manners and rude behavior of the newly-rich working men who'd earned millions by investing in the gold fields of Cripple Creek, those same holier-than-thous were often found bellied up to the bar, cheek-to-jowl with the previously mentioned lucky stiffs, and sharing the favors of the identical same girls in the bordellos over in Colorado City . . . an easy couple of miles west of alcohol-free Colorado Springs . . . where underground tunnels connected the gin mills on the one side with the whorehouses across the street, thus saving the reputation of many a proper gent.

Charity Moon was posing as a daring young socialite from New England, who was vacationing alone out west. She'd attracted the attention of a showy young dandy named Mapleton Sheryl Jones—'Mapes' to his closest friends—who was out west "At the urging of the Palmers, Penroses and Tutts, *Seeking to acquire a few mining interests for the family, my dear,*" in Mapes' own words to her.

The Jones family was old-line Philadelphian, with roots going all the way back to the first Quakers who founded the city in the late seventeenth century. In the following two hundred years, the Sheryl, Mapleton and Jones families had all prospered mightily during that bountiful time of no income taxes and much less government. The fortune was vast, well tended and watched close by familial elders and their minions . . . a duty which was about to fall upon Mapes, who was the last heir. Whether he was up to the task—or not—was still an open question, but when Charity Moon cruised through the Broadmoor Casino one warm evening in July, she made him for a mark. A big dumb goose, with his wealth on casual display and privilege taken for granted. Mapes never could've guessed that he was falling into a honey trap devised by a team of expert swindlers to separate him from a chunk of his family money . . . he thought he was in love. And he knew better. He'd been taught from birth to beware of strangers befriending him, but when the love bug bites, the infection it leaves behind will not go away. A young man in his mid-twenties like Mapes, stood no chance against the likes of a beguiling temptress with the charms of Charity Moon.

At first she flirted, then she played hard to get, until at last, about five weeks after their first meeting at the Casino, when Mapes was almost mad with lust, Charity allowed him to seduce her. Before he knew what had happened, he was head over heels for Charity, because Mapes—a man with no prior sexual experience—wasn't just hooked, he'd been harpooned.

Meanwhile, Charity's partner without a conscience, Frank Rogers, had been in Colorado Springs for a week. He'd met with Bunyan, Delbert McKnight, who was passing himself off as a mining engineer, and surprise, surprise, he was damned good at it. The grift the two devised was simple and ingenious.

"I think it'll work, Del, with you, me and Charity all in on it together." Frank said.

The two men were sitting in a buggy that Bunyan had rented at the Midway Livery over on North Tejon Street, and driven out to the Garden of the Gods, where they sat among the giant pink sandstone rocks that looked like the dorsal fins of a whole school of Mesozoic leviathan sea monsters, intent upon chewing the northeast corner off of Pikes Peak. *The Shining Mountain Sitting Big,* as the Ute Nation called it, made a solemn and majestic backdrop to their conversation and provided a quiet reminder of the immensity of the world . . . and the insignificance of any single man.

"I'll put the ad in this afternoon," McKnight said. "Yuh want the mornin,' or evenin' paper?"

"The Evenin' Star, up in Cripple Creek is the one that has the most news about the goins' on over in the district—and it's the official newspaper of the town—so put it in there for three days. We'll look more legitimate that way. But *The Gazette,* here in town is where we need to run it for at least a week. I'll

have Charity point it out to the Mark. D'ya know what t'say?"

"In the ad?"

"Yeah."

"Minin' engineer seeks investors for provable claim in Cripple Creek District. Great potential. Low risk. Reply to Delbert McKnight."

"Sounds good . . . change provable to proven, and add this: *Option expires soon.* Put it just before your name."

"Good idea. Shudda thought of that myself."

"Where you stayin', in case I need to talk to you?"

"Alamo Hotel."

"Good choice. I've stayed there a few times myself. It fits your legend as a minin' man who's watchin' his pennies."

Del McKnight took off his dusty, sweat-stained brown Stetson with one hand, and scratched the back of his head with the other giant paw, then put the hat back on before he said anything. "Believe it or not Frank, this ain't my first grift, and it damn sure won't be my last."

"I know, Del. I know. It's just that the size of this one's got me checkin' on everythin' three or four times . . . makin' sure I made sure . . . an' didn't leave nothin' to chance."

The big man fished in his shirt pocket and came out with a plug of Tiger Tobacco. "Chaw?" he said to Frank, as he held it out in the direction of his fellow conspirator and partner-in-crime.

"I never chew. Thanks."

McKnight shrugged, and holding the mass of pressed black tobacco with both hands, stuck it in one corner of his mouth and bit off a chunk with his yellow teeth. He stuffed the remainder in the same shirt pocket, then began chewing on the wad of 'baccy he'd packed into one cheek like a chipmunk with a mouthful of sunflower seeds. He worried the mass of Virginia burley for several minutes, then leaned over to his left side, hawked up and expectorated a long stream of rich brown juice that hit the ground and splattered in all directions.

The big man was busy wiping his mouth on his shirt sleeve when Frank Rogers said, "Jee-zhus Kee-rhist Del . . . that's disgustin'."

"Mebbe so," Del said as he spit over to the side again, "but swallowin' a little bit every now and again keeps me regular."

"That's nice . . . don't do it in front of Charity, or the Mark."

"I may be coarse, but I ain't stupid. No grift ever goes as planned. Sometimes yuh gotta have a diversion . . . just in case."

"All well and good, but no chewin' or spittin' when we're closin' the deal . . . unless the Mark offers it to you."

"Sure."

Rogers pulled a gold cigarette case out of his inside pocket, took one out and lit up. "What do you have for paperwork?"

Del spit before he spoke. "Adolph fixed up everythin' we'll need. Lease papers, assayers report, survey maps . . . even some core samples. I got business cards and engineerin' certificate and résumé showin' I've worked mines all over the west."

Frank put his foot up on the dashboard and smoked for a bit, thinking about the operation. Halfway through the cigarette he said, "Tell me about the property."

Chapter Forty-Eight

Delbert McKnight spit, and shifted the chew to his other cheek before he started talking. He said, "Its west and a little north of Cripple Creek. Close enough to be part of the main caldera, but at an ample distance to give us some privacy to do whatever we want."

"What's a caldera?"

"The cone at the top of a dead volcano. Its a good place to look for gold."

"What about the property owner," Rogers said as he flicked his cigarette butt against some nearby boulders and watched, as it exploded in a shower of sparks.

McKnight grinned and said, "There ain't one, other than the US Government. Won't nobody bother us, long as we keep it small and to ourselves. Our biggest worry'll be spies and claim jumpers tryin' to muscle us off if they think we've got a real strike."

"Well, we'll just convince 'em otherwise," Rogers said with a smirk. "Ain't had much chance to show our sinister selves for a while. I miss it at times . . . the action."

Del spit again, took off his hat and wiped his forehead with his sleeve. "It's gettin' hotter than hell out here. We need to be goin' back. And don't be thinkin' about goin' renegade and shootin' the place up like John Wesley Hardin. That's all gone and Wes Hardin's been dead for five or six years now. Them desperado days is over and done with."

Frank Rogers sat up straight and looked Bunyan in the eye and said, "I know you're right Del. I just miss it is all, the action, the thrill, the feelin' you get after it's done and you get away and you're more alive than you've ever been in your life . . ."

"Yeah, and somebody's shot dead or dyin' and the law is right on yore ass. It ain't worth it no more."

"Well, some of my old *compadres* are raisin' a whole lot of hell down in Mexico."

"After we pull this one off, go on down there. See how yuh like it," Del said as he undid the reins and set the young gelding in motion with a snap of his wrists.

They took the long way back to the Springs, going the entire length of the newly-donated park and enjoying some of the most fantastic scenery in all of the country. Neither man spoke again until they passed the gigantic balanced rock at the southwest gateway and started down the hill that lead back to Colorado City. That's when Rogers said, "I can see why the Indians named it *The Garden of the Gods*. It's the damndest place I ever seen."

Del McKnight spit off to the side, and said, "Don't know as I'd use the word damn and God in the same sentence, but yer point's well taken. This's where the injuns come to pow-wow and parley, work out their arrangements. Wasn't no fightin' allowed in there, under penalty of death. This whole area, all the way over to Manitou Springs was sacred to 'em."

"Why?'

"'Cause they believed the Great Spirit, The Manitou, was asleep under the mountain, and the bubbles comin' up in the soda springs was from his breath, as he exhaled. But the Utes would fight to the death with the plains tribes—the Arapaho, Cheyenne, Sioux—to keep 'em from goin' up the pass . . . what we now call Ute Pass."

"Why not, what's so special about the pass?" Rogers said as he cupped his hands together and lit another cigarette.

"The Utes didn't want anybody else gettin' up into South Park, by the Eleven Mile Canyon. There's a salt flat there that the Utes controlled and they didn't want nobody else gettin' any without their say-so. Salt was really valuable and an important tradin' tool. All about money, I guess, or what passes for it."

The brown quarter horse was keeping a steady trot behind the expert driving of Delbert McKnight. Frank Rogers decided that trying to smoke in the wind wasn't worth it, and threw his tailor-made cigarette away. He said, "How come you know so much about this place Del?"

The big man didn't answer, but stayed cat-quiet as he pulled back on the reins and stopped where the road came to an intersection, after crossing Fountain Creek. He had to spit once again, then stuck a sausage-sized index finger in his mouth and threw the mass of glistening soggy brown tobacco away. He said, "I was born here, about this time of year. In a tent a little bit downstream from where we sit. My old man was a Johnny, come west after Lee surrendered, lookin' for a fresh start."

"He find it?"

Bunyan tapped the horses flank with the harness reins, turned them to the left and headed east, into Colorado City and back toward town. He kept his own counsel for a bit, as if he were once again measuring his words for an answer, then said, "Don't know. He left the two of us there just as the weather turned cold."

"In a tent . . ."

"Yeah."

Before he thought, Rogers said, "How'd you . . ."

Del cut him off, looked at him with eyes that could have started a brush fire and said, "Don't. She survived the only way she could and she cared for me until she died. I was thirteen."

They were coming down Colorado Avenue into the bar and brothel area, where brick two and three story commercial buildings made up the business district of Colorado City. Without thinking, Frank Rogers—who had as much natural cunning as a high plains coyote—said, "I guess that makes us two of a kind. I left home, two days after my Pa was killed. I was sixteen years old, never even knew my ma. She died givin' birth to my sister and me."

"Twin . . ."

"Yeah."

"What happened to your pa?"

"Somebody shot him in front of our house. Walked up from behind, and plugged him between the ears. Took out his right eye an' half his eyebrow."

"Did they catch the guy who done it?"

"No. They ain't."

"How'd 'ya know . . . you left the next day, didn't ya?"

Rogers felt like biting his tongue off and spitting it in the street. He said, "I. Just. Know. Let me off here. I'm thirsty and you hafta get those advertisements in the newspapers. We'll lie low for a few days until Charity gets the Mark to call. Stay outta trouble."

"Yeah," Delbert McKnight said, as he watched the man he knew only as Frank Rogers stride up the board sidewalk and into a drinking establishment called *The Charm of the West Saloon.* It was the place every sport in town knew was only the front for Gun Wa's opium den in the shack out back . . . and just a dozen or so big steps, from the beer, sawdust and blood of one world, to the smoke, dreams and extirpation of the soul in another.

Oh Shit, was all Del McKnight could think, as he drove on east into Colorado Springs.

Chapter Forty-Nine

After killing nearly ten thousand people, destroying hundreds of thousand head of livestock, and laying waste to crops across every state in the union, the most devastating heat wave in American history finally broke in late August of 1901. From the hundredth meridian out west, to the shores of the Atlantic Ocean, all creatures great and small experienced a profound sense of relief as the low pressure fronts pushed in and lowered thermometers all across the land.

In Cleburne, Texas, the wind began to freshen in the morning. It came out of the southwest, picked up in mid-afternoon and brought with it low clouds which gradually built into towering white and gray stratocumuli that were pregnant with moisture, and reached from horizon to horizon. As they crept eastward, the clouds covered the sun and dropped the temperature, while the faint booms of far off thunder could be heard in the distance and the scent of rain rode in on the air.

At the house on Featherston Lane, Mimi James was shelling pinto beans on the back porch when Ella Stringfellow came home from school with Carole and Evelyn in tow. After the two girls had greeted their mother and gone to change from school to everyday clothes, Mimi said, "Another one of them letters come that had to be signed for. I made my mark—like you showed me—but the mail man ask my name anyhow. I told him and he wrote it down then he left the thing. I put it on the desk in the library."

Ella sat down on the porch steps next to Mimi and began stripping beans from the dried husks. She said, "Thank you. I'll read it when we finish with these."

"That may be a while . . . there's seven more bushels after this one."

"We'll get the girls to help."

As if on cue, both girls reappeared and without being asked, sat down on the porch and began shucking with the adults. The four of them had been concentrating on pinto beans for a few minutes, when Mimi said, "It's gonna rain."

"Do you think the heat wave has broken," Ella said as she reached for more bean pods.

"Yeah, I do."

"Why, Momma," Evelyn asked.

"I don't know why, or how, or nothin' else about it," Mimi said, "but I've always knowed what the weather was gonna bring, an' so could my grandmother." She barely had the words out when there was a sizzle, a flash of lightning and an ear-splitting clap of thunder straight overhead that sent Duke the cat out from under the old buckboard—where it had been sitting by the barn, surrounded by cheat grass growing up through the wheels, ever since Mimi and her kids had used it to move from one life to another—and streaking for home with all the alacrity and enthusiasm of the recently scared shitless. He cleared all five steps of the back porch in a single leap and slid to a stop at the screen door with his tail puffed up like a bottle brush. Carole opened the door for him, and Duke stalked off into the gloom to recapture his dignity and restore his haughtiness, just as thunder boomed again and the downpour came at last.

"Hallelujah," Ella said, as the first precipitation in a hundred-plus days fell onto the baked and seasoned ground, where it was gulped down and swallowed by a parched and thirsty earth.

"Almost thought it would never come again," Mimi said as she stood and pushed the shelled beans further up the porch, where the moisture wouldn't reach. "Carole, you and Evelyn put these in the kitchen."

As the two girls did so, their mother moved the baskets of harvested pods to the driest place available while Ella remained where she was . . . sitting on the back steps . . . with raindrops falling all over her.

"Ella, ain't you gonna move?"

"No Mimi. I'm not. I want to sit here and let it come down in buckets on me, let it wash all the dust out of my hair and the grit from my eyes. I want to feel cool . . . and clean . . . for the first time since summer began and this damnable heat wave started."

Mimi just shook her head in resignation and went inside to start making supper. A full half-hour later Ella—soaked to the skin, with her tangled wet hair down around her shoulders, lips turning blue and teeth chattering—followed.

She was met at the mud room door by Mimi, who, with towels and a wool blanket in hand, said, "You are a crazy woman. Take off that wet dress—don't you track up my floor— and wrap up in these. I'll try to keep you from dyin' of a chill."

Ella giggled. "You make me feel like a little girl."

"Sometime you acts like one," Mimi said, then she snickered too. "Thanks be to the Great Spirit."

"It's hard to be grouchy, now that it's cooling off."

"It's a fact. We'll eat in a half-hour or so, just enough time for you to dry off an' change clothes."

"Yes'm."

"An don't forget the letter . . ."

* * *

It was another two hours before Ella found herself at her father's old desk, opening the second special delivery letter from Boyd Pirtle—also bearing an RPO postmark—with hands that were somehow damp, and a tiny bit nervous.

Dear Miss Stringfellow;

I have been delayed for the past ten days by an unforeseen side trip to Beaumont, the site of the huge oil discovery earlier this year, and where for reasons I have as yet been unable to determine, a certain Mormon Bishop was rather actively engaged in real estate dealings some twenty years ago, along the mouth of the Naches River. The properties there are all owned by a holding company whose origins are somewhat obscure, and I'm unable to determine just who the actual owners are. There was a flurry of activity before, and after, the date of the bishops untimely demise, followed by a five-year quiet period, after which another spate of intense transfers were effected with the actual ownership being more and more difficult to ascertain. The pattern was repeated ten years after that—the result of which is, those aforementioned properties are held by a series of interlocking offshore foreign corporations. Whoever owns all of the stock in them will remain a mystery, I'm afraid, because I have neither the time, resources, or the expertise to cut the Gordian knot the ownership problem presents . . . unless perhaps . . . you have other information? Are you, Miss Stringfellow, able to shine any light of truth on all of this?

I am, Ella thought *I could, but I won't.*

Pirtles letter went on . . .

> *In any case, I am en route to Houston for an overnight stop,*
> *then two days in San Antonio before finally, returning to*
> *Austin, where I will present my findings to Captain Newton*
> *and Governor Slater. Afterwhich, God willing, Will Posey and*
> *I will proceed with all haste up to Colorado in furtherance*
> *of the hunt for Frank Rogers, aka Chester Stringfellow. Until*
> *then, I remain, your obedient servant,*
> *Boyd Avery Pirtle, S.A. Texas Ranger HQ, Austin, Texas.*

Ella re-read the letter three more times before folding and putting it back in its envelope. Then she retrieved the first letter from the desk drawer and took both of them up to her bedroom, where she slept with them under her pillow. In the morning before breakfast the next day, she secreted them in the small iron safe her father had built into a hidden compartment in the closet, back when he was sleeping in the master bedroom Ella now claimed as her own. She checked her appearance in the mahogany cheval glass mirror that stood in one corner of the room, tamed a couple of loose hairs that had escaped her bun, smoothed her eyebrows with her pinky fingers and went down to join Mimi and the girls in the kitchen.

A hundred and eighty miles to the south, Boyd Pirtle was sleeping the dreamless sleep of the utterly exhausted, in his own room and in his own bed at Mrs. Orr's rooming house for the first time in three months.

Chapter Fifty

The heat wave, relentless travel and high pressure responsibilities— in addition to so many missed meals and often sub-standard road food—had all taken a toll on Boyd Pirtle. He'd lost twenty-five pounds and was suffering from periodic bouts of biliousness and irritable bowel syndrome, for which he was taking various tonics and so-called, self-proclaimed *"Miracle Cures,"* but nothing seemed to help. He was gaunt, looked like a scarecrow . . . and Will Posey was concerned about him.

It was raining hard by mid-afternoon that Friday in San Antonio, and the cloudbursts, once begun, continued unabated into the evening. The rising creeks, lakes and rivers delayed their train, causing the Rangers to arrive in Austin in the wee small hours of Saturday morning, where they had to hitch a ride with one of the brakemen, who was on his way home after coming down from Dodge City, Kansas on a double shift. He went out of his way to leave them at Mrs. Orr's rooming house in the drizzle and fog that came after the big rains.

"Many thanks, friend," Pirtle said as he climbed down from the carriage seat and retrieved his and Will Posey's gripsacks from the floorboards. Posey, meanwhile, was busy hauling a pair of high cantle saddles and his model 94 Winchester to the ground.

"Glad t'be able t'hep the Rangers," the Samaritan said, then nodded and drove off.

"What do yuh want to do now," Posey said, "it's only a little after three in the mornin'."

"Well, we ain't gonna go clompin' on in the house and wake 'em all up—scare the bejesus out of 'em. Put them saddles and gear on the porch. Mrs. Orr will be up in a couple of hours. We'll wait."

* * *

When she awakened at five-thirty to begin her morning chores, Vidabelle Orr was relieved that the heat wave had broken at last, but she could feel the chill and damp in her bones and joints. She was slow getting started with the daily routine . . . the biscuits were still just a lump of dough in the mixing bowl and the coffee only started to boil, when old Doc Wilton came stumping down the stairs on his handmade crutch and wooden leg. "Mornin' Doc. I'm afraid things are gonna be a bit slow today. Coffee's not ready yet."

"I'll just have a piece of bread if there is any. Do you know that there's a coupl'a bums sleepin' on the porch?"

"Not for long," she said as she grabbed her big wooden rolling pin and headed for the front porch door just as fast as her bulk would allow, with her Irish spirit showing in every one of her steps, and with blood in her eye.

But when she opened the door and came out on the veranda, she found Boyd Pirtle—covered with a rain slicker—asleep on the porch glider and Will Posey in a nearby wicker chair, guarding the man he'd follow into Dante's ninth circle, with a rifle across his knees. He said, "Mornin' Mrs. Orr. I see you've come armed. We'll surrender."

She smiled, "How long have y'all been out here?"

"Three hours or so. Boyd didn't want to wake anyone."

"I wish you had. It's too wet and chilly out here. Especially for him," she said, nodding at Pirtle. "I'm s'prised he ain't woke up. The man sleeps like a cat . . . one eye open all the time . . . day or night."

"We need to watch over him for a bit, he's exhausted, won't admit it, keeps drivin' himself. His gut's botherin' him too, he's lost a lotta weight, and he's been takin' too much of them patent medicines, tryin' to cure himself. I ain't sure they're workin', neither."

"We'll take care of 'im, get some good vittles in his body and a few days rest."

"That'd be good, but I don't think it's gonna happen. We gotta make a report to the Governor on Tuesday, and then as soon as he lets us loose, we're headed back up to Colorado, to try an' find Frank Rogers. He's obsessed with bringin' Rogers to justice . . . and although I doubt he'll admit it . . . he's infatuated with that Stringfellow woman up in Cleburne. He talks about her a lot, and writes letters to her too."

Mrs. Orr—who had a good heart, but was always eager for gossip—nodded sagely, as if privy to all that Posey was telling her. In actuality however, she was ignorant of anything having to do with her roomer's personal life, and was thrilled to the core, hearing such personal information. She said, "Let's get him inside and fed."

Posey touched his boss on the shoulder and called his name, waking Pirtle, who drew in a sharp breath and sat up, trying to get his bearings back in the damp gray dawn.

"Good day to ya, Boyd. You're the last person I expected t'find out here on the porch. Doc Wilton told me there was a coupl'a bums camped out here."

"Well, I've presented a better appearance for a fact," Pirtle said, as he rubbed the sleep from his eyes. "And good mornin' to yourself. How's Doc doin' by the way?"

"Same as ever. Windy. Still talkin' yer ears off. Ask him what time it is and he'll tell you who built the first clock, how it worked and how many gears was in it. By then, yuh can't remember what it was yuh asked him in the first place."

"Yeah, but he's also got a heart of gold. He'd give you the shirt off of his back and he's as smart as they come."

"All true, Boyd. Come inside, both y'all and I'll feed yez."

Chapter Fifty-One

By Monday morning, Pirtle was beginning to come around. After Mrs. Orr had stuffed him full of her home cooking for a couple of days and he'd slept in clean sheets in his own room and his own bed, his body was starting to recover, allowing him to regain some strength. He still had a ways to go . . . but it was a great way to commence a week that was destined for infamy.

Monday, September the second, was Labor Day. Vice President Theodore Roosevelt gave a speech at the Minnesota State Fair, where he uttered the immortal words: *Walk softly and carry a big stick,* in which he was referring to America's increasing hegemony in the western hemisphere and her growing military might.

Pirtle collected his notes and, with Will Posey and Wiley Newton assisting, assembled his report for Governor Slater. They worked on it throughout the day and evening hours on Sunday and Monday, wrapping up just in time to eat Mrs. Orr's sumptuous chicken dinner with all the fixings.

On Tuesday, September the third, Boyd Pirtle, accompanied by Will Posey and Captain Wiley Newton arrived at the Texas State Capitol building at eleven in the morning, where they were escorted straight into Governor Slater's office by his personal secretary, Milton Van Orden.

After greeting each of the Rangers by name, Governor Slater said, "As long as we're in the privacy of my office working on this crisis, I'd like to keep it on a first name basis. Outside of course, we'll stick with the formalities . . . all right?"

Wiley Newton smiled and said, "Sure Governor. Whatever you say."

The Governor shrugged. "I want all of you to be comfortable . . . and candid, that's all. And speaking of candidness, why are all three of you armed to the teeth?"

Pirtle spoke up and said, "It's what we do, Sir. We're always prepared to enforce law and order—anytime and anywhere—and maintain the peace. It's what we all swore to do when we took the oath to be Rangers. These are still dangerous times and we're always ready to get involved."

"Even now," the Governor said, "with all the science and progress the new century is bringing to everyone?"

"Especially now," Wiley Newton said. "Just hear what Boyd has to report . . . if it don't raise your hackles . . . nothin' will. He's uncovered a direct threat to the government. Maybe even our whole way of life."

"Is that true, Boyd?"

"Yessir. I believe it is. When you first sent Will and me on our mission, we had plenty of suspicions, heresay and anecdotal information, all of which was twenty or more years old. Most of what we started with was innuendo from Ella Stringfellow."

"And, I take it, her information proved to be reliable?"

"Much more than that Governor. It turned out to be an absolute treasure map that lead us in every case, step-by-step, right to the properties in question and left a crystal-clear paper trail, detailing title transfers to politically influential figures . . ."

"Such as governors?"

"Yessir. I'm afraid so."

"I don't want to hear this. Were they Republicans, at least?"

"'Fraid not, sir," Pirtle said. "We both know that anyone from Abe Lincoln's Grand Old Party has about as much chance of being elected to high office in Texas, as a stray rooster has of living past suppertime down in Slumgullion."

Governor Slater grinned and said, "You're right of course . . . but what a funny damned way of putting it. I'll have to remember that . . . use it in one of my speeches sometime. Hell, maybe I should have y'all writin' 'em for me."

Everyone in the room had a short chuckle, then Captain Newton said, "I hate to say this Governor, but you'd soon realize that Ranger Pirtle's a whole helluva lot better at kickin' asses, than he is at writin' speeches."

"That so, Boyd," Governor Slater said.

Before Pirtle could answer, Will Posey—who was most often as silent as a stone wall—said, "Governor Sir, I'll personally swear to that. I've been with 'im all summer and seen 'im in action before that, and tell yuh for a fact . . . he's a man of deeds. Not words."

"Guess I'm outvoted," the Governor said.

Pirtle unclasped his briefcase, which was stuffed to overflowing with evidence proving beyond any doubt that the Mormon Church had been trading real estate for US Marshals appointments for at least twenty-five years. The Service in all of the border states with Mexico, plus Utah, Colorado, Wyoming, Montana and Nevada had at least some Mormon Danites in charge of operations. The evidence was irrefutable and undeniable. "But," Pirtle said as he began to establish his chain of evidence, "one of the first facts we established in Amarillo, was that Mormon Marshals are enforcing all laws and orders on the books. It's just that they see their first duty as being to the LDS Church, and not the Federal Government of the United States of America. Their first responsibility, as they see it, is protecting the brethren. They answer to Salt Lake City, not Washington D.C."

"And that," Governor Hoyt Slater said, "is the red and beating heart of the problem. What we have here is a question of loyalty."

"There's also the matter of the separation of power between church and state," Milton Van Orden said. "This isn't the Barbary Coast, or the Ottoman Empire, where the church is the *de facto* government."

Governor Slater, who disliked—and seldom used—profanity said, "Well, be damned if this ain't a sweet pile of crap. Lay it all out for me, Mr. Pirtle . . . then we'll make plans to contact President McKinley. The Marshals Service is a Federal Agency. That makes it a Federal problem. It's not our responsibility. We're only the messenger."

And positive proof once more, Pirtle thought to himself, *just how gutless and self-serving politicians are. They won't take responsibility for a damn thing . . . fix anything that doesn't line their own pockets first . . . or serve our country. They just blather on about nothing and pretend to care, while all the while they're lying sideways in the public trough, getting fatter and fatter, always suckling on the public teat at citizen's expense. How I despise them all . . .*

Chapter Fifty-Two

As Boyd Pirtle, Governor Slater, Captain Newton, Will Posey and the Governor's secretary, Milton Van Orden were all huddled together at the capitol building in Austin, Texas, it soon became apparent to the Rangers that the Governor was most interested in making everything they'd brought to his attention someone else's problem. Despite the mountain of evidence, the names, dates and places all laid out in step-by-step chains of evidence, the Governor disavowed it all.

It was subtle at first. But as the afternoon wore on, the questions posed by the Chief Executive went from being inquisitive to downright confrontational. It was as if he was seeing Pirtle as the adversary instead of the advocate, and the dedicated Ranger didn't like it. He was starting to get angry, and was close to losing his temper. Seeing the frustration on his old friend's face, Wiley Newton said, "Let's break it off here, and resume tomorrow at the same time."

"I agree," Milton said. "It's been a grind. Boyd?"

"Yeah. I'm done for the day."

As he started gathering his notes and exhibits, the Governor said, "You can leave all of that."

Pirtle didn't stop, didn't look up, and didn't respond.

The Governor tried again. "It's fine if you leave everything."

"No," was all Pirtle said, as he stuffed every piece of the precious evidence back into his leather case and started to leave the room.

"I could order you to . . ."

"That won't be necessary, Sir," Captain Wiley Newton said, "I'll take care of this."

"See that you do. I won't tolerate insubordination, Captain. From anyone. Even highly-regarded officers."

Newton hurried to catch up with his Rangers, who were already down the stairs and halfway to the main door, despite Will Posey's bad leg. Seeing them, the Ranger Commander felt a profound sense of relief wash over himself as he thought, *This would be an awful notorious place for a gunfight . . .* He didn't catch up with the two of them until they were at the livery, retrieving their mounts. "Boyd," he said, "what was that all about?"

Pirtle said, "I don't trust him."

"He's our boss. He can order us to do whatever he wants."

"Only within the limits of the law, Cap'n . . . he can't order us to break it."

"Do y'all think he was breakin' the law somehow? I'm confused, Boyd. What exactly, has got ya so tight jawed? It ain't like yuh . . ."

Pirtle swung up in the saddle and took the reins from the stable hand. He said, "This," and pointed to the bulging dispatch case he had strapped over his shoulder in front of his chest. "This is what I'm fired up about . . . all this proof of criminality and guilt that Will Posey and I risked our lives—at the Governors request— risked our lives for in all kinda dismal circumstances through the heat an' misery of this past summer. I ain't leavin' it layin' around unguarded. Not up there. Not with that sonofabitch."

Captain Newton took the reins to his brown mustang and mounted up alongside Pirtle. As the three of them rode out of the stable together, he nodded at his number one investigator.

"Where to now," was all he said.

"Ranger headquarters," was all the answer.

When they arrived, Will Posey took charge of the horses, and dropped them off at the barn with the rest of the remuda that served the Rangers and caught the trolley downtown. He walked up the back steps and into Captain Newton's office, where the two senior Rangers were drinking coffee and sitting on either side of a battered old oak roll top desk talking.

"Your instincts have always been good Boyd . . . saved us from gettin' our tit in the wringer more n' once . . . but this's the Governor—the man in charge of the whole damn state of Texas—that y'all's talkin' about. Use yer head. He's someone above reproach by the very nature of his position."

Pirtle, who still had the leather dispatch case strapped to his side, was occupied rolling a cigarette with one hand. He stuck the finished coffin nail in the corner of his mouth and lit it, shook out the match and sucked down some smoke before he answered. "Every word you spoke is true, Wiley. I can't argue with any of it, but I think the man's bent. Something told me if I'd left that case and all them papers up there, I'd never see 'em again."

"Boyd, I think he was close to takin' 'em by force. You and Posey were already out the door when he lectured me about insubordination, told me he wouldn't put up with it from me, you or anyone else. I ain't sure, but I believe he was about to sic his personal hound after yuh."

"That guy Milton . . . against Posey, and me?"

"Don't kid yourself. Guys like him don't get where they are on looks or school grades alone. He's a bodyguard too."

"Interesting. Maybe I should interview him about his boss . . ."

"I don't think either one of 'em would let that happen."

"Prob'ly not, but that kinda goes to my point, don't it. Somethin' ain't right. All of a sudden, a change came over everythin' the Governor said and did."

Will Posey who'd been silent since returning to the cramped office, shifted in the low-backed bar chair he was sitting on and leaned forward. "I think I can help," he said, adding, "if it's okay to put my two bits in . . ."

"Of course," Captain Newton said. "Speak up. We'll take any help we can get. Say whatever yuh got t'say."

"It's just . . . I don't want nothin' to mess up my career in the Rangers . . ."

"Don't worry, Posey," Wiley Newton said. "Nothin' mentioned in here will get repeated."

"You have my word too," Boyd chimed in. "Tell us what you got to tell."

Will Posey nodded and said, "Thanks. It's just I never been around such important personages before and . . ."

"They ain't no better'n y'all."

It was apparent to both of the senior Rangers that their young associate was more nervous than they'd first realized. Pirtle said, "Will, speak. Get it out. We'll decide what to do with it."

Posey swallowed, and said, "Mr. Pirtle's right. The Governor's a crook. I seen it when y'all laid out the property deeds and transfers that we uncovered down around Brownsville, near the mouth of the Rio Grande. There'd been a dozen or more land swaps from Utah to Colorado to Texas, and each time there was either more value—mineral rights, water rights or a platted town—or a lot more land area. Square miles of it. It was when you were pullin' out maps and deeds, Mr. Pirtle, and the Captain was outta the room for a nature call. That Van Arden guy saw some legal forms from a law firm in Laredo. The letterheads said, *Wolfe and Blake* on them, and were all signed by somebody named James Carlos Blake. When Milton picked it up, he went ashen, his hand started to shake and his face got sweaty. There were several other items from the same lawyers in there and Milton looked sick to his stomach. He hurried over to the Governor's side and had a quiet word with him. Same result. That's when they took all of us down to lunch. But not before I got those documents and put 'em in a safe place while alla y'all were leavin' the room."

"Where's that," Pirtle asked.

"Right here," Will Posey said, and hiked up his pant leg to reveal a tall cowboy boot stuffed with legal papers of every type and description, most having the words *Wolfe and Blake* on it somewhere.

"Nice work, Will," Boyd Pirtle said. "Damned nice work."

Posey added, "From that point on, Governor Slater wasn't our friend no more."

Chapter Fifty-Three

While the Rangers struggled to overcome the entrenched and institutionalized forces of criminality down in Austin Texas . . . another pair of villains of the well-dressed, but low rent variety operating in Colorado Springs and the Cripple Creek Mining District of Colorado . . . were putting the finishing touches on the biggest scam they'd ever engineered; a swindle of epic proportions for both audacity and size. Based upon greed, they reckoned it was infallible. Simple too. They'd found a lustful, naive and wealthy young tenderfoot who wanted to buy a mine. The two con artists were doctoring one up for him, while the third member of their group—a nubile, pretty young whore named Charity Moon—was passing herself off as a college educated society girl on a summer fling, and she was fucking the lad to within an inch of his life. Charity enjoyed her work, was good at her job, and Mapes—Mapleton Sheryl Jones—was a happy happy lamb as he was being inexorably led toward financial butchery.

Frank Rogers, dressed up as an ersatz lawyer, and Delbert McKnight, a bogus mining engineer, were having a sit-down in one of the snugs at Johnny Nolan's Saloon in Cripple Creek. They were eating Cornish pasties—little folded over pie crusts filled with ground beef, onions, and potatoes, then baked to a golden brown—and drinking mugs of pilsner beer from Zang's Brewery in Denver.

Frank pushed his mug back with one hand, and pulled out a package of factory rolled cigarillos with the other one. He was about to light up, when Del McKnight said, "You care if I eat them," pointing to a pair of untouched pies on Frank's plate.

Rogers shook his head. "Help yourself. They're tasty enough . . . I just ain't real hungry right now."

McKnight looked at his companion with a critical eye as he chewed his food. He swallowed, took a drink of beer and said, "You ain't wantin' to eat 'cuz yuh been smokin' too much of that shit over at Gun Wa's. Opium messes with yer mind. It clouds yore judgment too. It's bad cess, an' besides that, it'll fook up yer reflexes and yuh can't afford to be impaired right now."

"Don't worry," Frank said, as smoke uncoiled itself, then slithered out of his nose and mouth, "I can handle it, and I'll be ready to take care of business when the time comes too."

"Sure yuh will," the big man said, as he bit the last pastie in half and swallowed it with a gulp.

Attempting to dial down the tension that had sprung up between them, Frank said, "You did good, findin' those old workin's up there. If I didn't already know better, I'd think it was a real, active mine . . ."

McKnight swallowed the last of the pasties, drank another mouthful of beer, belched behind his closed fist . . . and proceeded to lick all ten of his fingers, one by one. Finished, he fastidiously wiped both hands and his mouth on the red and white cloth napkin that came with the table setting, and dropped it in the middle of his plate . . . while Frank Rogers watched in utter amazement. Del said, "They're even more impressive now. I salted 'em over the last two nights, and I got a few nuggets to drop when he comes up tomorrow for an inspection."

"What's salting?"

"It means," Del said, as he reached over and helped himself to one of Franks little cigars, "that I replaced the buckshot in about half a dozen shells with gold dust. Then I went in after dark and blasted the reloads around in the mine workin's, so that it looks like there's a lotta lode-bearing veins of ore in there. And that, plus a few nuggets sprinkled around, along with the assay reports an' geology estimates I've made up, should be enough to have him pissin' himself with eagerness to write a big fat check to buy all the rights to the *Lock, Stock and Barrel Mining Corp.* of Colorado. Then the rest'll be up to yourself."

Frank leaned back in his chair and smoked, thinking about all of the complex steps that had brought them to this point. After a few moments of reflection to reassure himself that they'd done everything to insure a successful swindle, he said, "It looks like this is it then, until Friday, when we'll meet to close the deal."

"'Pears so. I'm meetin' Charity an Mapes here—around noon tomorrow."

"That takes care of Wednesday . . . what about Thursday . . . I don't want Mapes runnin' around loose, thinkin' a reasons to crawfish on us."

"I believe Charity Moon has a plan for that. She'll keep the laddie busy and tuned to a fever pitch if I know her. She'll have 'is nose to somethin' alright, and it sure as shit won't be no grindstone."

Frank ground out his smoke in the middle of his dinner plate, smiled, and said, "Damn, Del, you got a way with words. I can just see our darlin' Miss Moon, sittin' up on satin pillows in the bed, holdin' that rich young jasper by the ears, and directin' him as to how and where to satify her. She'll no doubt ruin that boy for life before she's done with him."

Almost always dour, Delbert McKnight cracked a slight grin, followed by a full-face smile and then a chuckle—which caused Frank Rogers to follow suit—and after another moment, both men were laughing out of control.

"Damn you Frank," Del said between peals of laughter, as he wiped tears from his eyes, "I won't be able to look at that edjit without thinkin' of his hairy ass stickin' up in the air while Charity twists his ears and rides the moustache right off'a his face." Which sent the pair of them into more gales of uncontrollable laughter.

When their storm of mirth finally blew itself out, Rogers said, "The tricky part of the whole thing's gonna be the conversion. Gettin' him off the idea of writin' checks, and on to the notion of payin' with cash . . . or gold."

McKnight relit his smoke, which had gone out while the two men were having their hoot. He shook the wooden match and tossed it on Rogers' plate, now doing duty as an ashtray. Del puffed, and said, "I'll set that up for us. You can help by sayin' somethin' to Charity, if yuh talk to her tonight. This whole grift is based on greed. That is, I told young Mapleton that I needed an investor, 'cuz I found out that the prospects worth a lot more than you, the lawyer, or the eastern society dame who inherited it realizes. And, that both a yez are willin' to take even less, on a cash on delivery basis. It won't be too awful hard to convince 'im that he's fookin' you and the legatee . . . when in fact it's Mapes himself who's takin' it in the shorts. There's a certain, ah, whatcha' call it, poetic irony in that, don'cha think?"

"It's poetic justice, or dramatic irony, that you're lookin' for . . . and where the hell didya come up with a word like *legatee,* Del? It ain't one I'd expect from you."

McKnight shifted in his chair as he got ready to get up. The big man looked Rogers in the eyes, and said, "This ain't the first time I fooked a person outta an inheritance," as he stood and started to leave the room. "See yuh Friday," were his last words as he went out the door.

Frank Rogers thought about dramatic irony all the way back down to Colorado Springs on the narrow gauge Cripple Creek Short Line, the railway whose scenery *Bankrupts the English language,* according to its advertising. But the closer he came to the city, the dimmer the view became to him, and the stronger the siren call of the couch, the lamp and the pill at Gun Wa's, where the lure of erotic opium dreams forswore all that was light and reason.

Chapter Fifty-Four

Will Posey began removing deeds, certificates, letters of transmittal, articles of incorporation, minutes of annual meetings, shareholder lists, tax receipts and a wide assortment of other forms, documents and notes from his boots—all of which bore the words *Wolfe and Blake, Attorneys at Law* on them somewhere.

Seeing the lot of paperwork all together, Pirtle said, "I thought those were trouble when we first located them, but I didn't think it'd be so great . . . or so quick."

"We always knew we'd come up against them again, sooner or later, Boyd. They've just been layin' low these last few years while Porfirio Diaz has the country by the throat."

Posey looked at the two senior Rangers in confusion. "What country," he said, "and who are these Wolfe and Blake guys?"

"It's a long story," Captain Newton said. "The short version is that the Wolfe's are a big family, half of which lives in Mexico and half in the U.S. Some are legitimate, some of 'em are criminal bad asses who don't recognize boundaries of any kind. Originally, they were part of an Irish brigade of U.S. Army troops that defected to Mexico during the Mexican War in 1845. The Blake's are their allies by marriage. The Rangers and Wolfes have tangled many times."

"Who won," Posey said.

"Nobody," Boyd Pirtle replied. "We've only ever fought to a draw. There's been a lotta skirmishes over the years, and we've all had our share of hits and misses, small wins or losses, but neither one of us's been able to knock the other out."

"The question is," Wiley Newton said, "what are we gonna do now, about the Mormons takin' over the US Marshals Service? The Wolfes will keep. They ain't goin' nowhere, but this situation with the corruption of state and federal officials is somethin' that won't wait."

"No," Pirtle said, "It won't. And I'd bet my bottom dollar that Milton Van Orden's already called down to Laredo and evidence is disappearin' right now, while we're talkin' about it. This stuff is gonna be the only proof that the crimes were ever committed."

"It also makes the three of us into prime targets for a bushwhackin'," Will Posey said.

"Well then, you'd better grow eyes in the back of your head, because you're the only bodyguard I trust enough to stand behind me," Pirtle quipped, then added, "and keep your powder dry, and guns oiled . . . because I believe it'll get worse before it gets better. But . . . what're we gonna do about tomorrow? We're still expected at the capitol by Governor Slater."

"I've been thinkin' about that," Wiley Newton said, "and here's my plan. I'll go to the Governor by myself and stall, tell 'im you've come down with the croup from all the talkin' yesterday and . . ."

"Make it the grippe. It's more believable—from sleepin' outside in the rain the other night—and it's communicable. The Governor won't want to take a chance on catchin' it. Hell, he may even send you away."

"Boyd, you are downright diabolical," Newton said. "How the hell d'ya think of things like that?"

Pirtle laughed, crossed his legs and started rolling a smoke. "You see, Will, what all that readin' does . . ." and lit up as the Captain continued.

"Anyways, I'll stall 'em, buy us as much leeway as I'm able. Prob'ly 'til next week sometime. In the meanwhile, Boyd, you an' Posey rearrange all them notes of yours and write up a summary tellin' the who, what, when an' where . . . as brief as yuh can. Then box it all up an' send it Special Delivery to President McKinley at the White House. Don't let it outta your sight until it's been taken in by the US postal clerk and he gives yuh a receipt."

"I'll do one better'n that. I'll put it into the Railroad Post Office Baggage Car on the fastest, most direct route I can find."

"Make sure they hafta sign for it at the other end. Have 'em send the notice back here, to my attention at Ranger HQ."

"Sure. Then what?"

"After that, you and Posey can be on your way to Colorado. I reckon y'all might leave here Thursday mornin' and be in Colorado Springs by Friday afternoon or evenin'."

"Are you sayin' we can go as soon as we get this evidence arranged and sent?"

"Yeah. I am. And Boyd . . . be sure and introduce yourself an' Posey to the Marshal, or Sheriff, or Police Chief, or to whichever law officers they got in charge up there, when the two of yez get into town."

"Okay Wiley," Boyd Pirtle said, as he put his cigarette out in the sand pail next to the desk that doubled as an ashtray and spittoon. "Will, would you gather up all the papers and meet me back at Mrs. Orr's. We'll work at her kitchen table. I got to go send a telegram."

"No need to move everything Boyd. Y'all can use my office. I won't be back here until I'm done at the Governor's tomorrow. Lock the door when you go, here's the key . . . less chance of losin' somethin', or havin' too many eyes on things."

"Good. It'll make the process go faster. I'll be back in a few."

As Pirtle and Newman started to leave, Will Posey said, "Mr. Pirtle . . ."

"Yeah Will?"

"Wouldya bring back somethin' t'eat? I'm starvin'."

Chapter Fifty-Five

Sixty leagues—about 180 miles—to the northwest of Austin, events on Featherston Lane in Cleburne, Texas were of a more mundane nature during the opening days of that first week in September, 1901. There, Mimi James and her children, Skipper, Carole and Evelyn Ruth, together with Ella Stringfellow, were all busy fourteen hours a day, harvesting, preparing and canning every edible stalk, stem, root, leaf, berry and fruit in sight, in order to feed all of them through the coming winter.

It was an entirely new experience for Ella, who'd always been indifferent to meal planning and preparation, or the stockpiling of food—even with her Mormon heritage—because her needs were so minimal when she was living alone. But with five persons in the house, and three of them growing youngsters, it was a whole different proposition. Ella was glad to have Mimi for a mentor; one who seemed to somehow possess all there was to know about how to survive. The woman had a knack for passing on her knowledge, and Ella was an apt, if not eager student who absorbed it all with the first telling. They were finishing up the last of a bumper crop of peaches, when the telegram came on Tuesday evening from Texas Ranger Special Agent Boyd Pirtle.

Miss Stringfellow, My duty here concludes Thursday 5 Sep 01 stop *Will leave same for Colorado Springs to resume hunt fugitive Rogers* stop *More when available* stop *BA Pirtle SA Texas Rangers* stop.

As soon as she read it, Ella's heart began racing . . . *Finally,* she thought, *finally after all this time, all the effort, the endless waiting, hoping and trying . . .* "Mimi," She said out loud from the front hallway where she stood clutching the message to her bosom, "Mimi, we need to talk. It's important . . ." *And it's gonna change all our lives* she thought, as she hurried back to the kitchen where Mimi, Skipper and the two little girls were washing utensils and cleaning up.

When Ella came into the room, Mimi was wiping down the surfaces of all the cabinets and work areas, while Skipper scrubbed pots, Carole dried and Evelyn put them away. On the table, four dozen quart jars of peach halves sat cooling and sealing themselves on clean linen dish towels. She said, "That is an impressive sight, Mimi."

"Be good eatin' too, until next summer's crop comes in."

Ella took a pair of white china mugs from the cupboard and made tea. She handed one to Mimi and said, "Would you come in the library with me? I need to tell you a few things."

"Of course," Mimi said as she took the mug, adding, "you kids finish up in here and go on upstairs to your rooms. You've got school tomorrow."

"I'll be workin' for Mr. Battle," Skipper said, "at the

lumberyard. We've got two gondolas of sawed timber and a boxcar of hardware to unload."

"I'll be up and get breakfast for everyone," Mimi replied. She followed Ella to the former office of Bishop Stringfellow, unable to shake off an intense feeling of dread.

Ella sat in one of the side chairs in front of her father's old desk, and Mimi took the other one—expecting the worst—but hoping for something a little less than devastating. She was dumbfounded instead, by what she heard next.

Ella took a deep breath . . . looked at the bay window behind the desk, where Duke the cat lurked among the ferns, Swedish ivy and spider plants, staring out as he surveyed all that which belonged to cats—and said, "I'm leaving."

"YOU'RE WHAT?"

"I'm going to Colorado. First thing tomorrow. I'm pretty sure Mr. Pirtle has located my brother, Chester."

"The one who's been missing for so long?"

"Twenty years. He disappeared the day after the day after my father was killed, right in front of our house."

"Two days . . ."

"Yes."

"Where in Colorado is he?"

"I think he's in Colorado Springs. That's where Mr. Pirtle said he was going on Thursday of this week. He put it in the telegram I just received. I don't know if that was an error or not, but he's never mentioned any specific place before. So I'm taking a chance and heading up there first . . . to see if I can find my brother Chester."

Mimi stared at the book-filled shelves that lined the walls, unable to speak for the moment, as her mind gyrated, twisting the endless bad outcomes she foresaw, all of which left her and her children homeless and destitute. After a few moments that seemed like ages, she said, "And how soon do you want us to get out of your house?"

Now, it was Ella's turn to be shocked. "What . . . did you say?"

"Will you want us to get out tonight?"

"Mimi James," Ella said, "whatever gave you an idea like that . . . what kind of a person do you think I am, anyway. Do you really believe I'd put a mother and three children out on the street, when I wouldn't let a young boy drown a stray cat?"

Mimi looked down at her mug, still full of tea in her hands, and without looking up said, "You needn't raise your voice Ella, I'm an adult. I just figured that with yore leavin', you wouldn't want us in the house no more. And I don't have no bad feelin's about it neither. I wanna know what to expect is all, and judgin' by my life so far . . . what I can look forward to is the awfulest thing that I think can happen."

Ella reached out and put her hand on the distraught woman's arm. "Mimi," she said, "listen to me. Nothing bad's going to happen to you or the kids if I can help it. The only way for you to leave here is if you want to leave . . . I don't know how long I'll be gone is all and there's some things about the place that I need to tell you."

"You're not wantin' us to go?"

"No. For the last time Mimi, No. N.O. means NO."

"I understand. What do you want me to do?"

"First of all," Ella said as she took a drink of tea, "I want you to utilize some of those extra rooms on the second floor as a boarding house, so you'll have an income in case I don't get back right away. I don't have any idea how long my trip will take, and I want you to treat the place like it's your own. Do you think you can do that? You ought to be able to get three or four boarders, don't you agree?"

Mimi put her tea on the desk and thought for a moment before she answered. "I believe so . . . Skipper will have to help me with the bookkeepin'. He's real good at his ciphers."

"I'll show him how to keep a ledger. It's not hard, as long as you stay up to date. Don't let things pile up. And I'll leave you some funds, for a kitty, to get everything started. There's a big iron safe hidden inside one of the feed stalls out in the barn to keep your money in."

"There is . . . I never knew . . ."

"You weren't supposed to know. No one is. The purpose of having a safe is to conceal and protect your cash and valuables; so the more people who know about it, the more people you'll have trying to break into it. Does that make sense?"

"Perfect."

"Good. There's a great many other things to tell you and not much time, so listen close and ask questions if you don't understand."

The two women spent several more hours together that Tuesday night, as Ella instructed Mimi in the basics of operating, maintaining and living in the big three story house on Featherston Lane. After satisfying herself that Mimi had all the information she needed to sustain the household, Ella packed and made her own preparations, which included raiding the cash hoards she had stashed about the property and getting out the .32 caliber Colt pistol she'd had since her father died. She checked to make sure it was loaded and working properly. Then she wrapped it and the soft holster among her intimate things. Some of the money she gave to Mimi, the rest she sewed into her clothes. She wrote a short resignation letter to the school board and library that Skipper would hand deliver for her. In it, she expressed regrets for the short notice of departure, but stated that the importance of finding her long-lost brother overrode all other considerations.

Chapter Fifty-Six

On Wednesday, September the fourth, 1901, Ella Stringfellow woke early, said her good-byes to Mimi and the girls, then Skipper dropped her at the depot, where she took the first shuttle from Cleburne to Dallas. Arriving before eight a.m., she telegraphed ahead for a reservation at what was supposed to be the number one, best and most luxurious hotel in Colorado Springs. Called *The Antlers,* it had been constructed by General William J. Palmer—the man who founded the city and built the Denver & Rio Grande Railroad—it was also where he housed and displayed his personal collection of hunting trophies. After receiving her wire confirmation, she purchased a first-class ticket to the Pikes Peak Region, which included her own private sitting and sleeping accommodations for the overnight journey.

She was excited to be making her first trip away from Cleburne and hopeful of finding Chester, but as the Ft. Worth & Denver City Railway passenger train left the station, Ella found that she was equal parts anticipation and apprehension. She was eager to catch up with her brother, but anxious too. What would she say . . . what would he say . . . would they even recognize each other after so much time had gone by. *Twenty years,* she thought, *twenty years and a thousand grievances . . . there'll be plenty to say . . . a lifetimes worth of words to speak.*

She watched the scenery rolling by, settled back in her seat and got comfortable for the seven hundred and fifty mile trip ahead. There'd be stops in Wichita Falls, Amarillo and Dalhart, Texas, then they'd steam across the barren flatlands of northeastern New Mexico before stopping in Trinidad and Pueblo, Colorado, then at last in Colorado Springs—after which the train would terminate at Union Station in Denver, the mile-high, Queen City of the Plains.

At Ranger Headquarters down in Austin, Boyd Pirtle and Will Posey were once again up to their elbows in paperwork. For the third time in less than a week, they were collating documents and organizing a paper trail that established a chain of evidence which proved that certain Mormon Church officials—starting twenty-five years earlier with Ella's father, Bishop Carl A. Stringfellow—had bribed and corrupted high government officials by trading LDS land for appointments to the US Marshals Service, and that a long-denied secret Mormon militia known as the Danites not only existed . . . they had been appointed to posts as federal law enforcement officers with far-reaching authority and powers of arrest throughout the western United States. Making the job even more tedious and time-consuming however, was the fact that Pirtle had to write letters of explanation for each incidence that detailed the method of collection, as well as notarized affidavits from himself and Will Posey. The work was exhausting, but by late afternoon they had all eleven cases sorted, numbered and arranged, put into individual sealed envelopes and then carefully packed into a wood shipping crate that Will Posey was closing with horseshoe nails and lead seals with embedded fine wires in them. As Pirtle's first letter explained, it was impossible to open the box without breaking the wires.

Captain Newton, who'd been in and out of the office ever since returning from his morning meeting with Governor Slater, watched as Posey wound the last wire and lead seal around the final pair of nails, then hammered them home. He said, "Whose idea was that," pointing to the place that Posey had just wired and nailed shut.

"Will's," Pirtle said.

"Damned if that ain't a good one son," the Captain noted. "Whatever gave yuh the idea?"

"It's how boxcars are closed," Posey answered.

Wiley Newton looked at the shipping crate, the address labels and the light ropes that looked like a cargo net Posey had tied around it, "Is it ready t'go?"

"Yeah."

"When are yuh leavin', Boyd?"

"Posey and I are goin' first thing tomorrow. We'll mail it when we get on the Ft. Worth train."

"Good. Don't let it outta your sight 'til then."

"Seriously, Wiley . . ."

"Sorry, Boyd. Heat of the moment."

"Don't worry Cap'n," Posey said. "We'll take care of everythin'."

In Cripple Creek, Colorado, the bustling mining town on the backside of Pikes Peak, Mapleton Sheryl Jones—the randy young scion and heir to a Philadelphia mercantile and real estate fortune—along with his consort, Miss Charity Moon, *femme fatale,* first-class seductress, and innocent looking but thoroughly soiled young dove, were being met by Delbert McKnight, a Denver bunko artist who was posing as a mining engineer. He was taking Mapes on a tour of a mine site that the untested green tenderfoot was thinking of buying. Unbeknownst to him, the mine, like the engineer, was as phony as a three legged duck. The site inspection would be their final performance before the swindlers went for the close, and extracted a bunch of his money from the gullible young man. That last job would be carried out by Frank Rogers, pretending to be a shyster lawyer who was representing a disinterested eastern society matron and widow.

But at that moment, Frank Rogers, aka Chester Stringfellow, was passed out on a couch in the back room of a notorious bucket of blood joint over in Colorado City. Called *The Pride of the West Saloon,* it was really a front for a Chinese opium den known as *Gun Wa's,* after its ruthless Oriental proprietor. Frank was just entering the second day of a three day binge . . . deep into lurid opium dreams . . . unaware that the past was about to reappear in his life . . . or that it would demand so great a retribution.

Chapter Fifty-Seven

The big workhorse Baldwin 4-6-0 locomotive chuffed, thumped and then jerked the ten car train into motion with a hiss of steam and a belch of oily black coal smoke, just as the sun was making its presence known over the eastern horizon in a dazzling display of all the pale-colored pastels in God's own paint box.

As he watched the city of Austin sliding past the open baggage car door and noted the riot of color in the dawning sky, Boyd Pirtle said, "I've always believed that the risin' and settin' of the sun over the plains is one of the greatest sights in all of nature. I never tire of it."

"It's a glory all right," Will Posey said, as he pulled the sliding door closed with a thunk, "but it don't make up for bein' eight hours late."

"All the rains has caused a lotta damage. I'd wager there ain't a railroad in Texas that's runnin' on time right now. We'll catch the Katy at Elgin, ride it on up to Ft. Worth and see what we see when we get there. Its gonna be another twenty-five or six hours from there to Colorado Springs, maybe more, no matter how we cut it."

"Are we gonna ride the whole damn way in the postal car?"

"No. Once we get that," Pirtle pointed to the wooden crate

they'd poured their hearts and souls into for the past three and a half months, and said, "into the US Postal System, we can ride in the Pullman."

"When are yuh gonna send it?"

"At Fort Worth. We'll have a layover and change lines again. I reckon we'll have time ta eat, go to the RPO and send it off."

Posey made his way over to where his boss was seated on a pile of mail bags and tried to make himself comfortable for the short, twenty-seven mile run to Elgin, Texas. He said, "How come it takes two hours to go such a little ways?"

Pirtle gave him the stink eye for a moment and said, "You'd have to ask the railroad gods. How the hell would I know . . ."

"Well here's another one then. After all we put into that box right there, do ya trust them post office people to get it where it's gotta go?"

"I've got as much faith in them as I do in every other facet of our government," Pirtle said as he shoved mail bags around and tried to make himself a place to nap, "especially when every person who touches, transfers, handles, or delivers it or has anything at all to do with that package . . . has to sign for it."

"You think they'll bother?"

"On a package from the Texas Rangers to the White House and the attention of President McKinley himself . . . you bet they'll do it, if they want to keep their jobs.

"I sure hope so. We've put an awful, awful lotta effort into gettin' what's in there . . ."

"That we did, but it's gonna be out of our hands as soon as we mail it," Pirtle said, as he stretched out and put his hat over his eyes, "and we have to trust others to do their job, same as us. Quit frettin' about it and wake me up when we get to Elgin." Less than a minute later he was sound asleep.

Wish I knew how the hell he does that, Will Posey thought as he lit a cigarette and watched the sun rise through the iron window bars on the armored door of the slow moving baggage car.

Two hours and twenty-five minutes later, the Houston & Texas Central Train No. 4 made entry into the brick-making village of Elgin . . . where Pirtle, Will Posey and the all-important package transferred over to the larger Missouri-Kansas-Texas or KATY line, that would carry them on to Ft. Worth—where they'd make one last transfer—a hundred and eighty miles north and a bit more than eight hours later.

When the train came to rest at the Ft. Worth station, Posey opened the door, looked out over the crowded platform and checked their surroundings before he hopped down with a pair of Gladstone bags in one hand, and a model 94 Winchester lever action carbine in the other. Pirtle followed, carrying the crate of case-files they were sending to Washington. He said, "I ain't been here in a while, so keep on the lookout for somewhere to eat. Somethin' decent. I'm sick of the kinda places where we have to fight the roaches for the food."

"Sure, boss. I'm so damned awful hungry, my backbone is rubbin' a hole in my bellybutton."

"Well, try not to die on me just yet, Will. We'll get yuh fed as soon as this's in the mail and the RPO is just over yonder," Pirtle said, as he walked toward the modest office with the small black and white sign over the door.

Inside was an ink and grime encrusted oak counter, with a clerk standing behind it who was wearing sleeve garters on a collarless seersucker shirt and a green see-through visor on his bald head. "Evenin' gents," he said. "What can I do for yez."

"Need to send this by special delivery," Pirtle said as he heaved the wire and rope-bound wooden shipping crate up on the counter where it landed with a thud. "With particular handling, to include the who, where, what time and how long for each person that touches it—beginnin' with myself and yourself—to be done in duplicate and returned to the attention of Captain Wiley Newton at Texas Ranger HQ in Austin, Texas. And in addition, I'd like a return receipt from the last person who touches it: the one who receives it at 1600 Pennsylvania Avenue."

"Certainly sir," the railroad postal clerk said, as he began pulling out forms and rubber stamps with a brisk efficiency, and writing on them in black ink with a steel nib pen. When he lifted the box and weighed it on a black cast iron post office platform scale, he frowned, looked at Pirtle and said, "You realize sir, that this item is gonna be pretty expensive . . ."

"I do," Pirtle said as he flashed his Ranger badge at the clerk and added, "and I hope you realize just exactly how important this item is. It's critical that it gets to its destination as fast as possible, without delays or problems. That's why I'm entrusting it to the United States Postal Service."

"Do not worry Mr. Pirtle. The Post Office prides itself on the reliability of its service, and the dependability and honesty of all our mailmen. We'll get it there for yuh. That's a promise."

"How soon will it go out?"

The RPO man pulled out a timetable, consulted it, checked his pocket watch, then said, "In exactly thirty-seven minutes, a Santa Fe express will stop here and take on coal, water, mail and passengers on her way to St. Louis. She'll leave here exactly thirty minutes after that, and your package will be safely and securely on board. It'll get transferred to one of the big eastern lines and delivered to the White House on Tuesday, September the tenth."

Pirtle looked the clerk in the eye and said, "Much obliged. Now my compadre can rest a little easier, and we can concentrate on the outlaws we're after."

"Glad to be of service," the clerk said, as he busied himself tallying up the charges for all the services the Pirtle had ordered.

As he was paying and getting a receipt, in order to get his money back from the Ranger Purser, Pirtle said, "Can you tell us where we can get a decent meal around here? We've had nothin' but gut-waddin' and road food—if anythin' at all—for the past couple of days. We've got two hours before our train leaves and I'd like to treat my associate, Ranger Posey here, to a nice sit-down supper with all the trimmin's."

"Sure can," the RPO man said. "The best place in town's just three blocks away. It's called *Billyrich's Steakhouse & Supper Club*. Guy who runs it's named Richard Lawler. Tell 'im Cecil sent yez. And try the chuck wagon beefsteak. You'll be glad you did."

Two hours and ten minutes later, at six o'clock on Thursday evening, as Ella Stringfellow settled into her room at the Antlers Hotel in Colorado Springs, Boyd Pirtle and Will Posey made themselves comfortable in a pair of adjacent Pullman seats on Ft. Worth & Denver City Railroad Train No. 1, running ten hours behind schedule due to all the repairs necessitated by the extensive damage from the heavy rainfalls of the previous week. When asked, the conductor told Pirtle that, barring any more natural disasters, they'd be in Colorado Springs by eight pm on Friday evening.

"Good thing," Will Posey said, as he lowered the back of his seat and stretched his legs. "It's gonna take me at least that long to break outta the food coma I'm in . . ."

Pirtle smiled and finished rolling an after-dinner cigarette with his left hand. As he lit it with a wooden kitchen match he pulled from his waistcoat pocket, he said, "I reckon old Cecil knew what he was talkin' about. That was one helluva feast. Enjoy it while you can though, 'cause God alone knows what tomorrow will bring."

Chapter Fifty-Eight

On Thursday, September the fifth, 1901, with Boyd Pirtle a day behind her, Ella Stringfellow was awed by her first sight of the Sangre de Cristo Mountain Range when her train crossed New Mexico, summited Raton Pass and made its descent into Trinidad, the coal producing town just over the Colorado state line. A Texas woman, born and bred in flat country, she'd never seen anything so grand. But an hour later, after a stop for people, fuel and water, when the Colorado & Southern passenger train moved through Walsenburg, he got her first glimpse of the magnificent Spanish Peaks . . . a pair of 12 and 13,000 foot volcanic mounts that jut up from the flatlands of the San Luis Valley . . . *Huajatolla*, the Native Americans called them: *The Breasts of the World*. They're visible for almost a hundred miles in every direction and they took her breath away. But there was still more to come . . . and Mother Nature was saving the best for last.

Ella was utterly captivated when her train steamed into downtown Colorado Springs and she got her first close and personal look at the towering might of 14,110 foot Pikes Peak, *The Shining Mountain Sitting Big,* as the indigenous Northern Utes called it. The granite pinnacle dominated the city and all of its surroundings as her luggage was retrieved and loaded into an open carriage, piloted by a liveried, top-hatted driver and pulled by a matched pair of black horses. As she sat in the rear-facing seat, the driver explained that the hotel had mysteriously burned to the ground in 1898, and the newly rebuilt Antlers had only just been reopened.

"What happened to all the hunting trophies?"

"You mean the stuffed heads . . ."

"Yes. The ones General Palmer took."

"Burnt up in the fire. And, if you don't mind me sayin' so ma'am, good riddance. All them poor critters, kilt for sport, all them eyes starin' down . . . give yuh the creeps. They was bad juju far as I'm concerned, and I'm glad they're almost all gone."

"You mean they're still some in there?"

"Yes'm. There's a pair of elk, a buffalo and a full-size grizzly bear in the main lobby."

"I've never seen any one of those creatures."

"Well ma'am," the driver said, as he pulled the barouche up to the front entrance, you'll see every one of 'em in a few minutes, but dead 'uns ain't nothin' at all like the real live beasts."

"Thank you, I'll certainly keep that in mind," Ella said, as she extended a gloved hand and was helped to descend. Then she tipped the driver a few coins and watched the bellman, who'd met them at the entrance, put her luggage on a wheeled cart and escorted her to the registration counter.

Ella gasped out loud when she passed the standing mount grizzly bear, which snarled down at her from its full ten foot height and displayed huge four inch claws on both of its extended paws. Even in death, the pair of elk exuded a gravitas that almost broke her heart. *What kind of man,* she thought, *could derive pleasure from killing such proud and magnificent creatures as these for lust, and call it sport? When God gave man dominion over the animals, I don't believe this is what he had in mind. Subsistence, certainly. We are, after all, carnivores and need meat to survive. But wanton slaughter is nothing less than a mortal sin.*

Last of the taxidermy was the huge head of an American Buffalo, whose presence only served to remind her that millions of their kind had been murdered—by so-called sportsmen, equipped with fifty caliber rifles of all makes, shapes and sizes—and their carcasses left to rot in the hot sun and endless winds of the high plains.

Her reverie was cut short by an officious little man with a carefully groomed and clipped moustache, wearing a pair of pince-nez eyeglasses perched upon his nose and standing behind the registration desk. He was straightening the lapels on his suit coat when he said, "May I help you Madam?"

"Yes," Ella replied. "I'm checking in. My name is . . ."

"Madam," he interrupted, "this is a proper hotel, and we . . ."

"And I am a proper woman, here on behalf of my entire family, to locate my missing brother. I have a reservation, a confirmation, and furthermore, I resent your insinuation and your manners. Why don't you send over your superior—and I am sure there are many—but your immediate supervisor will do, for I will not speak with such a rude and impudent lackey as yourself."

Behind her the bellman, dressed for glory in the Antlers official maroon and silver livery, was staring straight down at the floor while pinching the bridge of his nose in an attempt to choke down his laughter.

The red-faced clerk, publicly stripped of whatever dignity he'd come to work with that morning, was sucking for air and trying to think up a snappy comeback at the same time, but wasn't having much success with either. That's when a distinguished older gentleman in a black swallow-tailed coat and gray striped dress pants stepped in. He said, "That will be all, Maurice. Go help the maître d' in the dining room."

"Immediately, sir," the humbled fop said, as he left with his head down and fists clenched.

"My name is Mr. Caldwell," the man said. "I'm the Manager and part-owner of the hotel with General Palmer. I apologize for the rudeness of that employee, and I assure you . . . it will never happen again."

"I accept your apology . . . and thank you. But please, don't let that man lose his job because of what just transpired."

"No, he won't . . . but he'll be reassigned. And your reservation?"

"Stringfellow."

Caldwell searched the reservation book and said, "Ah, yes. E. Stringfellow, Cleburne, Texas. For how many nights, may I ask?"

"Indeterminate. Possibly as many as thirty. It depends on how successful I am in finding my brother. He disappeared twenty years ago, two days after someone shot and killed my father . . ."

"I'm sorry for your loss. Did they catch the murderer?"

"No. The case was never solved."

"I can only imagine how difficult that must have been for you. What's your brother's name?"

"Chester. Chester Stringfellow."

"And why do you think he's here . . ."

"He's been sending money to me . . . anonymously. A Texas Ranger traced it to a bank in the region."

"Well," Mr. Caldwell said, as he turned the registration book around, handed Ella a desk pen and pointed to the place for her to sign, "with the gold strike up in Cripple Creek, we have no end of banks in the city. Banks and churches abound here . . . I suppose because the newly rich need a place to keep their money, and another one to pray that they'll get it back when they want it. Welcome to Colorado Springs, Miss Stringfellow, I hope your visit is both enjoyable and fruitful."

"I'm certain it will be," Ella said as she returned the pen to its well and accepted the key to a luxury room high on the west side of the hotel, where the balcony afforded her a heart stopping view of the most famous mountain in the country.

A half-hour later, as she settled into her temporary quarters, Ella found herself marveling at the rich splendor of her surroundings and wondering . . . *How do I go about finding a lone individual in a city of some twenty thousand souls . . . when I don't even know a single solitary one of them?*

She turned the question over and over in her mind throughout the afternoon, evening, and a long, restless, sleep-deprived night. It wasn't until Friday morning—while she was drinking coffee on her private deck—that the answer came to her. When it did, her life changed forever.

Chapter Fifty-Nine

Late Friday morning, September the sixth, 1901, Texas Rangers Boyd Pirtle and Will Posey were aboard a Colorado & Southern passenger train, bound for the city of Colorado Springs. The line had simply changed its name at the Texas-New Mexico border, because both railroads were owned by the Burlington System, but only allowed to operate for certain distances, and the town of Texline was the end of one and the start of the other. The Springs was where Pirtle was hoping to finally capture a notorious fugitive and killer named Frank Rogers; a man born and baptized Chester Stringfellow, Ella's twin, missing for the past twenty years.

As the train—which had taken on water, coal and a helper engine pushing from the back at Raton, New Mexico—was making its way up and over 7,834 foot Raton Pass, the two Rangers were a little less than eight hours from their destination. They'd eaten an early lunch of sandwiches and glasses of draft beer, and were relaxing in the parlor car, where Posey was about to light a cigar and Boyd Pirtle was preparing to take a nap.

Posey fired the end of his Colorado Claro, got a glowing cherry red coal going at the tip, and puffed. He looked at his boss through a cloud of cigar smoke and said, "How do you do that?"

"Do what, Will."

"Fall asleep in an instant. You can do it anytime and anywhere. I've watched yuh."

Pirtle sat up and said, "Training. I taught myself to do it when I was in the war."

"How?"

"Necessity mostly. That and trial and error. We never knew whether we were gonna go, stay or fight. After a while it just became natural. If yuh got a chance to eat or sleep, you took it, because the next thing you knew, we could be standin' and fightin' for our lives and there wasn't no tellin' beforehand and how long it'd be. Days sometimes."

"So, yuh taught yourself . . . just like that."

Pirtle stared at him for several moments before he said, "Not exactly. Have you ever been so tired that you started seein' things?"

"What do yuh mean?"

"Hallucinatin'. Seein' things that ain't there, 'cause you're so damn exhausted that your brain freezes up. Quits workin'. Pretty soon you're duckin' down from imaginary things that just don't exist."

"No. I ain't. But how's that got anythin' to do with what I asked yuh?"

"It's when I taught myself to take combat naps. We'd been at it with the Yankees for nigh on two days without a letup, at a place known as Chickamauga, in Tennessee. Some called the fight "the Gettysburg of the west," because it was so big. It was a sure-enough scrap, that I can tell yuh. Anyway, we fought and fought and fought. Three days in all. I never got a wink the first two days, damn little to eat and hardly any water. By the third day, I started seein' things that weren't there. Phantom Yankees . . . infantry, cavalry, artillery . . . things that didn't exist, and things that couldn't exist, flyin' through the air and comin' outta the ground. Most of my company—boys I'd grown up with and had known all my life—was dead or maimed. That's when a sergeant from Alabama named Caywood grabbed me by the arm durin' a lull in the fightin' and told me to lay down and rest. Said he'd look out on guard and wake me in a bit so he could nap. We did that two or three times each and ever since then, I can go to sleep anytime or place."

"How do yuh wake up?"

"That, I don't know, but I do. If I want to get up at a certain time, I look at my watch beforehand and tell myself to wake . . . and I do."

Posey looked out the window as they crested the top of the pass and began picking up speed, descending into Trinidad. He turned, glanced at his companion and said, "Are you sayin' that you can tell time in your sleep?"

Pirtle sighed, looked at the end of the Pullman Car they were traveling in, then back at Will Posey. He said, "I don't know the answer to that either. I don't think so . . . but if I want to stop sleepin' at a certain point, I will if I think about it before I let myself relax."

Posey stood, held the backs of alternating seats and made his way to the rear of the car, where he tossed the soggy remnant of his stogie into the communal spittoon that rested beside the exit door. When he returned, he took his seat opposite Boyd Pirtle and said, "Dang, Boss. All this time together and I never would've even guessed that you were able to do that in your unconscious. It's an impressive talent, for a fact."

Pirtle locked eyes with his bodyguard and protégé. "Truth is Will . . . what I just said to you is more than I've ever talked about anything to do with the war and my little part in it. I don't like rememberin' it, and I don't wanna mention it again . . . even with yourself. Understand?"

Posey flushed, turning red from his neck to his ears, embarrassed by the intimate nature of their conversation and the frankness of the answers Pirtle had given . . . as well as the glimpse he'd been given, of the festering wounds that still infected his mentor's psyche. He said, "Perfectly. Boyd."

Pirtle took out his fixings, and began rolling a one-handed cigarette. As he was licking the paper, he said—with a burst of that uncanny instinct and insight he had—"And before you ask me, Caywood bled to death in my arms after bein' gut shot by a Yankee sniper who had hit him with a .54 caliber Minnie ball. It happened a few hours after he'd saved my life . . . and I never even learned his last name. I've always regretted that."

Will Posey excused himself at that point and went for some fresh air on the platform between cars, while Boyd Pirtle smoked his cigarette and looked off into the middle distance with the thousand yard stare that only those who've seen the elephant ever possess.

Chapter Sixty

The train was making its slow and noisy way into Trinidad Station, with the engineer laying on the steam whistle and the fireman ringing the hundred pound brass engine bell that was mounted under the headlight, when Will Posey returned to his seat and found Boyd Pirtle reading from one of his notebooks.

When the young Ranger sat down, Pirtle looked up and said, "How's the weather out there," as he closed the journal and returned it to the inside coat pocket of his suit coat.

"Warm and sunny." Posey said, over the clanging, hissing and screeching of the big iron horse coming to rest, adding, "Are yuh findin' anythin' new in there," and pointed with his chin at Pirtle's pocket.

"No. I'm not. As a matter of fact, all I'm findin' is more of a mystery every damn time I go through my notes. At this point, I ain't even sure if Conan Doyle and Sherlock Holmes himself could figure it all out. There just ain't enough information."

Posey squirmed around on his seat, trying to make six-feet, four-inches and two hundred thirty pounds fit comfortably in a five-foot, eight-inch space while accommodating a gun belt, holster and a .44 caliber Colt revolver at the same time. He finally turned sideways and extended his bad leg on the seat beside him. He sighed, rubbed his thigh to ease the ache, and said, "Well, I ain't Sherlock, that's for damnsure. But, maybe I can offer some insights . . . based on my vast law-enforcement experiences and a thorough soakin' up of all your valuable law-enforcement lessons."

Boyd Pirtle grinned, then laughed. He said, "Sure. Why not. We've got several more hours aboard this slow-assed train, maybe we can put them to good use," as he reached in his pocket and retrieved the case notes. "The problem I have, has to do with my first meetin' and interview with Ella Stringfellow, and it's been naggin' at me ever since." He opened the small leather book and handed it to Will Posey.

"You want me to start from here?"

"Yeah. Then we'll talk."

After going over the first three pages, Posey marked his place with his index finger, looked up and said, "Is there anythin' in particular you want me to concentrate on?"

"Yeah." Pirtle said. "Pay close attention to what she says about her father's murder."

Posey nodded and resumed reading, while his boss busied himself with a day-old copy of the *Amarillo News* someone had left on the seat across the aisle from them.

Thirty minutes later, Will Posey closed the journal, handed it back and said, "'Pears to me that there's a lot about the where, when and how of it, but not very much about the who or why."

Pirtle took the leather book and tucked it away. As he folded the newspaper and put it back on the adjacent seat, he said, "You're right. There's not. That strike you as odd?"

Will Posey gazed out the right side windows at the flatness of the high plains and the endless blue skies, then through the left side windows at the foothills that marched up to the towering Rocky Mountains . . . thinking . . . before he answered. "No. It don't. It's been twenty years after all, and nobody was ever accused, much less brought to trial. So no. I don't think it's unusual."

Pirtle started to get out the makings for rolling a cigarette, changed his mind and put them away. He said, "Have you got any more of those stinkers, like you was smokin' a while ago?"

"As a matter of fact I do," Posey answered. "They come in bundles of four and I only had one of 'em." He took a pair of cigars from his shirt pocket and offered one to the senior Ranger, who accepted it with a nod of thanks.

When they'd lit up, Pirtle puffed a couple of times and picked a flake of tobacco from his lip with the same hand that held the cigar. Then he said, "As soon as we know why, we'll know who. Any ideas?"

"Sure. Three come to mind right away. Somebody who hated Mormons. Somebody he skinned in a real estate deal. Could have even been the Mormons themselves, 'cause they found out he was cheatin' 'em."

Pirtle blew a smoke ring and nodded again. "All good choices, and to those we can add the usual suspects: business rival, love interest, organized criminals like our bad boys in Laredo and Brownsville, and then, there's Chester."

"Damn. I shudda thought of him first, 'specially with his doin's as Frank Rogers."

"Yeah," Pirtle said. "I like him for it myself . . . except for the why. That's been botherin' me non-stop. I can't figure out why he'd do it."

"It's also easy to overlook, when everythin' else points to him. Do we even have to know why someone did somethin' in order to prove they done it?'

"No. You're right . . . we don't . . . but we'll always get to who did it a lot faster if we know why. Knowing why also makes our case more watertight. You don't ever want to deprive someone of their liberty, or their life, then find out later that yuh got the wrong man. It's hard to undo—sometimes it's impossible—and it's devastatin' to your conscience. You never get over it."

"I believe yuh. It's an experience I don't ever want to have," Posey said from behind a cloud of smoke.

Pirtle, stone-faced as the Sphinx, and enigmatic as the oracle at Delphi said, "Yeah. Well sometimes you just don't have a choice."

Will Posey, usually as enthusiastic and curious as a young puppy, was smart enough to let the conversation lapse into silence and contented himself with his smoke and the scenery as the train crawled through the foothills toward the steel-making city of Pueblo . . . where a telegram awaited them with news that would change everything. At the same time, in the seat opposite him, Special Agent Boyd Pirtle struggled with his inner demons as he thought about the life he had led, some of his ill-advised deeds, and a few other of the crimes he had seen done in the name of the public good.

It's a helluva list, he mused, *and keepin' the peace just ain't what it once was. That's for damn sure . . . and now that I think on it, I don't know if there's a place for an old campaigner like me in this new, modern century . . . and I ain't sure I care.*

Chapter Sixty-One

Ella Stringfellow was enjoying the warm and sunny morning on the balcony of her west side hotel room. She was drinking coffee, nibbling on toast and writing a letter to Mimi and the kids when she heard the clippity-clop tattoo of a lone horse, accompanied by the cacophony of several hundred glass bottles jiggling in dissonance and disharmony. She looked down at the rear entrance to the hotel and saw a white milk wagon pulled by a brown horse. As she was about to turn back to her correspondence however, furtive movement at the back of the wagon caught her eye. The canvas door flap moved, a head peeked out, then a ragged-looking man with no shoes crept down and tip-toed to the back door of the Antlers Hotel, while the milkman drove away.

The delivery doors for the hotel faced west and were raised, so that the teamsters could back up to the dock, where the wagon bed was even with the floor of the hotel. The big doors only opened when a delivery was going in, or refuse was coming out. For staff and all else, access to the hotel was via a reinforced door that faced south, positioned atop a set of four steps and a large stoop, which was where the shoeless man—dirty and disheveled, his clothes in tatters, his face and hands filthy, his hair matted and bloody—stopped and with slow deliberate caution, checked his surroundings one last time before slipping inside, which gave Ella Stringfellow a perfect view of him. She nearly upset the inkwell in her excitement as she leaned over the banister, craning her neck for a better perspective, but leaving no doubt in her mind, that even dressed up like a Yankee drummer, Ella was certain she was looking at her missing brother, Chester.

Half my life, she thought, as she gathered her writing materials and hurried inside to properly dress before leaving her room. *More than half my life, I've wondered about your whereabouts or I've been looking to find your own self . . . and now I've done it. Glory be and hallelujah! We'll soon be having an interesting meeting and a long overdue discussion, you and I . . .* She giggled then, as she put on her most conservative and modest clothes: a long black skirt and tight-waisted white blouse that buttoned to the neck, then topped it all with an onyx necklace featuring a carved brooch at her throat, and a short black jacket with embroidered sleeves and placket, that buttoned at the waist and flattened her chest. Looking at herself in the mirror as she pinned up her hair and held it in place with a pair of tortoiseshell combs, she decided that the only word that could be used to describe her appearance was . . . *Formidable.*

Ella gathered her things in a small drawstring purse and headed for the lobby, looking for the bellman who'd escorted her into the hotel the previous day. His name was Howard, and she found him at one end of the check-in counter, talking with another bellman.

When he saw her waiting, Howard excused himself and came over. "Hello, Miss Ella. Are you finding everything to your satisfaction?"

"Yes," she said. "But, I was wondering if you would do me a favor . . ."

"Of course. How may I help you?"

"I believe I just saw my brother, the one I've come here to meet, but I don't have his room number. Could you possibly check the registry for me? I'll give you a handsome tip . . ."

"I can handle that. What's his name?"

"Chester. Chester Stringfellow."

Howard looked around the lobby, but no one was paying attention to them. He said "Wait out front, on one of the benches. I'll be right there."

Ella crossed in front of the grizzly bear, went through the revolving door and took a seat in the shade, where she could watch the trolley cars, pedestrians and horse-drawn vehicles as they went up and down Pikes Peak Avenue in the hustle and bustle of city commerce.

After a few minutes Howard came out and walked over to her. "I'm sorry, Miss Ella. I went back to the Fourth of July. There's never been a Chester Stringfellow that stayed here."

"But I just saw him. I know he's here," she said, and thought for a moment, before she had a flash of insight about something Boyd Pirtle said, back in May. "What about Frank Rogers? Is he in residence perhaps?"

"There's a Franklin D. Rogers in 337. He's a lawyer from Denver. Splashy dude. Fancy dresser. Big drinker and big tipper. All the bellmen know him."

"Wears his hair parted down the middle and fancies long porkchop whiskers?"

"That would be the man."

"Room 337?"

"Yes'm."

"Thank you Howard. You've done me a great service," Ella said, as she placed five silver dollars in his outstretched palm. "Would you please keep this between us?"

"Discretion is my middle name."

"And could you tell me where I can make a long-distance telephone call?"

"Certainly," the obliging bellman said, as he pocketed the tidy sum she'd just passed over to him.

Twenty minutes later, Ella Stringfellow was talking to Wiley Newton in Austin, Texas on a static-filled line from a booth in the Antlers Hotel lobby in Colorado Springs. Holding the receiver to her left ear and leaning forward to speak directly into the bakelite mouthpiece on the end of its metal gooseneck arm, she said, "Ella Stringfellow. I'm in Colorado Springs. I want to speak to Mr. Pirtle. Boyd Pirtle. He's a Special Agent there."

"This is his boss, Captain Newton. Pirtle's not here."

"Can you get a message to him?"

"I might, if it's important."

"It is. Do you know who I am?"

"Yes. I do."

"Good. Tell him I've located the man he knows as Frank Rogers. He's at the Antlers Hotel here in the Springs. Room 337. No telling how much longer."

"Don't do anythin'. Pirtle is on his way. He'll be there by eight o'clock tonight. Don't approach Rogers. He's a dangerous outlaw and murderer. He's . . . Hello . . . Hello?" The line was dead. Ella Stringfellow had hung up.

Chapter Sixty-Two

There ain't no possible way around it, Frank Rogers thought as he assessed the damage that unknown assailants had inflicted upon his face, *I'm fucked up for a fare-thee-well and gone . . . and that's the plain fact of it.* He'd been savaged—probably with a wooden club, or a piece of lead pipe. His right eye was purple and swollen shut. When he forced the lids open, blood and pus dribbled out, the sclera looked like pulped red-pudding and he had no sight, only a sense of light. A quick glimpse in the mirror with his one good eye was all it took to realize that he'd been blinded. A wave of nausea swept over him and he retched into the nearby toilet with his hands on his knees, his face inches from the bowl.

Finished, he stood and gulped air, then set about discovering the rest of his injuries. There were many . . . he'd been beaten from head to toe. He had a one-inch cut in his right eyebrow, his left cheek was swollen, bruised and probably broken, based on the tenderness he felt there. Left ear torn, bloody, swollen . . . jaw out of alignment, several teeth loose, two missing . . . arms, torso and legs bruised, sore, and throbbing with unadulterated pain from the clubbing he'd taken. In addition, he knew there was a sizeable lump and gash at the back of his head. His fingers came back with blood on them when he touched himself there. *Probably where they first hit me,* he thought. *Funny, I don't remember much of anything.*

After three days of non-stop reveling, he smelled like a rutting goat in a garbage pile. He had to clean up, and he needed to eat. He thought about room service, about ordering breakfast, then stripped off his ruined clothes while the bathtub was filling. He'd have to hurry if he was going to make his meeting with Mapes and Delbert McKnight, where they'd complete the sting and get the money. He took a slug from the bottle of laudanum he had in his luggage in an attempt to ease the pain, and slid down into the hot water with a sigh.

The next thing he knew, someone was calling his name. He thought he was dreaming at first, but then the voice came again, louder this time, saying his name, his old name . . . the one he'd left behind all those years ago.

"Chester!"

Something jabbed him then, something cold and hard, just in front of his right ear. His eyes sprang open and he heard the double click of a single action pistol going to full cock.

"Do. Not. Move." The voice said. "Do not twitch, fidget, or speak unless I tell you to. Do you understand . . . nod if you do."

He did. He couldn't see his assailant who was on his blind side, but he could tell from the pitch of her voice that it was a woman. He knew too that she was angry, by the unrelenting pressure she was keeping on his temple . . . he could feel the tremor in her wrist and arm . . . and wished that the fogginess in his brain would clear out, so he could think straight and try to figure his way out of the situation. It wasn't happening though. All of his thoughts were in slow motion. He stayed still and waited.

It didn't take long. She said, "Why? Why Chester? Why did you do it . . ."

And he knew then, that it was his twin sister, Ella. He wondered for an instant, why it took him so long. "Why what, Ella?"

"Finally figured out who I am. Well good for you. Now tell me why, damn you."

"Why I sent you money?" He said, in a bid to buy time.

"No. I don't care why you did that. I have it all saved by the way, and I'm going to give every last cent to the Women's Suffrage Movement."

"Don't matter to me," he said, "it all came from different jobs I done."

"You mean robberies?"

"Con jobs. That's what I do now. Take money from those with too much of it, by usin' their own greed against 'em."

"All the more reason the Suffragettes deserve to have it. Tell me why you left and why you did what you did."

He thought about lying. He thought about the shame of getting killed naked, in a bathtub full of dirty water . . . *At least Wild Bill and Wes Hardin got it like men, sittin' up in a saloon drinkin' and playin' stud . . .* He said, "After Daddy was killed, I figured I'd be next. And so far as the other's concerned it was Daddy's idea, said it'd make a man outta me."

"At twelve years old . . ."

"What he told me."

"Well, maybe you can meet up with him in Hell and talk about it," Ella Stringfellow said, as she pulled the trigger and watched with detachment as the ninety-five grain, .32 caliber bullet splattered her brothers blood, bone and brain matter up the tiled wall. *Funny,* she thought, *I expected it to be louder than that.* She watched the gore ooze down the white tiled wall and dribble into the bath water as the body sank below the surface. She dropped the pistol on the floor, stood and went back to the bedroom where she took a seat on one of the overstuffed chairs, opened a book of poems by Emily Dickinson and prepared to wait as long as it took for Boyd Pirtle to show up.

Chapter Sixty-Three

Ranger Special Agent Boyd Pirtle was still talking with his protégé and bodyguard, Ranger Will Posey, about the interview he'd conducted back in the late spring of the year with Ella Stringfellow. That was when she'd revealed that her father, Bishop Carl A. Stringfellow, a founding member of The Church of Jesus Christ of Latter Day Saints—and the architect of an outrageous plan to protect and preserve that neonatal, controversial and persecuted church by infiltrating the U.S. Marshals Service throughout the western United States—had been mysteriously shot and killed, twenty years earlier. The murder was never solved, and her twin brother Chester disappeared two days later. Pirtle had gone on to prove that the killer he'd been pursuing for close to a decade, an outlaw named Frank Rogers, was in fact the missing brother Chester, but was unable to prove that he'd killed his father.

Will Posey said, "It's complicated all right, and maybe that's where we're goin' wrong. Maybe Rogers is like William Bonney, and he just plain enjoys it. He likes killin'. Simple as that, there's your why."

Pirtle looked at the young Ranger and said, "You never cease to amaze me Will. Ever hear of Occam's razor?"

"No. What's a razor got to do with what we was talkin' about?"

"It ain't a thing, it's a theory. It says that the best solution to a problem is usually the simplest one. You may have just put your finger on the why . . . when you compared Frank Rogers to Billy the Kid."

"Where'n hell didja come up with that?"

"Dunno, exactly" Boyd Pirtle said, "I musta read it somewhere or other," as the eight car consist behind the 4-6-0 Baldwin locomotive banged, clanged, huffed and screeched their way into Union Station in Pueblo, Colorado for a two and a half hour layover.

The engineer and brakeman had barely brought the train to a standstill when Posey said, "There's some kind of commotion goin' on outside. Look there at the platform."

Pirtle glanced toward the trackside waiting area where people were gathered in groups, talking, gesticulating and crying. It took another few minutes for the news to get to them that a couple of hours earlier—while the two Rangers worked the details of a twenty year old cold case and their train grinded its way up from Trinidad to Pueblo—the unthinkable had happened at the Pan-American Exposition in Buffalo, New York. President McKinley had been shot, once in the chest and once in the abdomen, by an anarchist named Leon Czolgosz, using a .32 caliber Iver-Johnson pistol he'd purchased at a Buffalo hardware store. The news was incomplete, but it appeared that the President was still alive and clinging to life, while his assailant had been captured and put in jail.

The Rangers were stunned. As they walked into Union Station looking for a place to eat however, they had no time to discuss the news before Pirtle heard his name called.

"PIRTLE. BOYD PIRTLE. TELEGRAM FOR MR. PIRTLE. PIRTLE . . ." the Western Union man hollered out as he moved through the crowd of travelers and news seekers.

"Pirtle here," the Ranger called to attract the messenger's attention, and he headed straight to the pair of men in cowboy hats.

The telegraph clerk glanced at the Winchester carbine Posey was carrying, but said nothing, noting that both men were also armed with Colt revolvers.

Boyd Pirtle, seeing the man's unease said, "We're lawmen. Texas Rangers. We're on the trail of a notorious bad man," as he flashed the silver star on the inside of his lapel. "You have a message for me . . ."

"Yessir. If you're Mr. Pirtle."

Pirtle drew a deep breath, gave the Western Union man a squint eye and said, "Yeah. I am," as he held out his hand, palm up.

His delivery made, the man turned to leave while Pirtle tore the envelope open and scanned the short message from Wiley Newton. EMERGENCY CALL ME NOW STOP, were all the words it contained, but they spoke volumes to the recipient. Pirtle interrupted the clerk with a hand on his arm. "Take me to your office," he said.

The telephone and telegraph lines were jammed with talk of the President, but after fifteen minutes of pulling rank and cajoling operators and their supervisors, Boyd Pirtle managed to get through to Ranger Headquarters in Austin, Texas and Captain Wiley Newton. There were no pleasantries or wasted words. As soon as the phone was answered, he said, "Wiley it's Boyd."

"Ella Stringfellow called here earlier this afternoon. She said she's in Colorado Springs and that Frank Rogers is in room 337 at the Antlers Hotel."

"That's it?"

"Yeah. She said she didn't know how long he'd be there, but she saw and positively identified him as her brother."

"Anything else?"

"No. She hung up."

Pirtle was using the telegraph office manager's phone. He grabbed a pad of telegram forms, tore off a page and started writing. "Antlers Hotel, room 337 . . . that right?"

"Yeah," came Newton's voice over the scratchy phone line.

"How long ago was it that you spoke to her," Pirtle said.

"Couple of hours."

Pirtle looked at the clock on the wall, "We're forty miles and about three and a half hours south of there if we stick to our schedule, but maybe I can hitch us a ride or somethin'."

"I hope so. I'd hate for that sonofabitch to slip away from us again."

"Don't even think that Wiley. And don't call anybody up there. I wanna nail that murderin' bastard myself."

"As you wish. Good luck and stay in touch."

"Yeah."

Chapter Sixty-Four

Thirty minutes later, with a stroke of pure Scots-Irish luck and the help of a congenial Station Master named Darrell "call me Dusty" Abbott, Boyd Pirtle and Will Posey had hopped aboard a freshly rebuilt 2-8-0 American Locomotive with a pair of hostlers and their firemen who were delivering three engines and coal tenders from the repair shops in Pueblo to the Denver Train yards, where they were urgently needed as replacements. As such, they were given high priority and clear track, all the way through to Union Station in the Mile High City.

The trio of locomotives, along with their tenders, were hooked nose-to-tail, making a short but heavy consist which required an engineer in both the front and rear cabs. Most of the motive—or pulling—power would be supplied by the leading unit, but the rearmost one had constant boiler pressure and steam up at all times during the run, so that it could push whenever needed.

The two Rangers were squashed into the cabin of the lead locomotive with a hostler-engineer named Jack Reynolds, a tall sinewy man wearing a seersucker hat that had a set of goggles attached, overalls, a pair of heavy leather gauntlets and a red bandana tied around his throat. His fireman was a husky young man in his twenties named Shane Graham, who looked to Pirtle to be a perfect specimen to recruit for the Rangers.

Jack Reynolds said to Pirtle, "Mr. Abbott told me you're a Special Agent for the Texas Rangers and that you're after an outlaw who's up in Colorado Springs."

"Yeah, we are. Me'n Posey over there, almost had 'im four years ago, but he escaped at the last second. We've chased him ever since . . . How long will it take us to get there?"

"The Springs?" Reynolds said, "We'll be there in half an hour or less. We'll go just as soon as the yard men finish switchin' us up onto the main line and that red light yonder goes green."

Pirtle said, "It's forty miles from here to where we're goin'. There ain't no way to get there so fast. Hell that's more than a mile a minute."

"Wouldya bet a dollar on it," Reynolds asked.

"That you can't make it to the Springs in half an hour or less? Yeah. Betcha a buck."

"You're on Mr. Pirtle."

The semaphore arm went up five minutes later and showed a green light. Reynolds gave two short blasts of his steam whistle, released the Johnson bar and the big drive wheels started to turn as black smoke poured from the stack. Twenty-seven minutes later Pirtle was handing over a dollar and thanking Jack Reynolds for the ride, while an ashen-faced Will Posey climbed down to the ground and received his rifle and their two bags from the fireman. Pirtle came next and was barely on the ground in the middle of the Colorado Springs trainyards when the locomotive started to move. Two toots of the whistle later the six unit train was making speed and disappearing past Colorado Avenue.

A shaken Will Posey said, "That was the fastest I have ever traveled. How can yuh go so damn fast and not die . . ."

Pirtle stepped across the rails as they made their way to Sierra Madre Street. He said, "I don't know, but you didn't. Now you need to be thinkin' about what's gonna happen when we get into the hotel over there. Can yuh? We may be in a gunfight in a few minutes. That bad-assed bastard inside ain't gonna surrender easy, if at all. He knows we got too much on 'im, and he'll go to the gallows. So, can yuh Will . . . forget about the one and think about the other. Both our lives may depend on it."

"Sorry Boyd. You're right. And don't worry, this leg's an every day reminder of what Rogers did to us at the bank in Clarendon. And if it comes to shootin', I'm ready."

"Good," Pirtle said. "Let's see if we can get in that door right there."

Their luck was still holding. Just as they mounted the four steps, a man in a kitchen coat came out. Pirtle caught the door before it latched and they were inside.

"Put your star on the outside," Pirtle said, "And act like you own the place."

As both men pinned their silver Texas Ranger badges on their left chest, Posey said, "Are we gonna let the hotel folks know what we're up to?"

Pirtle was busy checking his single-action Colt, looking under the loading gate to make certain all six rounds were in their place. He spun the cylinder, closed the gate and holstered the revolver. He looked at his protégé and said, "Are you ready to go get this guy?"

Posey said, "Shouldn't we tell somebody we're here?"

"Who . . . tell who, Will?"

"I dunno . . . Town Marshal or the Sheriff maybe, or the people runnin' the hotel?"

"And take the chance on one of 'em slippin' the word to Rogers and have that sneaky bastard get away again . . . no. I don't think so, I'd much prefer grabbin'—or killin'—our quarry first, and lettin' the other authorities know last, on the theory that it's easier to get forgiveness afterwards than permission beforehand. And besides, what've we got to lose other than our freedom and jobs, or our sacred honor as Rangers?"

For a moment, Posey looked liked someone just shot his dog, but then his features softened into a grin. He said, "Well shit, since that's all there is to it, let's go get the sorry sonofabitch."

Pirtle looked up, into the eyes of his subordinate—who was a whole head taller—and said, "Thanks for backin' my play, son. And I want yuh to know that I'm takin' full responsibility for everything if it all goes to Hell in a handbasket, or I come up dead. There's a letter in my coat pocket exonerating you for whatever happens here tonight. It states that I ordered you to do it. You'll have a long career with the Rangers. I talked to Wiley about it before we left."

"You act like you're gonna die."

"No. I ain't plannin' on nothin' like that, but I want to make sure I've done my job to the best of my ability, no matter what happens. So let's go find the stairs to the third floor and put a Ranger endin' to this outlaw's career."

Chapter Sixty Five

As Ella was reading from her book of poetry by Miss Dickinson, a tipped in page written in her own fifteen year old hand fell out. It was a passage from Aeschylus, an ancient Greek playwright. Carefully copied on a single piece of stationary, it read:

Pain that cannot forget
falls drop by drop
Upon the heart
and in our despair,
Against our will,
There comes wisdom
Through the awful
Grace of God

Ella's hand trembled and a tear fell from her left eye as she recalled some of the incidents leading up to her rendition of that particular text, and her response to them. *The humiliation I felt then still hurts,* she thought, *and the shame still burns . . . as does the desire for absolution and at the same time . . . vengeance.*

Her reverie was interrupted by footsteps in the hallway that stopped at the door, followed by a heavy knocking. "Who is it," she said. There was no answer, only more furious banging at the entrance. She waited. Then the knob turned, the door pushed in and Boyd Pirtle stepped into the room, followed by another man she didn't recognize.

Pirtle had a .44 caliber Colt pistol in hand, a Ranger badge on his chest and looked ready to shoot it out. The other one was younger she noted, and carried a revolver in one hand, a rifle in the other. That man holstered the handgun and took up a strategic position on the wall alongside the entrance, from where he could cover the whole room.

Pirtle saw Ella and said, "Where's Roger's?"

Ella pointed to the closed bathroom door. "In there, where I shot him. He's dead."

Pirtle was careful, opened the door just a crack at first, then wider as he got a glimpse at the carnage inside. There was a dead man in the bathtub, blood on the wall, and an old pocket pistol on the floor. He took a look at the man's face—making sure it was Rogers—then felt his neck for a pulse and picked up the handgun. He sniffed the barrel, smelled the burnt gunpowder and returned the weapon to the place he found it.

Coming out, Pirtle closed the door and said to Will Posey, "He's gone. Shot once in the right temple. Body's cool, not cold. Been dead for a few hours. Go look if you want, but don't touch anything."

Posey crossed the room and eyed the scene in the tub, then closed the door and took up his post again without saying a word. He still had the rifle in his hand as he watched and waited, looking to his mentor for a clue as to what came next.

Pirtle took a seat opposite Ella Stringfellow in the corner of the large room, where a loveseat, low table and a pair of side chairs were located. He said, "This is my associate and fellow Ranger, Will Posey. He knows who you are. I am pleased to see you again, but not so much with the circumstances. What's happened here . . . and why are you in Colorado Springs?"

Ella smiled at him and said, "And I you, Mr. Pirtle. Much has happened since last we spoke. As to how I'm here, well, your most recent telegram mentioned this city. I deduced that this was probably where Chester was located. It was pretty simple actually. After that I bought a train ticket and came. It was only blind luck, or perhaps divine providence, that I spotted my brother."

Sitting with his left foot on top of his right knee, Pirtle got out the makings and began to roll a one-handed cigarette. He said, "But why the violence. What's happened here?"

"Here is the result, not the reason."

"Now, I'm really confused," Pirtle said as he finished making his smoke and lit it up with a wood kitchen match he scratched on the sole of his boot. "Would you mind explaining it a little more?"

Ella shifted in her seat, closed her book and handed a loose page to the Ranger. She said, "It's a long story . . . and an indelicate one I'm afraid. If you'll read this, I'll tell you the reason I copied it out . . . it's from a Greek tragedy and it was written before the time of Christ."

It took just a few seconds for Pirtle to examine. Finished, he looked up and said, "This is a compelling—and disturbing—piece of verse. When did you write it and why?"

Ella shifted on her chair again as she looked at a spot behind him and to Pirtle's left. Holding her quivering chin up she said, "I was fifteen years old at the time and finding solace in the town library by losing myself in literature. When I first saw the passage, I thought it was a message from God . . . a communication about atonement . . ." she trailed off at that point and stopped talking.

Pirtle smoked for a moment, then said, "You mean like Christ on the cross, paying for all mankind's sins?"

"No," she said, her eyes flashing with indignation and anger. "What it meant to me was blood atonement. *Whoever harms a Mormon shall pay in blood,* the unwritten creed of the LDS church—as enforced by the Danites—also known as the Mormon Militia. It was giving me the permission I needed, by telling me that blood atonement was just as applicable for women as it was for men. Women are not an underclass Mr. Pirtle, and we are not chattel."

Pirtle uncrossed his legs leaned forward on his chair and said, "Permission to do what?"

Ella Stringfellow looked down at the floor for a moment, then raised her eyes, and looked straight into Pirtle's. "Kill my father and my brother," she said.

An experienced interrogator who'd conducted tens of dozens of criminal interviews in his career, Pirtle was no longer surprised by the perfidies of his fellow man, but Ella's soft spoken and matter-of-fact delivery was stunning. He disbelieved his own ears at first and said, "I want to make sure I heard you correctly. Would you say that again," and crushed out his cigarette on the porcelain ashtray in the center of the table.

"Which part?"

"Just the last one."

"About permission to kill my father and brother?"

"Yeah."

"Well, I just did, didn't I?"

Pirtle put his elbows on his knees and cupped his chin in his hands. He said, "Yes. I guess you did. And the only questions that leaves is . . . why . . . and how?"

Chapter Sixty-Six

Ella answered the Ranger's question with one of her own.

"Have you wondered, Mr. Pirtle, why I have never married? I'm an intelligent, reasonably good-looking woman in the prime of her life. I'm attractive to men, and I've had more than my share of suitors . . . I should be surrounded by my own children and wed to a strong, hard-working Mormon man, don't you think?"

"Yes." Pirtle said. "And yes to every one of your questions. Personally, I find you most fair and often wondered why some Prince Charming hasn't come along and captured your heart, then swept you from your feet and carried you off to his castle somewhere, to live happily ever after. So, why Miss Stringfellow, why haven't you?"

She looked up at the ceiling for a moment, then down at the floor where her teardrops splashed on the parquet. She said, "Because I am not chaste, Mr. Pirtle. My father took that from me when I was nine years old. Said he was going to teach me to be a woman and he kept giving me lessons four, five, even six times every week. After about a year, he brought Chester in, at first to watch, then, a couple years later, to participate and *to make a man of him,* Father said. And my lessons continued, only then, there were twice as many, day after day, week after week, month after month, and year after year. There are many, many ways, Mr. Pirtle, in which the female body can be violated and I have been abused countless times in all of them."

Her tears were now a flood. She was sobbing and gasping for air at the same time. A stone-faced Will Posey handed her a clean, white, ironed and folded handkerchief, then went back to his post without a word and resumed studying the pattern on the floor like his life depended on it.

It took several minutes for Ella to compose herself, during which time neither of the men spoke. When she was able to go on, she said, "I was petrified I'd become with child. But, God bless dear Mrs. Ince, she looked after and cared for me throughout the ordeal, and showed me how to take care of my body. I am certain that she offered herself in my place, but my father said that miscegenation was a vile abomination in the eyes of God and the church, and told her that if she ever said anything to anyone about what was going on in the house, he'd call a trader he knew down in Mexico, who'd come get her in the middle of the night and take her to Brazil, where human slavery was still practiced. She was powerless and terrified, as was I."

Pirtle asked if she needed a break.

"No," Ella said. "I don't. This is the only time I've ever told the entire tale, and I want to get it over with."

"Go ahead then," Pirtle said, "and stop whenever you want." Ella nodded, said, "Could I have some water please?"

Without a word, Will Posey went into the lavatory and got a glass from the drainboard of the sink, filled it with tap water and took it to Ella, never looking at the bathtub or the body.

"Thank you," Ella said, as she received the glass and drank, while Posey went back to his station by the wall and Boyd Pirtle busied himself rolling another smoke.

Ella sipped, then put the glass on the table and folded her hands together in her lap. She drew in a breath and resumed her narrative. "By the time I was fifteen, I was ready to take my life, because my despair was so great and my depression so deep. I was being used as a concubine and a sex slave, and I had to make it stop. I couldn't take any more of their insatiable attentions. I felt I was worthless, no more than a harlot, a thing to be used and discarded; something vile, morally depraved, base and dirty. I couldn't get clean, no matter how much I scrubbed, no matter how often I washed, and no matter how hot the water or coarse the soap."

Ella stopped at that point to dab at her eyes and take another drink of water. She took a deep breath and resumed her confession. "I purchased the pistol in there," pointing to the bathroom, "at the dry goods store with monies I pilfered from my father and the household, and I intended to shoot myself in some public place in order to embarrass him and the LDS Church. I stopped for one last look at the library, the only place on earth where I felt comfort, safety and serenity . . . and to say goodbye to all the books I loved so well."

Ella's eyes were shining as she looked at Boyd Pirtle and said, "But then I opened an edition I'd never looked at before and found the message from God. I wrote down the passage and stuck it in a poetry book and made plans to take things into my own hands, and so I did Mr. Pirtle, and so I did. When the opportunity presented itself a few weeks later, I came up behind him and, without hesitation or remorse, I put a bullet in the back of his head. He died instantly. And he died in the gutter where he belonged. He was a pig and my only regret is that he never knew who killed him. Everything else is as I told you when we first met. That's the entire story."

"What about Chester," Pirtle said, as he finally put a match to the cigarette he'd made and forgotten about while he listened to Ella give her account. He shook the match and tossed it into the same ashtray that held the remains of his first one.

"Chester," she said. "I think he knew somehow—twins often have an uncanny sense of each other—that he was next. He wasn't strong enough to force himself on me without our father helping him. I always intended to track him down, but somehow time just got away from me. When he started sending checks however, everything flooded back and I found that my desire for vengeance was stronger than ever."

"Why would he send money?"

"To assuage his conscience."

"Do you think he had one," Pirtle said as he stood up.

"Maybe not. Probably not. But I can't think of another viable reason."

"Me neither," the Ranger Special Agent said, "but now, much as it pains me, I'm gonna have to arrest you for capital mur . . ."

"Wait a minute," Will Posey said, "I don't think that ought to happen."

Chapter Sixty-Seven

Boyd Pirtle turned to the younger Ranger. "What did I just hear you say?"

"I didn't stutter," Posey said. "This woman ain't gonna be arrested for nothin', if I can help it."

"She's a murderer."

"Yeah. So are you and so am I."

"We were enforcin' the law and doin' our sworn duty. And besides which, they were all bad guys."

"Are you certain of that Mr. Pirtle? You positive they were all guilty of the worst crimes, or were they just some dumb-asses who got talked into somethin' they didn't think through . . . like them three you hung in Ft. Worth, back in ninety-seven?"

"Bad luck, stupidity . . . wrong place, wrong time . . . all makes no difference to me. They broke the law. She broke the law. Break the law, get caught, pay the price. It's as simple as that."

"Maybe it used to be, back in the frontier days, but I think it's a lot more complicated now. If there's anything I've learned by bein' around you, it's to use my head. And my head is tellin' me that it'd compound the evil and be a terrible miscarriage of justice to put this woman in jail, when them scallywags down in Austin are doin' what they're doin' and gettin' away with it."

"She's still a murderer and she still broke the law," Pirtle said.

"The way I see it, see that same situation . . ." Will Posey shot back, "is that there's the law . . . and then there's justice . . . and they ain't the same thing . . . never was and never will be. She, Ella Stringfellow herself, all by her lonesome self, delivered justice by stoppin' an obcenity and rightin' a terrible wrong. The law is there to set things straight, but sometimes it don't, can't or won't and besides which, this here's a whole different animal."

"That don't make sense."

"There ain't nothin' to be gained from arrestin' this woman. You're just pissed off cause she beat yuh to it. I say we write it up as a self-inflicted death, hang the Bishop's murder on Rogers and let this woman live out her life in peace. She's suffered enough."

"I'm right here," Ella Stringfelllow said, "I can hear everything you're saying and I don't want to be talked about like a day-old loaf of bread."

"You surprise me, Will," Pirtle said, "and I want . . ."

Whatever Boyd Pirtle was going to say next was interrupted by heavy footsteps thudding down the hallway, and a moment later the door was crashed open by an enraged giant of a man. He was shouting at the top of his lungs about "Killing a no good hop-head fookin' bastard named Frank Rogers who'd failed to show up as planned and fooked off the biggest fish they'd ever had . . ."

The giant stopped in his tracks when he saw the silver star on Boyd Pirtle's chest. That's when Delbert McKnight made the biggest mistake of his life and went for his gun.

The big man was fast, but Will Posey was faster. McKnight's .45

caliber Smith & Wesson had just cleared its holster when a huge, 275 grain bullet from Posey's Winchester hit him smack dab in the center of his chest. The round blew out his heart, knocked him five feet backwards and killed him instantly. Delbert McKnight was a corpse before his body hit the floor, but somehow, he managed to pull the trigger of the pistol in his hand as he fell and the projectile struck Boyd Pirtle in the abdomen . . . where it ripped a tornadic path through his liver and severed his spine as it exited the middle of his back.

Paralyzed from the waist down and bleeding to death, Pirtle fell to the floor in a heap, while Will Posey took the gun from McKnight.

Ella Stringfellow was recoiling in shock from the sudden noise and violence, as well as the sight of so much blood. She gasped, covered her mouth with one hand and pushed herself backwards in the chair—as if trying to put as much distance as possible between herself and all the death in the room—but she did not scream or cry out.

After disarming the unknown assailant who stormed in, Posey rushed to the man who'd become like a father to him. "What can I do to help yuh, Mr. Pirtle," he said, as he held the old Ranger.

"Nothin' Will. It's my time. That bastard has killed me." Pirtle was laying on the floor in a widening puddle of blood and growing weaker with every breath. "Never thought I'd end like this . . . it's up to you to carry on Will . . . my kind of policin' is over and done. It went away with the Old West."

Posey had to bend down, and put his ear close to the dying man's face in order to hear his voice.

Pirtle said, "And Ella Stringfellow should be . . ." But he never finished whatever he was going to say. His voice gave out, then he took one last rasping breath as the spirit left him . . . and he died.

There wasn't time to mourn or carry on, Posey realized. He'd miss the man for the rest of his days, but that would have to come later. He said, "Miss Stringfellow I stand by what I told Mr. Pirtle: there's law and there's justice. I believe in both and I also believe we've got to find the balance somewhere between 'em. Now go. This place'll be swarmin' in a few moments and you shouldn't be here. Do good things with your life and be thankful you knew a man like Boyd Pirtle. There won't ever be another like him."

Chapter Sixty-Eight

Will Posey was in the process of putting fire to his last Colorado Claro. As he puffed, and spun it around with one hand and applied the match with the other, he said, "Damned if this ain't like old times Boyd. Here we are, ridin' together in the baggage car of another slow-assed train, headed towards home and takin' forever to get there."

Pirtle didn't answer.

Posey shook the wooden kitchen match and pinched it between his thumb and forefinger to make sure it was safe before he tossed it toward the door and watched it settle on the boxcar floor. He smoked for a time, and blew some rings in the air to amuse himself, while the minutes dragged on, the train clattered along and the miles passed. One. By. One.

He could have ridden in comfort in one of the Pullmans, but Posey chose instead to stay in the baggage car and go as freight alongside the coffin of his mentor, friend and role model, Texas Ranger and Special Agent, Boyd Pirtle. "It's not that I'm sentimental or nothin', but I figured it'd be our final ride together and my last chance to talk to yuh in private . . . there's several things

I've got to say . . . plus a few to tell."

"First, I want to thank yuh for the letter you wrote. It was one of the first things the Springs detectives collected—that and the other letter from Captain Newton namin' you as a special agent—and they was nice enough to photograph 'em for their case files and return the real ones to me. They're right here in my pocket, along with your Ranger star. I ain't sure, but I don't think there's very many of them hand made silver ones, and I didn't want somebody to steal it for a souvenir."

"No don't worry. I'll put one on yuh before it's lowered. I won't let 'em bury yuh without a badge, but it'll be one of the new ones like mine. I'm gonna have your name engraved on back of the old one, and wear it in your honor. I reckoned you'd like that and it'll keep you close to. . ." Posey had to stop talking for a bit, in order to rub his eye, which was watering from a stray cinder or something. When he got it out, he pinched the bridge of his nose for a moment, then went on.

"So . . . while you were down at the undertakers . . . I was closin' out our case regardin' Frank Rogers, aka Chester Stringfellow."

"What's that? No. She didn't. He's planted in the indigent section of the city cemetery as Frank Rogers."

"Yeah. I thought it was a fitting end too, and I'm glad you approve."

Posey stopped his narration then and busied himself for a few moments in the process of relighting his cigar. When he had it going, he took a few puffs and resumed talking. "It's an odd thing to say, Boyd, but I can feel your presence right now—even though I know you're in God's hands and this here is just an empty shell—it's like your spirit is right there, talkin' to me, and it's a comfort. A great comfort."

He stood, and swaying like a sailor in mild seas, Posey made his way to the big sliding door to look out of the little barred window, but the scenery was featureless, the land flat and lacking of any topographical details that he could identify. He guessed they were in New Mexico, somewhere north of Clayton, still hours and hours from Austin, with dusk settling on the landscape.

Posey went back to his seat on the pile of mailbags beside Pirtle's simple pine coffin. Putting his hand on the unvarnished lid, he said, "It turned out that that big bastard who shot yuh was a known felon from Denver. He was a thug and leg-breaker who was mixed up with a gang of thieves and bunko artists up there. Several of the Springs lawmen knew of 'im—but funny thing— he ain't never been arrested, or even charged with nothin'. Stinks to high heaven, don't it? A known badman . . . but untouchable. There's talk of widespread corruption in high places in Denver, and rumors of a wee bit of it in Colorado Springs too, but nothin's bein' done about it. His name was Delbert McKnight, by the way, and he's dead—on account of I put one in his chest."

Posey shifted his position and moved several of the canvas bags in an attempt to gain a measure of comfort, and delay the last part of their informal debriefing. He sighed and said, "Which leaves only Ella Stringfellow to tell yuh about."

Posey puffed on the stump of his cigar for a few moments while he thought about what to say next. It didn't take long. He said, "I cut her loose. She was gone before anybody else got on the scene, and the investigating officers were happy to accept my word as a sworn officer of the law and a Texas Ranger. I put Rogers down as a suicide, when you and me was closin' in on him, and I laid the murder of Carl Stringfellow on him too, with some promptin' and a lot of innuendos, plus some circumstantial evidence. They were all happy to help clear a twenty year old cold case, too. I think they were paddin' their records some, but so what. Who cares? Nobody. Because one murderous bastard, as you put it is out of business forever and a child rapist will never do it again . . . never hurt another little one. Maybe Frank Rogers paid for a murder he didn't do, but we both know he did a bunch of others he never answered for, and I'm good with that. My conscience is clear and I'd do it again because justice was served. The law may have come up a little short in this case, but it won't on the next, or the one after that and knowin' it lets me sleep good at night."

"As for Ella Stringfellow, she's the one who's done all the sufferin' and nobody came to help or rescue her . . . the one who was supposed to be her main defender was her ultimate abuser . . . so she avenged herself. I hope she can live out the rest of her life in peace and comfort. And I hope too, that her wounds heal with time and the scars aren't so hurtful any longer."

Will Posey stopped talking then, and rode in silence alongside Boyd Pirtle's remains as the train rumbled into the gathering night and ever closer to his final resting place down in Austin— the old-west, heart of Texas.

Epilogue

When the train pulled in to Austin Station on Saturday, September 14, 1901, Captain Wiley Newton was waiting with an honor guard of Rangers and the news. William McKinley, America's twenty-fifth President, had died that morning and Theodore Roosevelt had been sworn in as the new President. The country was in mourning.

The assassin Leon Czolgosz was executed in the electric chair on October 29, 1901 at the state prison in Auburn, New York.

Mapleton Sheryl Jones—in spite of the utter disapproval of his family—was married to Miss Charity Moon on November 10, 1901.

Ella Stringfellow returned to Cleburne, and together with Mimi James, opened a boarding house for young women. She remained an ardent supporter of the Suffragettes and was a life long advocate for women's rights.

The Blonger-Duff gang continued to swindle honest—but greedy—folks out of tens of thousands of dollars.

On Sunday September 15, 1901, the body of Boyd Pirtle was laid to rest alongside his wife Genevieve, in Austin's Oakwood

Cemetery, with lawmen from every corner of the state in attendance. Also paying their respects were Civil War veterans, judges and politicians, including the sitting governor, who gave a brief eulogy. It was said to be the largest funeral ever held in Austin.

Doroteo Arango rode out periodically from his northern Mexico hideout to loot, rape and pillage the haciendas, banks and ranches of the rich and powerful, honing his men and their skills until he made a name for himself during the Mexican Revolution as Poncho Villa. Tomás Urbina was his second in command until his death.

Although he did his best to hide it, Captain Wiley Newton was devastated by the death of his friend and longtime fellow Ranger, Boyd Pirtle. He found himself thinking more and more often about a quieter life and the benefits of a peaceful retirement while still able to enjoy it.

Will Posey was also in a mental fog after the loss of his mentor and guiding light. He was at Ranger HQ in Austin, where he sat at a desk doing paperwork, day after day, hoping for a new field assignment and despairing when none came, week after week. Then, on Monday, October 14, 1901 he received a phone call . . .

"Hello, is this Texas Ranger William Posey?"

"Yes it is."

"This is the operator. Please hold for the President."

President of what . . . Posey thought, as he listened to a series of whirrs, clicks and pauses, followed by a bang . . . then an unmistakable voice.

"Will Posey? This is President Theodore Roosevelt. I understand we have a problem with the US Marshals Service out there . . ."

Author's Note

Dear Reader;

Would you please take a few moments and leave an honest review of *UNFORSAKEN* on Amazon and Goodreads . . . your comments are greatly appreciated and incredibly important . . . because that's how our stories are able to reach more readers like you.
And if you really liked the book, kindly get a friend to buy one, as we need all the help we can get!

Thanks for the help . . . and thanks for reading my book.

John Dwaine McKenna
Colorado Springs, Colorado

Acknowledgments

Unforsaken could not have been written without the indispensible help of two women. The first is my wife, June, whose genealogical research found the newspaper ad which begins the novel. The second is Lora Lee Brown, my indefatigable assistant who types, spell-checks, keeps the appointments straight, answers the mail, makes us laugh at just the right moments ... and keeps my foot out of my mouth at all times.

A special thanks to Steve Patterson at the Colorado Railroad Museum in Golden, Colorado who helped the author keep Pirtle's train schedule accurate and mostly on time.

And many thanks to Don Kallaus for building such beautiful books, Jeff Kallaus our online wizard of all things internet, our other readers, friends and usual suspects who help, encourage and support: Mike Curley, Dwight Haverkorn, Barbara Nickless, Bob Will, Linda Commando, Frances Brown w/a Claire Gem, Betsy Cary, Skip Mooney, Joanie Mooney, Jim Ciletti, Alta Dunst, Don Cesare, Terry Ross, Craig Ross and Dale Ross.

Last, a very heartfelt thank-you to all the antecedents and descendants of the Orr and Lynn families, whose roots lie deep in the Scots-Irish heart of America.

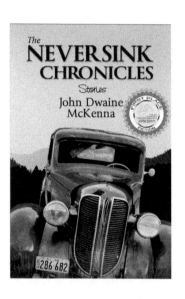

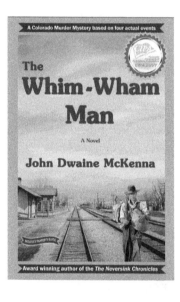

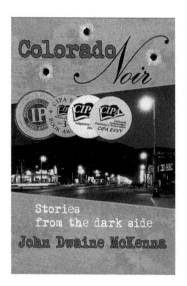

Biography

John Dwaine McKenna is the multiple award-winning author of *The Neversink Chronicles, The Whim-Wham Man,* and *Colorado Noir.* He's a member of the Colorado Author's League, and his newspaper column, *Mysterious Book Report* appears weekly in the *Tri-Valley Townsman* and online. He and his wife June are long-time residents of southern Colorado.